MW01716711

The Advocate's Trigger

Legal Suspense Murder Mystery

Teresa Burrell

Silent Thunder Publishing

This book is a work of fiction. References to real people, events, establishments, organizations, or locales are intended only to provide a sense of authenticity and are used fictitiously. All other characters, and all incidents and dialogue are drawn from the author's imagination and are not to be construed as real.

Edited by L.J. Sellers

Book Cover Design By Madeline Settle

ISBN: 978-1-938680-62-5

Library of Congress Number: 2026910040

San Diego, CA

Dedication

To Allie, my great niece and my trusted assistant. Your kindness, strength, and unwavering heart make you truly special. You give so much of yourself to others, always with kindness and grace. I'm grateful for you every single day. Your big heart, your strength, and your tireless spirit inspire me more than you know, and I am so proud of the woman you've become.

Acknowledgements

A special thanks to **Kim Vincent** for suggesting the title.
My Loyal Beta Readers:
Beth Agejew
Vickie Barrier
Dianne Biscoe
Denise Bowman
Lisa Boyles
Melanie Cardullo
Michael Farmer
Darby Farmer
Lori Grace
Julie Howard
Dianne Jensen
Crystal Kamada
Sheila Krueger
Linda Langille
Janie Livingston
MaryAnn Schaefer
Colleen Scott
Alice Shepherd
Carolyn Silberman
Tracy Weber
Denise Zendel

Chapter 1

Monday afternoon, 3:45 pm

"Mateo Alvarez never arrived at the Venables' foster home." Filippa, the social worker, sounded young and worried on the phone.

Sabre Orin Brown, Mateo's juvenile dependency attorney, stopped walking.

"What do you mean?" Sabre asked. "He should've been there two hours ago."

She stood in the narrow hall outside Department Three, files tucked under one arm. She heard a bailiff laugh at something someone had said.

"I don't know," the social worker said. "The Venables called and said he wasn't there at two. They waited. They called again at three, and again a few minutes ago. Still nothing."

"Who transported him?"

A pause, while papers rustled. The sound of someone looking for an answer instead of knowing it.

"County transport," Filippa said. "Routine transfer."

Routine. Sabre hated that word. "Which vehicle?"

"I'll have to check."

"You should already know," Sabre kept her voice level. "Was he picked up?"

"Yes," the social worker said quickly. "He was logged out of Polinsky at one-fifteen."

"But not logged in at the Venables'?"

Another pause. "That's correct."

Sabre shifted the files against her hip and turned toward the stairwell. "Did you contact the transport company?"

"Yes. I called dispatch."

"And?"

"I didn't get an answer."

Sabre stopped at the top of the stairs. "It's three-forty-five. This isn't after hours."

"I know," the woman said. "I left a message and sent an email."

"When?"

"About twenty minutes ago."

"You waited twenty more minutes to call me?" Sabre didn't try to mask her irritation.

"I thought it might be traffic," the social worker said. "Or a wrong turn. These things happen."

"No. They don't. I want the transport log pulled now," Sabre said. "Vehicle number, driver name, route, and timestamps. Do not mark this as a delay."

"Sabre—"

"Now." She ended the call and pushed through the stairwell door.

Mateo Alvarez was fifteen. Quiet. Smart in a watchful way. He'd learned early that attention could be dangerous, but invisibility was worse. Sabre had met with him on numerous occasions. The last time was after a prior placement collapsed under the weight of promises the system couldn't keep. He hadn't cried. He hadn't complained. He'd asked one question. "Where am I going next?"

She hadn't known the answer then.

By the time Sabre reached the parking structure, her phone was vibrating again.

"I pulled the vehicle ID," Filippa said. "Unit 417."

"Who was the driver?" Sabre asked.

"It's a contracted company. County-approved."

Of course it was. "Have you heard back from dispatch?" Sabre asked.

"No."

"Still no one answering?"

"No."

Sabre stopped beside her car. "Where is the vehicle now?"

A pause. "It's not showing," the social worker said. "The GPS went offline about twenty minutes into the route."

Sabre briefly closed her eyes. "Offline how?"

"I don't know. It just dropped." Some panic in her voice now.

"Vehicles don't just drop," Sabre countered. "What route was logged?"

"The standard freeway, southbound. Exit at Valencia."

"That's ten minutes from the Venables'," Sabre said. "Where was the last ping?"

"Near the frontage road."

Sabre opened her car door but didn't get in.

"Call the police," Sabre commanded. "Tell them we have a missing minor during transport and a contractor who isn't answering the phone."

There was a long hesitation on the other end. "Sabre—"

"Never mind. I'll call. You start checking local hospitals."

She ended the call, got into her car, and started the engine.

Missing during transfer didn't happen without some kind of noise. And not without someone responding when the phone rang. Mateo Alvarez hadn't arrived because either the vehicle had been in an accident or someone had taken him somewhere else.

Chapter 2

Monday afternoon, 3:54 pm

Sabre pulled onto the shoulder before she reached the freeway. She wanted to call Vinny DuBois, but he was a homicide detective, and Mateo Alvarez was just missing. She hoped it would never come to that, but she was scared for the boy.

She dialed the non-emergency number instead.

"San Diego Police Department," the dispatcher said. "How can I help you?"

"This is Attorney Sabre Brown. I need to report a missing fifteen-year-old boy who disappeared during a county-supervised transport from Polinsky to a foster placement."

There was a pause, brief but noticeable, as the dispatcher processed what Sabre had just said. "When was the boy last seen?"

"A little after one this afternoon," Sabre said. "He was logged out of Polinsky Receiving Home and placed into a county-contracted transport vehicle. He never arrived at his placement."

"And you're reporting this now because...?"

"Because the transport company isn't answering its phone, the GPS on the vehicle went offline mid-route, and the county can't account for the child. They're calling it a delay," Sabre said. "It's not a delay."

That earned her another pause. A keyboard clicked this time.

"Can you come into the station?" the dispatcher asked.

"I'm already on my way."

~~~

The station was busy in the way police stations always were with controlled noise, people moving with purpose, the low-level tension of things going wrong in different directions. Sabre checked in at the front desk and was told to wait.

At five-foot-four she didn't look imposing, but she carried herself like someone who expected answers. Her brown hair was well past her shoulders now, and she dressed in a navy-blue suit and high heels and always carrying a stack of files whenever she was in the courthouse. Right now, she was empty-handed.

JP, her mate and private investigator, was already there. She had called him on her way. He stood near a side wall, coffee in one hand, phone in the other, scanning the room with a quiet attention that came from years of noticing what other people missed. Tall and broad-shouldered, he wore jeans, boots, and a black Stetson hat. He carried himself like a man who had seen trouble and didn't intend to be surprised by it again.

JP looked up when he saw her. "You called it in yourself," he said. Not a question.

"I didn't want the situation sitting in county limbo." Sabre joined him at the wall.

"Good," JP said.

A familiar voice cut in. "Well, this isn't where I expected to see you two today." DuBois approached, jacket off, badge visible, looking more curious than concerned. He was five-eleven, solid without being imposing, the faint curve of a long-earned belly pressing against his dress shirt. His full head of salt-and-pepper hair was thick and stubborn,
~~~

refusing to thin despite years of homicide stress. His tie was loose, sleeves rolled once at the forearms, the posture of someone who had been at work longer than expected.

He gave JP a nod, the corner of his mouth lifting slightly. "McCloud," he said, the nickname automatic. It was a reference to the old television cowboy detective JP resembled in both wardrobe and stubborn streak. Then the detective looked at Sabre.

"Missing kid," Sabre said.

DuBois' expression shifted. "Who's got it?"

"According to CPS, it's Detective Miller," Sabre said. "I haven't met him yet. JP has had some dealings with him in the past."

DuBois nodded. "He's solid, and he doesn't scare easy."

As if summoned, a man in his forties stepped out of a nearby conference room, folder tucked under his arm. His sandy hair was cut short, his tie conservative, and his jacket close at hand, like a man who believed procedure was not a suggestion but a structure.

"Sabre Brown?" he asked.

"That's me."

"I'm Detective Oscar Miller." His handshake was firm and professional. "Hi, DuBois, JP." He nodded at the two men, then turned to DuBois. "Are you involved in this?"

"No. I just saw my friends and stopped to say hello." He glanced over at Sabre and JP. "Whatever they say, listen carefully. They both tell it like it is and are not prone to exaggeration. Although, sometimes you have to decipher what the cowboy says. He talks funny."

JP looked at DuBois. "Aren't you supposed to be retired?"

"I'm six months from a beach chair and a fishing pole."

JP laughed. "Yeah, right. You've been threatening that for years."

Sabre smiled. "Thanks, Vinny."

Miller gestured toward the security entrance. "Let's talk."

In his cubicle, Miller listened without interrupting as Sabre laid out the timeline, the pickup, and the logged transfer. She highlighted the dropped GPS tracking signal and the failure of the transport company to answer calls.

Miller leaned back in his chair and exhaled slowly. "This should've triggered a response already."

"Yes," Sabre said. "It should have."

Miller picked up his desk phone and dialed. The call rang, and rang, and then went to voicemail.

"It could be after hours for them now, but it wasn't when I called," Sabre said.

"I know," Miller said. "That's a problem."

JP shifted forward. "Where's their yard?"

Miller looked at him. "I can send a unit."

"I'm going anyway," JP said.

Miller studied him for a beat. "Did you forget you're not law enforcement anymore?"

"I know, I'm retired," JP said. "But I'm a private investigator now, and I'm thorough."

From the doorway, DuBois cleared his throat. "He's also annoyingly hard to stop."

Miller's mouth twitched. "All right. I'll go with you. But before we go, Sabre, can you give me the *Reader's Digest* version of how Mateo came into the system?"

"Both parents have long criminal records and drug history. The father was a gangbanger."

"Was?"

"Mateo's mom claims he's dead. We have no proof of that, but Mateo believes it."

The detective stood, grabbed his jacket, then paused and looked at Sabre. "Are you going home?"

"Yes," Sabre said. "But I'll keep my phone on me."

~~~

The transport company's yard sat behind a chain-link fence in an industrial strip where the lights were dim and
~~~

the buildings indistinguishable from one another. JP parked behind Miller and killed the engine.

No lights were on inside, and when they checked the door, it was locked.

While Miller checked the gate, JP walked the perimeter. Part way around the yard, he climbed over the fence, looked around, and walked back to where Miller was standing on the other side.

"What the hell are you doing?" Miller asked.

"I'm looking for the vehicle they used to transport Mateo."

"You can't be in there. We don't have a warrant."

"I don't need a warrant. I'm trespassing. Do you want to arrest me?"

"Just get out here."

JP climbed back over. "There are several vehicles here, but not the unit that was assigned to Mateo."

Miller's jaw tightened. "Which means it didn't finish its route."

The detective pulled out his phone and dialed again. The call went straight to voicemail.

"Somewhere, a county-contracted vehicle that should've been parked, logged, and accounted for is still missing," JP said. "And so is Mateo Alvarez."

Chapter 3

Monday, 5:03 pm

The yard was too quiet. JP stood at the chain-link fence and let his eyes travel past it, through it, the way he'd learned years ago. Empty yards lie by omission. There was no routine, no rhythm, no human error to measure against expectation. Just locked gates and the sense that someone had decided not to be available.

The evening summer light was the kind that lingered longer than it should, washing everything in a pale gold that made shadows look harmless when they weren't.

Miller stood a few feet away, phone to his ear, jaw tight. "Still voicemail." Miller ended the call and slipped the phone back into his pocket.

JP nodded. "You'd think they would have cell phones they could answer. Which means they're either incompetent or hiding."

Miller didn't respond to JP's comment. He didn't need to. "Okay," Miller said. "We treat this case like a missing juvenile, because that's what it is."

He climbed into his car, flipped open a folder, and started making calls. JP leaned against the hood and watched traffic slide past the industrial strip. People were driving home, windows down, radios on, unaware that a fifteen-year-old kid had vanished.

Miller called his supervisor. "I need the last GPS ping for vehicle Unit 417 with Western Youth Transport."

Miller's face tightened as he listened. "Frontage road access near Valencia," Miller repeated. "That's nowhere near the placement." Miller hung up and looked at him. "We're going to the last ping."

"Good," JP said.

Miller hesitated half a second, probably considering protocol and liability, then nodded. "Let's go."

~~~

The frontage road baked under the lingering sun, concrete throwing heat up at them even though the air had begun to soften. Summer stretched the day out, refusing to let darkness rush in. The light made everything clearer, and somehow worse.

Miller pulled onto the shoulder just past an access gate. JP parked behind him. The freeway thundered overhead, steady and indifferent.

JP stepped out and took a moment. Not looking, just listening. Beneath the roar of traffic was the softer noise of wind in scrub brush, the distant clatter of something loose against concrete.

"They could've pulled off here," JP said. "For any reason."

Miller nodded.

A patrol unit arrived minutes later, lights off. The young officer climbed out, his eyes alert.

"Detective Miller?" he asked.

"That's me. We're looking for a missing fifteen-year-old boy. The last GPS ping in the transport vehicle was here."

The officer glanced around. "Is he a runaway?"

Miller's attention flipped briefly to JP, then back to the officer. "That's not our working theory."

JP didn't say anything. He just looked down the embankment, where the ground dropped unevenly toward a drainage canal that disappeared under the overpass.
~~~

Miller pointed to the patrol officer. "You stay along the shoulder and work down. Anything you see, don't touch it. Call it."

"Yes, sir."

Miller turned to JP. "Stay where I can see you."

JP gave a noncommittal nod and started down the slope anyway, careful with his footing. The dirt was dry and summer-loose. No recent rain to blur or wash anything away. That mattered.

He moved diagonally, eyes trained on what didn't belong—a crushed cup, a broken bottle, and fast-food debris.

Then he saw the strap. It was half-hidden in the brush, navy blue nylon torn clean through, the break too sharp to be from wear. JP stopped moving and raised his hand. "Detective," he called.

Miller climbed up from lower on the slope, boots slipping slightly, and crouched beside the strap without touching it.

"It looks like it's from a backpack," JP said quietly.

Miller pulled on gloves, picked up the strap, and examined the stitching and the tear. "It looks like a hard pull as opposed to something dropped or something taken." He bagged and pocketed the potential evidence.

JP pulled out his phone and stepped away a few yards. Miller stayed put, staring at the drainage path that ran darker beneath the overpass. JP could feel it in his chest, not panic or fear, but the quiet certainty that whatever had happened here hadn't ended quickly. He hoped it hadn't been Mateo's life.

"We found something," JP spoke low into the phone.

"What?" Sabre asked.

"A torn backpack strap near the last ping," JP continued. "It looks like it was ripped."

"What color is it?"

"Navy blue."

"I called Polinsky and got a description of Mateo's clothes. He wore a black sweatshirt, blue jeans, lime green shoes, and carried a navy-blue backpack."

"So, the strap could be his."

"Any word on the vehicle?"

"No. And the company is still not answering. I'll keep you posted." JP hung up.

Miller's expression tightened. "What was he wearing?"

JP's head snapped up, then he repeated the description from Sabre.

Miller glanced back toward the strap. "Navy-blue backpack."

"It's a common color and doesn't prove it's Mateo's," JP said.

"No," Miller agreed. "But it doesn't help us pretend it's nothing either."

The patrol officer called to them from a distance. "I've got something else." He was near the drainage access.

JP didn't wait.

Neither did Miller.

The sun still hung above the freeway, bright and indifferent, as they moved toward the darker stretch beneath the overpass, where the daylight thinned, and whatever else had been left behind waited to be found.

Chapter 4

Monday evening, 5:29 pm

The canal smelled like wet concrete and oil, even though it hadn't rained in weeks.

JP moved carefully down the slope beneath the overpass, the ground dry and gritty under his boots. The evening sun spilled in at an angle, illuminating the canal's edge in long, pale bands before disappearing into shadow. It would be dark soon.

The patrol officer stood several yards ahead, rigid. "Right there." He pointed at something deeper in the shadow. "I didn't touch it."

JP followed the line of sight and felt a tightening in his chest. Not panic. Not yet. Just the steady awareness that this was no longer a routine search.

A shoe lay near the edge of the canal. It looked to be about a size nine, a teenager's bright green sneaker.

JP walked over to it. The fabric was dusty but intact. There were no scuffs, no broken brush, nothing that suggested a frantic run.

"The lace was loose, but that doesn't mean much. So many of these kids wear them untied."

"That's true." Miller crouched nearby, careful not to disturb anything. "Is there just one shoe?"

"Yes, sir," the officer said. "I don't see the other."

Miller angled his flashlight so the beam cut into the shoe's interior. The opening was smeared with dark, dried blood.

JP exhaled slowly. "That's not from running."

Blood inside the shoe meant it had come off first. Or that Mateo hadn't been moving when he was hurt. Either way, it didn't match a stumble or a fall.

Miller, still crouched, took photographs, marked the location, then called for the tech team. "We need to search this whole area."

JP stepped back and pulled out his phone.

Sabre answered on the first ring.

"We found a green tennis shoe," JP said. He didn't soften his voice. Sabre didn't need that.

"That's what he was wearing."

JP looked back at the shoe. "There's blood inside it," he said. "Not on the outside."

Another pause. Longer this time. "That doesn't sound good," Sabre said.

JP watched as the evidence techs arrived and began their quiet work. Photographs. Markers. Careful movements.

Up above them, traffic rolled on. Summer pretending nothing had changed.

Down below, with one green, bloody shoe, the truth was starting to surface, but it wasn't finished yet. And until it was, JP wasn't about to stop looking.

~~~

Monday evening, 5:59 pm

By the time the evidence tech cleared the canal, the sun had begun its slow slide west. JP stood near Miller's car while the detective logged his last photos. "Where to next?" JP asked.

Miller didn't hesitate. "The dashcam footage from the vehicle, if they have it."

They drove back toward the station, traffic thickening as commuters poured onto the roads. JP watched the traffic
~~~

and thought about how easy it was for a single vehicle to disappear in plain sight, just another box on wheels in a city full of them. A van like that, plain, forgettable, could move through all of it without anyone noticing. That was the problem.

At the station, Miller moved quickly. He made the calls that triggered the next tier of response, one to his watch commander, one to county contracts. Then he logged into his system and pulled the transport company's file.

"The county contract requires dashcam," Miller said, scrolling. "Forward-facing at minimum, but it has to be internal if the vehicle carries juveniles."

"Then it recorded something," JP said. "Even if they don't want us to see it."

Miller called the transport company again, and it went to voicemail. He ended the call and didn't bother to hide his irritation. "I'm done asking."

He didn't wait on the company. Instead, he went through the county. Ten minutes later, they were at a secure workstation in a contracts office down the hall. A county liaison logged them into the transport oversight portal. No fuss, no delay, just a quiet understanding that this had already crossed a line, and a child's life was at stake.

"Contractors are required to upload dashcam footage to the county server," the liaison said. "Usually end of shift. Sometimes sooner if there's an incident."

Miller didn't look up.

"This qualifies," he said.

The liaison nodded and pulled up the file list.

Vehicle 417 – Forward Cam – Partial Upload

The video came up grainy at first, then stabilized. The view was from a forward-facing dashcam, so they could see the freeway traffic. Nothing was out of place.

"Timestamp?" Miller asked.

The liaison clicked into the metadata. "The recording starts at 13:18," he said. "Release from Polinsky logged at 13:15."

"Run it."

They watched the vehicle merge into traffic onto the freeway. Normal speed. Normal spacing. No sudden movements.

The van took an exit. They watched it slow and then turn onto the frontage road.

"Pause," Miller said. The image froze. "Back it up two seconds."

The liaison did. "Go ahead. Run it."

The video continued for another minute, then jumped.

The timecode skipped forward. Not a glitch. A clean break.

JP leaned in. "That's not buffering."

"No," Miller said flatly. "That's a gap."

"How big?" JP asked.

The technician checked. "Eleven minutes."

Miller's jaw tightened. "That's not an accident."

"Nope. That's your window," JP said.

The video resumed, and the vehicle was moving again. No sudden jolt. No obvious incident. Just motion, as if nothing had happened.

"We need to watch to see where the van goes," JP said.

They continued to watch as the van drove onto the freeway and toward the transport company. Then it stopped.

"Is that it?" Miller asked.

"Someone just turned it off, just as they do at the end of the transport."

"Except this time, the delivery wasn't over." Miller stared at the screen. "What about internal footage?"

The technician hesitated. "There isn't any."

Miller didn't raise his voice. "Under this contract, with juveniles, internal cameras are required. There should be a separate upload."

The technician loaded up a second file marked Vehicle 417—Interior Cam. He clicked but got nothing. Just black. He tried again with the same result.

"Is it corrupted?" JP asked.

"The camera was never on," the technician said.

JP sat back.

Someone had intentionally not recorded any of the video evidence.

Miller stood. "Print everything. Logs, timestamps, access records. I want to know who touched this footage and when."

"Yes, sir."

Miller stepped away and pulled out his phone. JP knew who he was calling.

Sabre answered immediately, and the detective filled her in. After a pause, Miller said, "We don't have proof of what happened yet."

JP felt the weight of that word, *yet.*

Miller ended the call and looked at JP. "I'm authorizing a wider search radius."

"Good," JP said. "Because if Mateo's alive, he didn't walk far without a shoe."

Chapter 5

Monday night, 6:35 pm

On the frontage road, Miller parked farther down, and JP eased in behind him. This time, they were closer to a dirt turnout that looked like it had been used often enough to forget it wasn't official. The kind of place delivery trucks pulled into when drivers needed to check directions, or to wait, or maybe meet someone.

JP stepped out and automatically scanned the ground before he moved anywhere. Once he'd learned how much was written in dirt and dust, he'd stopped trusting clean pavement.

Miller walked up beside him. "This area wasn't part of the initial sweep."

JP nodded. "It wouldn't be. It's not obvious unless you're looking for a vehicle that didn't belong."

They moved slowly, parallel to the road, eyes down. The shoulder transitioned from cracked asphalt to packed dirt and gravel.

JP stopped. "Hold up."

Miller halted immediately.

JP crouched, careful not to step closer than he had to. In the dirt, just off the edge of the turnout, were tire impressions, clean enough to read if you knew what to look for. "These tracks aren't county."

Miller bent beside him. "You sure?"

"Yeah," JP said. "County fleet uses standard all-seasons. These are wider, have deeper tread, and are more aggressive."

Miller studied the pattern, then looked toward the road. "It could be a truck."

"Could be," JP said. "But not a county vehicle."

Miller stood and called it in. A half hour later, an evidence unit pulled up and taped off the area.

JP stayed where he was, letting the technicians do their work. Photographs. Measurements. Casts. The quiet, methodical process that turned dirt into fact.

"Are you thinking someone made a transfer?" Miller asked quietly.

JP didn't answer right away. He watched the tech press material into the impression, careful not to blur the edges.

"I'm thinking there were two vehicles," JP said finally. "Unit 417 pulls off. Something happens during that eleven-minute gap. Then both vehicles leave, maybe together, maybe not."

Miller's mouth tightened. "With the kid?"

"Yeah," JP said. "With Mateo."

Miller looked back toward the drainage canal, then farther down the frontage road where it curved out of sight. "What about the shoe and the backpack strap?"

"Maybe he tried to get away but didn't."

"And then he was turned over to the other vehicle, and they drove off. The gap gave them plenty of time." Miller exhaled slowly. "I'm calling it."

He didn't need to explain what he meant.

"Detective Miller," he said when his supervisor answered. "Based on evidence recovered, I'm reclassifying this as an abduction of a minor."

JP listened to the clipped exchange, the formal language that carried real weight once it was said out loud.

When Miller ended the call, he sent photographs of the tire marks and the area. "They're sending someone to evaluate this area. We'll keep looking here. Maybe we'll find other evidence."

"Or Mateo."

Soon, patrol officers arrived and spread out along the frontage road, methodical and quiet. Radios murmured. Boots scraped. The tone of the search had shifted, no longer hopeful, but not yet hopeless.

JP stayed near the canal.

The K-9 unit worked the scent from the green shoe. The dog moved steadily at first, nose low, tail level, then slowed as it reached the darker stretch past the overpass. The handler coaxed gently. The dog circled once, then pulled hard toward the canal wall.

JP followed with Miller close behind.

"What've you got?" Miller asked.

The dog strained toward a narrow section where the canal dipped lower, partially hidden by a bend in the concrete. The handler followed, flashlight cutting through shadow.

And then JP saw him. At first, it didn't register as a person. Just a shape where a shape didn't belong. A dark bundle pressed against the canal wall, half in shadow.

JP moved fast but carefully, heart hammering hard enough to feel it in his throat. "We've got the kid," he called out.

Miller was beside him in seconds.

Mateo Alvarez lay on his side, knees drawn up, one arm twisted beneath him. His face was bruised, lips split, and one eye swollen nearly shut. Dried blood streaked his temple. His shirt was rumpled and filthy, his chest barely rising with shallow, uneven breaths.

"Mateo." JP dropped to one knee. "Hey. Mateo."

The boy didn't respond. JP reached out, hovering before touching, then gently pressed two fingers to the side of Mateo's neck.

"He has a pulse," JP said. "It's weak, but it's there."

Miller was already on his radio. "We have the juvenile. Alive. Repeat, juvenile located, alive but critical. We need medics at the drainage canal under Valencia, now."

The word *alive* landed like a physical force. JP swallowed and leaned closer. "Stay with us, kid," he said quietly. "You did the hard part."

Mateo's eyelids fluttered. His lips moved, but no sound came out.

JP felt something tighten hard in his chest.

"Don't move him," the K-9 handler said, already backing away to give space. "Let medical do it."

"I know." JP stayed calm even as his hands shook.

Sirens cut through the steady roar of freeway traffic above them, close, urgent, growing louder by the second.

JP pulled out his phone and called Sabre. "We found him."

A sharp intake of breath on the other end. "Alive?"

"Yes," JP said. "Barely, but yes."

For a moment, Sabre didn't speak. JP could hear her breathing, controlled but unsteady.

"Where are you?" she asked.

"Drainage canal near the frontage road," JP said. "The medics are coming."

"Let me know where they take him," Sabre said.

"I will." JP ended the call as paramedics rushed in, equipment clattering, voices tight and professional. They worked quickly, cutting away fabric, checking vitals, fitting an oxygen mask over Mateo's mouth and nose.

JP stood back, hands clenched at his sides.

"Blood pressure's low," one medic said. "He's been down a while."

They lifted Mateo onto a stretcher, securing him carefully, shielding his face from the jostle as they moved.

As the stretcher disappeared up the embankment toward the waiting ambulance, JP finally let himself breathe. Mateo

Alvarez had been taken and hurt. But he was alive. And that changed everything.

Chapter 6

Monday night, 9:22 pm

The hospital smelled like antiseptic and coffee that lingered from the cafeteria that had just closed. Sabre stood inside the sliding doors and forced herself to breathe before moving forward. She'd learned long ago that hospitals had their own gravity. Once you stepped in, time bent, minutes stretched, and news landed harder.

JP stood near the elevators, jacket still on, hands loose at his side. "They've got him stabilized," he said quietly.

"That's something," Sabre said.

She hadn't believed it when he first told her, not fully. She believed it now because she could feel it, because the fear had shifted shape. This wasn't the hollow terror of not knowing where a child was. This was the sharp, focused dread of knowing where he was and how bad it might be.

They took the elevator up together without speaking. The ICU doors were locked, but a nurse buzzed them through after checking their IDs. The hallway beyond was dimmer, quieter.

Miller was already there, standing near the nurses' counter, speaking to a doctor in blue scrubs. He turned when he saw Sabre.

"He's unconscious," the doctor was saying. "We don't know yet if it's from head trauma, drugs, or both. Probably a combination."

"What drugs?" Sabre asked.

Miller cut in to introduce them. "This is Sabre Brown, Mateo's attorney, and her investigator, JP Torn."

The doctor glanced at them and nodded. "We have a preliminary tox screen that shows sedatives in his system. They don't appear to be recreational levels."

"So, someone gave them to him," Sabre said.

"That's the most likely explanation," the doctor said. "We're running a full panel. We'll know more soon."

"Is he stable?" Sabre asked.

"For now," the doctor said. "But he's not waking up yet."

Sabre nodded. She'd been bracing for that.

"Can we see him?" JP asked.

The doctor hesitated. "One at a time. Briefly."

Sabre went first. Mateo seemed smaller than she remembered. He was wrapped in white sheets, wires and tubes mapped across his body with clinical precision. An oxygen mask covered his mouth and nose. One eye was swollen and bruised dark. His hair was matted near his temple, where dried blood still clung despite someone's attempt to clean it.

Sabre stopped just inside the entry. She had stood beside children like this before far too often. Each time it stripped something away that never quite came back. She moved closer and rested her hand lightly on the bed's rail. She didn't touch the boy. She never touched without permission, not even now.

"You did nothing wrong," she said quietly. The reassurance was a habit, but it mattered. "None of this is on you."

Mateo didn't stir.

Beside her, the machines breathed and beeped, indifferent to words.

When Sabre stepped back into the hall, JP was talking with Miller.

"I'll have an officer posted," Miller said. "And the staff knows not to release information."

"Good," Sabre said. "How soon?"

"Already ordered. Someone should be here shortly. I'll stay until then."

A nurse approached, clipboard tucked against her chest. "We were told to collect his clothing," she said. "For evidence."

"That's right," Miller said. "Make sure each item is bagged separately. His shoe, the backpack remnants, everything. We need to preserve chain of custody."

The nurse blinked, then nodded. "Of course." This was obviously not her first victim.

Sabre turned to Miller. "Please get me copies of the tox results. And I want written confirmation that the county had custody of Mateo from log-out to discovery," Sabre added.

"You already know they didn't." Miller studied her face. "You're already thinking about liability."

"I'm thinking about responsibility," Sabre countered. "Someone will try to frame this as an overdose or a runaway who made bad choices. I won't let that start here."

Sabre leaned against the wall for the first time since she'd arrived. The adrenaline was wearing thin now, leaving something heavier behind.

"He's alive," JP said gently.

But alive wasn't the same as safe. And it wasn't the same as justice. Somewhere between Polinsky and this hospital bed, someone had decided Mateo Alvarez was expendable. Or invisible. Or both.

Sabre pushed off the wall and straightened her shoulders. "They tried to make him disappear," she said. "They failed."

Miller met her eyes. "Now we figure out who thought they could. In order to do that, I need to know everything you know about this young man starting with who would want to kidnap this kid?"

She glanced toward Mateo's room, then back at Miller. "There's history."

"There always is," Miller replied.

Sabre shifted slightly. "This isn't his first time in the system."

Miller pulled out a small notebook. "Why was he in?"

"Let's step out of the hallway just in case he can hear us."

"Good idea."

They walked to the first waiting room and sat back in a corner. There were only two people at the other end, and they seemed to be caught up in their own issues.

"He came into the system because of neglect," Sabre said. "His mother has a substance abuse history, meth, mostly. She has some theft charges and probation violations. She got him back once after a clean stretch, but it didn't hold."

"Where is she now?"

"She went back into custody last fall, but the social worker said she was recently released. She has made no attempt to see Mateo."

Miller scribbled something down. "Maybe she has decided to get him back on her own this time."

"That's possible."

"And you said the father may be deceased?"

"That's the word on the street."

Miller looked up. "That usually means there's a story. Let's hear it."

Sabre took a breath. "Rafael Alvarez is self-proclaimed gang affiliated. Long record—assault, weapons, narcotics, domestic abuse. Not someone the court was ever going to hand a child to."

"Did he try?"

"Twice."

"And?"

"Denied both times," she said. "He couldn't stay clean. Couldn't stay out of trouble. Couldn't show stability."

Miller nodded. "And then he disappeared?"

"About four years ago. No body. No confirmed death. Just... gone."

Miller leaned back slightly, processing.

"And the mother tells the kid he's dead."

"Yes. She told everyone that."

"Were there any threats from the father regarding custody?"

Sabre nodded once. "On at least two occasions he told the court he'd take the kid and run."

Miller's eyes lifted. "When?"

"The second custody attempt several years ago."

"And nobody followed up on that?"

"They did," Sabre said. "Then he disappeared. And in all fairness, he made threats to lots of people—social workers, judges, cops, his attorney, me."

The couple at the other end of the room left.

"Did he carry out any of them?"

"Actually, he did. At least we think he did. A social worker had her car demolished and then he'd whisper things to her about it that no one else could hear."

Miller closed his notebook. "Gang ties," he said. "History of violence. Threat to abduct the kid. Then the kid goes missing."

Sabre met his eyes. "It fits."

"If he's alive," Miller said, almost to himself, "this would be the way to do it. Quick grab. No witnesses. No ransom."

Sabre felt tightening in her chest. "He's not a fit parent."

"That's not usually what stops them."

"But why would he drug him, beat him up, and leave him to die?"

"I can think of lots of reasons. Like maybe the kid didn't want to go, and that set him off. Maybe he hired someone to do the job, and Mateo fought them. Who knows?"

Miller slipped the notebook back into his pocket. "I'll start with Rafael Alvarez. We'll see if he ever really went away. And I'll find out where the mother is. More often than not, these cases turn out to be someone very close to home."

Chapter 7

Tuesday morning, 8:05 am

The transport yard looked different in early daylight. JP didn't like the company. It wasn't personal; he wouldn't like any company that moved kids and hid when something went wrong.

He parked across the street this time instead of pulling up to the gate. He sat for a moment with the engine off, watching the place wake up around him; roll-up doors halfway open, a delivery truck idling, someone inside laughing at something.

Yesterday, the silence had felt intentional. Today, the noise felt performative.

When the office lights came on, he crossed the street and walked up to the door. It was unlocked now. A small bell jingled when he pushed it open.

A forty-something woman sat behind the front desk, reading glasses perched low on her nose. She looked up, startled. "Yes?"

"I'm looking for someone," he said.

She gave him an amused look. "Isn't everyone?"

JP flashed his private investigator's badge. "I'm looking for information about one of your drivers."

Her shoulders stiffened. "Which one?"

"The one who drove unit 417 yesterday afternoon," JP said.

She hesitated. "That's Western Youth Transport," she said, as if JP might have wandered into the wrong office by accident. "We contract out, but we manage the logs."

"I know," JP said. "Who was driving it?"

She adjusted her glasses. "Why?"

"A fifteen-year-old boy didn't arrive at his placement," JP said. "You may have heard. I assume your company was notified."

Her mouth tightened. "I heard something."

JP waited. Silence did the work for him.

"I left early yesterday," she said finally. "I wasn't feeling well."

"What time?" JP asked.

"About two-thirty," she said. "Maybe a little after."

"Before the vehicle was supposed to return?" JP asked.

"Yes," she said quickly. "But that's not unusual. We don't wait for every unit to check back in."

JP nodded. "Who relieved you?"

"No one," she said. "It was a light day."

"And you haven't heard from the driver?"

She shook her head. "No. He hasn't been in this morning, either."

"What's his name?" JP asked.

She reached for a clipboard, flipped through a few pages, then slid it toward him. "Luis Mendoza. He's a contract driver."

JP verified the name without touching the clipboard. "Has anyone talked to him since yesterday?"

"I called his cell," the receptionist said. "I left a message but got no response."

"When did you call?" JP asked.

"This morning. As soon as I got in."

"What time did you get in?"

"Seven," she said. "Maybe a few minutes after."

"What kind of a vehicle is unit 417?"

"A white minivan. That's mostly what is used for that kind of transport."

"Has it been returned?" JP asked.

Her lips pressed together. "It's still not back."

"You understand how that looks," he said.

"I do," she said quietly. "And I don't like it."

JP studied her for a moment. She wasn't defensive, or evasive, but she looked tired. Worn in the way people got when they realized they'd been standing too close to something dangerous.

"Did anything unusual happen yesterday?" JP asked. "Any schedule changes? Any late assignments?"

She thought for a moment. "The route was normal, but the pickup was added late."

"How late?"

"It was after lunch. And it was marked urgent."

"By who?" JP asked.

She shook her head. "I don't know. That came from Operations."

"Who would I talk to there?"

She looked at her computer, clicked a few things, and said, "Try Carl. Here's the number." She wrote it down on a sticky note and handed it to JP.

"Thank you." He paused. "It would be a big help if I could get a little more information about the driver."

"I can't give you—"

JP cut her off, his voice calm. "I'm not asking for anything sealed. I just want what you already have in case someone comes looking later."

She hesitated. Then she stood. "Hold on."

JP watched her disappear into the back office. He didn't move, didn't touch anything. People noticed that.

She returned with a thin folder and set it on the counter without opening it. "This is all I can give you. Onboarding paperwork and a copy of Mendoza's ID. Contact info too."

JP didn't open it yet. "That's enough."

"You didn't get it from me," she said.

JP met her eyes. "You don't want to be the last one holding the file when someone asks why no one looked."

She swallowed and nodded.

"Thank you." JP handed her his card. "If you hear from Mendoza, or if he shows up, please call me. If you're not comfortable with that, then call the police immediately."

"I will," she said. "I promise."

JP picked up the folder, stepped back toward the door, then paused. "One more thing," he said. "Did anyone access the vehicle logs after you left?"

She frowned. "Not that I know of. But I wasn't here, and I don't really know how they schedule. I mostly just answer phones."

JP gave her a tight smile and walked out. He leaned against his truck and flipped open the folder.

Luis Mendoza. Contract driver. ID photo clipped to the inside cover.

JP studied the face. It was unremarkable, which would make him harder to pick out of a crowd.

Emergency Contact: Rosalia Mendoza, Sister. The address was listed but no phone number. *That seemed odd.*

JP exhaled slowly. Mendoza's last known address was an apartment off Imperial. He closed the folder. This guy wasn't a ghost. He was a man who had been hired, trusted, and handed a child. And now, everyone was pretending they didn't know where he'd gone.

Chapter 8

Tuesday morning

JP drove to Imperial with the address note folded in his pocket. He didn't rely on GPS for the last few blocks. He liked to see neighborhoods arrive, to feel the shift when an area stopped being commercial and started being lived in. Mendoza's address sat right on that line, too close to traffic to be private, too tucked away to draw attention.

The apartment complex was older than it looked and more worn than it admitted, evidenced by three stories of stucco with hairline cracks running like fault lines and railings patched instead of replaced.

JP parked near the back, engine off, windows down. There was no police tape and no activity that suggested anyone had come looking yet.

He got out and walked the perimeter first, slow and casual, like a man deciding whether this was somewhere he wanted to live. Trash bins were full but not overflowing. Mailboxes were dented but not pried open. And no sign of broken glass. Mendoza hadn't fled in panic.

JP climbed the stairs to the second floor and stopped in front of the number from the file. He listened for a moment and heard nothing. He knocked once, firm but polite. No answer. He waited a full ten seconds and knocked again. Still nothing.

JP tried the knob. It was unlocked. He leaned in, peering through the crack as he eased the door open just enough to glance around. The place wasn't ransacked. It wasn't abandoned either.

A mattress lay directly on the floor, stripped but not gone. Boxes lined one wall, half-packed, labeled in marker, like someone who hadn't expected to leave so soon but had been ready if necessary. Clothes folded into stacks instead of hanging in a closet. There were no photos and no personal decorations. A life designed to be moved.

JP closed the door and stepped back. He knocked on the neighboring unit. A woman answered, safety chain still latched, her eyes cautious but curious.

"Hi," JP said. "I'm looking for Luis. He lives next door."

Her expression changed, not to confusion, but more like recognition. "He moved out," she said.

"When?" JP asked.

"Yesterday," she said. "It seemed real quick. I mean, he hadn't mentioned moving."

"So, you don't know where he was going?"

She shook her head. "No. But someone picked him up."

"Someone he knew or like an Uber?" JP asked.

She hesitated. "It was a woman he seemed to know. I would guess family, but I can't be sure. I know he has a sister, but I've never seen her before. She looked worried. I could tell."

"How?"

"She was trying to get him out of here fast."

"What did she look like?"

"She had pink hair. Other than that, I couldn't tell you."

That ought to narrow the search, JP thought. He nodded. "Thank you."

He stepped back and leaned against the railing, looking down into the parking lot.

Mendoza hadn't vanished on his own. Someone had gone to him, someone who already knew where to find him and didn't need to ask questions.

Back in his truck, he opened Mendoza's file to the emergency contact: *Rosalia Mendoza.* JP started the engine and pulled out onto Imperial, already narrowing the field. Family didn't usually hide people forever. They just bought them time.

~~~

The sister's house sat at the end of a short block that didn't go anywhere important. JP parked across the street and cut the engine. He took a moment to let the neighborhood settle into him, the sound of a lawn sprinkler ticking somewhere down the block, a screen door slamming two houses over, a radio playing faintly through an open window. Everything seemed normal.

The small duplex was tidy in the way people kept things when they expected to be back. Curtains were open, the porch was swept, and a child's plastic tricycle leaned against the railing like it had been abandoned mid-thought.

JP watched the front door. Ten minutes passed without any action. He got out and walked the length of the block, slow and unremarkable. There was no movement at the windows, no cars pulling in or out, and no neighbors paying him any attention. That mattered too.

JP crossed back to his truck and leaned against the hood, checking the address again, even though he already knew it was right. He looked for signs of a sudden departure—trash pulled early, mail piled up, lights left on—but found none. Whoever lived here hadn't fled. They'd just stepped out.

JP waited another fifteen minutes. A delivery truck rolled by. A woman walked her dog past him without a second glance. Somewhere behind the duplex, a gate creaked and settled, but still nothing at Rosalia's.
~~~

JP exhaled and rubbed the back of his neck. If Rosalia Mendoza had picked up her brother, he didn't appear to be in her home right now. But that didn't mean this place wasn't important. People came back to what they trusted.

JP didn't knock. He wasn't ready to tip his hand yet.

He got back into his truck, pulled away from the curb, and drove on. He'd be back.

Chapter 9

Tuesday morning

Sabre finished her morning calendar and stepped into a quiet corner outside the courtroom. She pulled out her phone and dialed.

"Rady Children's Hospital."

"This is Sabre Brown," she said. "I'm counsel for Mateo Alvarez. I'm calling for an update."

"One moment."

A click. A transfer. "ICU."

"Hi, I'm calling about Mateo Alvarez."

"He's stable," the nurse said. "Still under sedation."

Sabre leaned lightly against the wall. "Is he conscious at all?"

"No," the nurse said. "Not yet. They're keeping him sedated while they monitor swelling and pain."

Sabre nodded, absorbing it. "Any change since admission?"

"Stable is good," the nurse said. "No setbacks."

Sabre let out a quiet breath. "Okay," she said. "Thank you."

She ended the call, walked to her car, and drove to Polinsky Receiving Home.

~~~

Polinsky looked the same as always. Too clean. Too bright. The kind of institutional calm that existed because chaos had been scrubbed out of sight, not because it didn't happen.
~~~

Sabre signed in at the front desk, clipped on a visitor badge, and waited while the security officer called upstairs.

She didn't sit. Waiting patiently made things feel optional. This wasn't.

A supervisor met her at the elevator. Marisol Palmer was in her early thirties, with hair pulled back tight and tired eyes. "Hey, Sabre. I heard Mateo was found."

"Alive," Sabre said. "Barely."

Marisol exhaled. "Thank God."

Sabre didn't respond. Gratitude came later, after truth.

They walked together down a hall Sabre knew by heart. Some doors were shut, some half-open. Voices were low, and somewhere a television played cartoons.

"Do you remember the driver?" Sabre asked. "What he looked like?"

The social worker hesitated, thinking it through instead of answering too quickly.

"Yeah, a little," she said. "He wasn't anyone I recognized. Not one of the regular county drivers."

"What do you remember?"

"He was average," she said. "Maybe mid-thirties, medium height. He was Hispanic. He had dark hair. It was short but not styled."

"What about his build?"

"He was lean, like someone who's on his feet a lot. Not bulky."

Sabre nodded. "Anything else stand out?"

The social worker frowned slightly. "He seemed nervous," she said. "Not shaking or anything, but distracted, like he didn't want to be here long."

Sabre's eyes sharpened. "How so?"

"He didn't make much eye contact," she said. "He kept looking past me, toward the lot. I don't know. It just felt off."

"What was he wearing?"

"Work clothes. A plain shirt. I think it had a logo on it, but I didn't catch what it said."

"Did he have facial hair?"

"A little bit," she said. "Like he hadn't shaved that morning."

Sabre nodded slowly. "Would you recognize him again?"

The social worker hesitated. "If I saw him in person, maybe."

"That helps. And I need to know everything Mateo did and said before he left here," Sabre said. "I don't need what's in the file. I need what you remember."

Marisol nodded. "I figured."

They stepped into a small conference room. Marisol closed the door behind them.

"When did you last see Mateo?" Sabre asked.

"As he was picked up," Marisol said. "He was sitting by the lockers, like he always did."

"Alone?"

"Mostly," Marisol said. "There were other kids around, but Mateo kept to himself."

Sabre set her file on the table but didn't open it. "Did he say anything?"

Marisol hesitated.

"That wasn't a no," Sabre gently prodded.

"He asked if his transfer was still happening."

"That's not unusual," Sabre said.

"No. But he asked it twice."

Sabre felt something tighten. "What did he say the second time?"

Marisol looked down at her hands. "He said, 'I thought I wasn't supposed to be going yet.'"

Sabre stayed very still. "Those were his words?"

"Yes."

"Did you ask what he meant?"

"I did," Marisol said. "He shrugged and said he might be confused."

Sabre nodded. "What else?"

Marisol took a breath. "There was a delay in the paperwork. Not long, but noticeable."

"What kind of delay?"

"The transfer order was already in the system, but there was an update."

"An update to what?"

"The child name field," Marisol said quietly.

Sabre didn't blink. "Whose name?"

Marisol hesitated again, longer this time.

"I don't remember the name," she said. "I remember thinking it was strange because it changed back."

Sabre felt her pulse pick up. "Changed back from what?"

"From a different youth," Marisol said. "The other name flashed on the screen for just a second."

Sabre sat back. "Do you know who made the change?"

Marisol shook her head. "No. Those edits come from the county side. We don't have permission to make them."

"Do you have access logs?" Sabre asked.

"Yes. But I didn't pull them."

"I'll need a copy of the original transfer request and the revision."

Marisol swallowed. "Sabre... if someone made a mistake—"

"This wasn't a mistake." Sabre's voice had gone cold. "Mistakes don't change themselves back."

Marisol nodded slowly. "There's something else."

Sabre waited.

"Mateo was watching the transport van," Marisol said. "Not like the other kids. He wasn't scared. He was... focused."

"Focused how?" Sabre asked.

"Like he recognized it," Marisol said. "Or something about it."

Sabre closed her eyes for a brief second. "What did he say?"

"He asked who else had gone out in that van recently. I told him I didn't know."

"Did you?" Sabre asked.

Marisol hesitated. "Not officially."

Sabre stood. "Marisol, I'm going to be very clear. A child was nearly killed. If there is anything else you remember, anything, you need to tell me now."

"I can't think of anything that will help."

"Did he say anything else before he left?"

"When the van pulled up, he mentioned something about another kid riding in that same van."

"Who was the kid?"

"It was a child who rode in that van a week ago," Marisol said.

"What is his name?"

Marisol shook her head. "I can't give it to you."

Sabre didn't hide her frustration. "Why not?"

"Because that child is under active juvenile probation supervision," Marisol said. "And if I give you his name without clearance, I violate confidentiality, and I lose my job. You know that."

Sabre considered that. It wasn't fear. It was procedure. "Then give me something I can lawfully work with," Sabre said. "Age. Case type. Anything."

Marisol nodded. "He's older than Mateo. Mid-teens. Delinquency case, not dependency. And he's been moved more than once in the last month." She took a breath. "Mateo was just saying that it was the same van. I don't know how that can help."

"It probably won't, but we don't know that. It's worth checking." Sabre opened the door. "Pull the access logs. Preserve everything before someone tries to *clean up* the system."

"Will do."

Chapter 10

Tuesday morning

Parents were always the first place to look when a child had been abducted.

Miller sat at his desk, the glow of his monitor flattening everything into lines and facts. Mateo Alvarez. Fifteen. Dependency case. Prior removal. Returned once. Removed again.

He clicked into the mother's file. Brandy Alvarez. Recent release, three weeks. He pulled up her extensive history, which included narcotics, possession, theft, and probation violations. Nothing was surprising. What mattered was what she'd done since she got out.

He ran her through local contacts. There was a note from patrol. *Frequenting prior residence area. Seen on Euclid. Known associates still active.*

Miller frowned. People who were trying to get their kids back didn't usually go back to the same streets that cost them those kids in the first place. On the other hand, people also went back to what they knew. That didn't make them guilty. It just made them suspect.

He picked up the phone. "Get me a unit on Euclid," he said. "I want eyes on Brandy Alvarez. If she's there, bring her in."

~~~

An hour later, Brandy Alvarez was in Interview Room Two. Miller watched her through the glass before going in.
~~~

She was in her early thirties. The hard years showed. Her hair was pulled back tight like she was trying to hold something together that didn't want to stay that way. Her posture was defensive but not scared. That mattered.

He stepped inside. "Brandy Alvarez," he said, taking the seat across from her.

She looked up immediately. "You're the detective?"

"I am."

"Where's my son?"

Miller held her gaze. "He's still in the hospital."

Her eyes searched his face, looking for something he wasn't giving her. "You think I took him," she said.

"Did you?"

"No."

"Where were you yesterday between one and three in the afternoon?"

"At my friend's house. Franny Kirk. She lives in my apartment complex. We had lunch together."

"At her house?"

"Yes."

"What did you eat?" Miller asked.

"Chicken sandwich."

Miller nodded like he was picturing it. "What time did you get there?"

"A little before one. Maybe twelve-thirty."

"How long did you stay?"

Brandy looked up, like she was thinking. "Until about three or four."

"Was anyone else there?"

"No. Just Franny."

"I have a few other questions."

She exhaled sharply but didn't argue.

"Three weeks out," he said. "That's how long you've been out of custody?"

"Yeah."

"You went straight back to your old neighborhood."

"I know people there," she said. "That's not a crime."

"No. It's not." He paused. "Have you seen Mateo since you got out?"

Her expression shifted. "No."

"Talked to him?"

"No."

"Have you made any plans to see him?"

Her jaw tightened. "I was trying to," she said. "The system doesn't make that easy."

"Have you made any attempt to reach the social worker?"

"They make it hard." She studied him now, a little less defensive, a little more uncertain. "You think I'd hurt him?"

"I know," he said carefully, "you've had him removed from your custody before. I think you know how this system works. And I think if you wanted to get around it, you'd know how."

She shook her head immediately. "No," she said. "It's not like that."

He watched her. There didn't appear to be panic or calculation in her voice. Anger, yes, and frustration, but not control. Still, that didn't clear her. She could be a good liar. But it didn't convict her either.

"Have you been in contact with anyone who might know what happened to him?" Miller asked.

"No."

"What about Mateo's father?"

"What about him? He's dead."

"How do you know that?"

"Everyone knows."

"How did he die?"

"Someone killed him."

"Who?"

"I don't know. I just heard he got killed. That's all I know."

Miller moved on. "Do you know of anyone from your past who might think they're helping you by taking your son?"

She hesitated.

Miller caught it.

"I know people," she said. "That doesn't mean anything."

"It might," Miller said.

Her shoulders tightened again.

"You people did this," she said. "You moved him, and he got hurt."

"That's not what happened," Miller said evenly.

"That's exactly what happened," she shot back. "The county takes kids, moves them around, and then when something goes wrong, you start pointing fingers." Her voice cracked slightly at the end.

Miller let her talk.

"If my son is hurt," she continued, "if something happened to him because of this—"

"Ms. Alvarez, your son *is* hurt. He's in the hospital, which you would know if you made any attempt to see him."

She leaned forward, eyes sharp again. "I'm getting a lawyer," she said. "And I'm suing the county."

"That's your prerogative."

She sat back, arms crossed, breathing hard.

Miller stood.

"You should've made sure he got where he was going," she said.

He didn't respond to that. He stepped out of the room and closed the door behind him. In the hallway, Miller paused. Brandy didn't feel like the driver of this. But she didn't feel clean either. Too many ties. Too many people around her who could step in, thinking they were doing her a favor, or something worse.

He pulled out his phone. "Run everyone she's been in contact with since release," he said. "I want names, numbers, locations."

He ended the call and glanced back at the interview room. Brandy Alvarez sat alone, staring at the table. Angry. Frustrated. And maybe telling the truth, but he wasn't sure she was capable of that.

Chapter 11

Tuesday late morning

By the time he reached the freeway, JP was dialing Carl. If the receptionist had told him the truth, and JP believed she had, then the answers he needed were one layer deeper, with someone who understood how the routes actually worked.

"This is Carl," a man answered. "Operations."

"This is JP Torn," JP said. "I'm a private investigator working with an attorney on a juvenile case."

There was a pause. Probably not resistance, but calculation.

"What do you need?"

"I need to know how driver substitutions work," JP said. "Specifically, Unit 417."

Another pause, shorter this time.

"Okay," Carl said. "I can walk you through that."

"Thanks. Start with who was supposed to drive the unit."

"The regular driver is Ken Gibson. He's been with us a while. He has a clean record. He would normally have had that route, but he called in sick late morning, sometime before noon."

"Who filled in?" JP asked.

"Luis Mendoza," Carl said. "He was on call."

"Did you assign him?" JP asked.

"No," Carl said. "He volunteered as soon as the request went out. He said he was nearby and available. He'd driven that route before."

"How often?" JP asked.

"Once. A few weeks back."

"The same vehicle?" JP asked.

"Yes," Carl said. "Unit 417. We use a lot of the same vehicles for the same routes. It makes the paperwork easier."

JP felt the pieces line up quietly, the way they did right before things got ugly. "So, Mendoza wasn't scheduled. He stepped in."

"That's right," Carl said. "Which isn't unusual."

"It is if he wanted that particular route," JP said.

"That's true."

"So, whoever set this up told him to be ready, stay close, answer the phone, and take the run."

"That's what it looks like."

"Was there anything odd about the substitution?" JP asked.

Carl thought. "No supervisor sign-off. Just the standard checkbox."

"Who approved it?" JP asked.

"The system," Carl said. "If both drivers are cleared, it goes through."

"Meaning, no human review," JP said.

"That's correct," Carl said. "It's designed for efficiency."

JP nodded. Systems like that worked great until someone decided to exploit them. "Has Mendoza checked in since yesterday?" JP asked.

"No," Carl said. "He hasn't answered his phone, and he didn't report this morning."

"And the vehicle?" JP asked.

"Still missing. We reported it as soon as law enforcement started asking questions. We didn't know it was missing until then."

JP believed him. Carl sounded like a man who wanted this solved, not buried. "One more thing. Did Mendoza request that route, or just the shift?"

Carl was quiet for a second. "He asked about the route. Specifically."

JP closed his notebook. "Thanks. You've been helpful."

"I wish I could've stopped it," Carl said. "I'm sorry that kid got hurt."

After the call ended, JP sat for a moment, letting the facts settle. Luis Mendoza had volunteered for a specific route in a specific vehicle at a specific time. That wasn't opportunity. That was intent. And intent meant motive.

JP started making the kind of calls that didn't go through offices or dispatchers, calls that went to people who knew how to find someone who didn't want to be found.

Luis Mendoza had wanted that van. Now JP wanted him, and he knew where to start.

JP knew people who knew how to get information. He didn't ask how. He just knew it would be accurate. He sat at his desk, legal pad open, and made the first call without looking at the number. Muscle memory.

"Yeah?" a man said.

"Frank," JP said. "It's me."

A short laugh. "You only call when someone's gone sideways."

"Fair," JP said. "I'm looking for a driver. Contract work. Goes by Luis Mendoza."

"That his real name?" Frank asked.

"Real enough to pass paperwork," JP said. "Not real enough to show up when he's supposed to."

Frank hummed. "What did he do?"

"He pulled a transport van he wasn't scheduled for," JP said. "A kid ended up in the ICU."

The line went quiet. "Send me what you've got," Frank said.

JP texted over the basics: name, description, photo, phone number, vehicle assignment, and last known road corridor.

JP made the second call. "Winnie," JP said when the line picked up. "You still doing skip traces?"

"That depends," she said. "Is it someone who doesn't want to be found? Or someone pretending not to be found?"

"Both," JP said.

She laughed. "That's the fun kind. What's the angle?"

"He's an on-call transport driver," JP said. "He picked up a kid for delivery, but the child never made it to the house. He's a no-show today, and the vehicle is still missing."

"What about the kid?"

"He's in the ICU now."

"That's not right," she said. "Text me what you know."

JP did.

The third call went to a man who didn't answer on the first ring. Or the second. JP waited.

On the fourth ring, the call clicked through. "You've got ninety seconds," the voice said.

"Eddie," JP said. "I'm burning about thirty of those."

"Make it count."

"Looking for a guy who drives vans and doesn't like attention," JP said. "Might've crossed into your world by accident."

Eddie snorted. "Nobody crosses by accident."

"Fair," JP said. "The name he's using is Luis Mendoza."

Silence.

JP didn't push. Eddie hated being pushed.

"Lots of people use that name," Eddie said finally. "I've heard it used more than once for different people."

"How recently?"

"Last couple weeks," Eddie said. "In my world, someone uses a name and ID until it doesn't work anymore. That one's still kicking around."

"Any idea where Luis Mendoza sleeps?" JP asked.

Eddie laughed. "No one like that sleeps in one place."

"Any idea where he parks?" JP asked.

Another pause.

"There's a strip behind an auto body shop off Imperial," Eddie said. "People rotate vehicles there when they don't want them tied to an address."

"That's a start," JP said.

"Your ninety seconds are up. Send me a photo."

"Will do. I appreciate you," JP said.

The line went dead.

JP's phone buzzed with a text.

Frank: *The name's not clean. It gets used a lot by others. The license exists with a photo match, but last address doesn't. He's moved a lot, Arizona, Nevada, then here. No long stays. No credit trail worth a damn.*

JP: *Any associates?*

Frank: *One number keeps popping up. A woman. Not family. Calls spike when he's in transit. A lot of messaging and calls back and forth.*

JP: *Can you ID her?*

Frank: *Working on it.*

JP closed the phone and stood. He grabbed his jacket and keys. The auto body shop was a place to start.

~~~

The strip off Imperial looked the way Eddie said it would—quiet and convenient, the kind of place vehicles came to disappear without making a scene.

JP parked a block away and walked, hands loose, eyes on alert. The auto body shop was buzzing, its roll-up doors partway down and tagged with layers of old paint. Behind the building, a narrow service lane ran like an afterthought, cracked asphalt, weeds pushing through seams, no cameras that cared enough to be obvious.

He spotted the van halfway down the lane—white, older model, with a county-style body. But it wasn't marked.
~~~

JP slowed, taking it all in. The van could be the right one. It was the same size and had the same roof rack mounts as the others he'd seen at the transport yard.

The unit number was gone. The license plates were gone too, front and back.

JP stepped closer, careful not to touch. Where the unit number used to be, the paint was fresh enough to still catch the light. The plate mounts were bare, screws missing, edges clean. They'd been recently removed.

JP pulled out his phone and called Miller. "I may have found your transport van," JP said.

"Where?"

"Behind an auto body shop off Imperial," JP said. "It's a white van with no unit number and no plates. And it matches the body type of the company's other vehicles."

"I'm on my way," Miller said. "Don't touch anything."

"Wouldn't dream of it." JP stepped back and waited, watching the lane like someone who belonged there.

A few minutes later, Miller pulled in with a patrol unit behind him. Miller got out first, eyes already scanning. He circled the van once, then again more slowly. The detective crouched near the rear quarter panel and ran his fingers just shy of the dent.

"This matches," Miller said. "There was damage reported on this vehicle from last month." Miller straightened and looked at him. "How'd you find it?"

"I went looking."

"That's not an answer," Miller said.

JP smiled faintly. "It's the one you're getting."

Miller studied him for a moment. "Do you have a source?"

"Even a blind hog finds an acorn now and then."

Miller sighed. "You're not going to tell me, are you?"

"Not today."

Miller looked back at the van, already shifting gears. "The crime scene's mine now. And if you're right about this being 417... "

"Then you've got evidence," JP said. "And someone's running out of places to hide."

Miller nodded. "Are you going to stick around?"

JP was already backing away. "I've done my part."

Chapter 12

Tuesday late afternoon

The other child who had ridden in Unit 417 didn't take long to find. Sabre stood at the counter in the records office, the clerk clicking through screens with the kind of practiced indifference that came from seeing everything and reacting to none of it.

"Unit 417," Sabre said. "One week ago. It was a transport out of Polinsky."

The clerk typed. "Got it. The kid refused placement and ran."

Sabre felt a small tightening in her chest. "What's his name?"

The clerk angled the monitor. "David Nguyen. Sixteen."

Sabre wrote it down. "Where is he now?"

"Juvenile hall. He was picked up two days later for breaking and entering."

"Who is his attorney?"

"Eric Gunderson."

Sabre walked out and called Eric. "I need a favor."

"That depends," Eric said. "Is it going to ruin my afternoon or just complicate it?"

"Complicate," she said. "Five minutes with your client. David Nguyen."

"You're chasing something?"

"Yes." She gave him a quick synopsis of what was going on.

"Fine," he said. "I'll meet you there."

~~~

Juvenile hall was louder than the courthouse. Metal doors. Echoes. Voices bouncing off concrete.

Eric was already there when she arrived, leaning against the wall outside the interview room, sleeves rolled, tie loosened. He gave her a quick smile.

"You look like you're not here for a casual visit," he said.

"I'm not."

He pushed off the wall. "David's a runner," Eric said as they walked in. "Doesn't like rules. Doesn't like placements. Doesn't like much of anything."

"Does he like talking?"

Eric shrugged. "Depends who's asking."

They stepped into the room together. David came in a minute later, escorted by a deputy. He glanced at Eric, then Sabre, then back to Eric.

"What's this?" he asked.

"You're talking to her," Eric said. "I'm here if you need me."

David dropped into the chair, slouched, wary, but not hostile.

Sabre didn't waste time. "You were transported last week," she said. "From Polinsky."

His eyes flickered. "Yeah."

"And you ran?"

A faint smirk. "I didn't like where they were sending me."

"Please walk me through it," Sabre said. "From pickup to when you got out."

David shrugged. "They picked me up. Drove for a while. Stopped at a light. I opened the door and bailed."

"That's it?"

"That's it."

"No stops before that?"

"No."

"No one met the van?"
~~~

"No."

Sabre leaned forward slightly. "Think about it. Was there any delay? Any reason the van would've slowed down before that light?"

David shook his head. "Just traffic."

"Did the driver say anything?"

"He yelled when I jumped," David said. "But he didn't chase me."

"Did you see him clearly?"

"Not really. I didn't care what he looked like."

Sabre held his gaze for a moment longer. "You're sure it was just you and the driver?"

"Yeah," he said. "Just me."

Eric, sitting beside him, gave the smallest nod. He believed him.

Sabre sat back. "Okay," she said.

David frowned slightly. "Is that it?"

"That's it."

He stood, already done with them. "Good luck," he muttered, probably not meaning it.

The deputy led him out.

Sabre thanked Eric and then replayed it all in her mind. One week ago, with the same van, same system, but nothing. There was no second man, no stop, no deviation. Marisol had been right. The lead she thought might break something open had gone nowhere.

~~~

It was time to take another approach. Sabre drove back to her office and decided to move forward with the assumption that the answer would be smaller than expected. People wanted reasons to be dramatic. The truth usually wasn't.

She sat at her desk with Mateo's file open and began with his history. What a child had been before something went wrong mattered more than what they'd been labeled afterward.
~~~

Mateo's record was thin, his parents, on the other hand, filled more than one folder. That alone told her something. He was fifteen years old, a dependent of juvenile court with multiple placements, none of which were catastrophic. He had no history of violence, no drug or gang indicators, no serious behavioral incidents, and no recent write-ups. Nor was he a kid who collected grudges.

She scanned school reports next. His grades were uneven but improving. Teachers described him as withdrawn but polite when engaged. No record of fights or suspensions. One note from a counselor stood out: Struggles to assert himself. Tends to avoid conflict.

That didn't scream retaliation.

Sabre called Mateo's last foster placement, Nancy Fermin, the one that had been disrupted most recently. The foster mother sounded tired, not defensive. "He was a good kid," the woman said. "He didn't cause trouble. I don't know why he'd run."

"He didn't run. I'm asking about conflict. Was anyone angry with him?"

"No," the woman said slowly. "If anything, he was the one who got pushed around."

"By whom?" Sabre asked.

"Other kids mostly," she said. "Nothing big. Some name-calling, but he ignored it."

Sabre wrote it down anyway. Small things mattered, until they didn't. "What about online?" she asked. "Social media, maybe?"

"He doesn't really use it," the foster mother said. "He didn't have a phone. He was a bit odd in that respect. He didn't really want one. I don't know of any social media accounts. If he had them, he didn't use them here. He wasn't much for the computer, only used it if he had to for homework."

Sabre thanked her, ended the call, and leaned back in her chair. No digital footprint meant no digital enemies.

She made two more calls, the first to the school administrator and then to the case aide. She got the same answers. Mateo didn't provoke. Mateo didn't retaliate. Mateo didn't escalate.

She pulled up juvenile incident reports in Mateo's last couple of zip codes. He didn't have a record, but she looked for anything that might possibly tie to him. She found nothing that suggested coincidence with intent.

Sabre rubbed her eyes and turned back to the file. If someone had wanted to hurt Mateo specifically, it should've shown up somewhere. But there was nothing loud enough to justify his sedation, assault, and abandonment.

She thought about the injuries again. The blood in the shoe. *What did it mean? Was it rage? Revenge? A plan gone wrong?*

She picked up Mateo's photo, one that had been taken a few months ago. The background was neutral, his shoulders slightly hunched, and his eyes were guarded. He was just a normal kid in the system. Not a kid who threatened anyone or cost any extra money. Had he somehow stood between someone and what they wanted?

Sabre closed the file. There were cases where motive jumped off the page, but this wasn't one of them. Which meant if Mateo had been taken on purpose, it wasn't because of who he was unless Miller's hunch was right and it was one of his parents.

But if it wasn't because of who he was—Sabre stopped herself. She wasn't ready to think what that implied. Not until she knew what JP had found on his end.

For now, she wrote one last line on her legal pad: *No obvious gain in hurting Mateo.* And under it: *Which makes the harm itself the question.*

She closed the file and turned off the lamp.

Somewhere in the ICU, Mateo Alvarez was still unconscious. And somewhere else, someone was probably hoping he never regained consciousness.

Chapter 13

Tuesday late afternoon

JP started where violence usually started, not with paperwork or court files, but with people who carried grudges long after they should. If someone had hurt Mateo Alvarez on purpose, the reason probably existed outside official records. Perhaps it was an argument, a debt, or a misunderstanding that grew teeth.

JP decided to drive around instead of calling. He learned more that way. The neighborhood around Mateo's last placement was quiet in the late afternoon, with stucco houses, sun-bleached lawns, and kids riding bikes. Too normal to hide anything big.

Sabre had spoken on the phone to the foster mother, Nancy Fermin. JP wanted to see what the neighbors had to say. He parked and walked up to the house next door to the Fermin's.

The woman who answered was in her sixties with sharp eyes and a guarded posture. She didn't smile, but she didn't shut the door either.

JP explained who he was, then said, "I'm asking about Mateo Alvarez. He's fifteen, and he lived next door until recently."

Her expression softened. "There's always lots of kids at that house. I know it's a foster home, so they come and go. Some are good, some not so much."

"What about Mateo? Did you know him?"

"Yeah, he was one of the quiet ones. Cute kid. Always polite. I didn't know him that well, but my granddaughter did. They were kind of friends." The woman abruptly called out, "Penny."

A young girl with soft curls came to the door. The grandmother explained who JP was and said, "Tell him what you know about Mateo."

"Like what?"

"Do you know of anyone who might've been angry with him?" JP asked.

The girl shook her head. "Not really. He wasn't the one who caused trouble."

"But he had trouble with someone?"

"Sort of."

"Tell me what happened."

She pointed down the street. "Some teenage boys live in that house. They're older and loud. They'd mess with Mateo sometimes."

"How?" JP asked.

"Calling him names. Taking his hat. That sort of thing," she said. "He mostly ignored them."

That tracked with what he had already heard. "Any fights?" JP asked.

"No," she said. "Except one time, he shoved one of them when the guy got too close. That was it."

"Did the kid get upset?" JP asked.

"He was embarrassed. I don't think he expected it."

JP's attention sharpened. "What's his name?"

"Dylan."

"Which house?"

"The yellow one, across the street."

"What does Dylan look like?"

"He's tall, with bushy brown hair." She made a face. "And he wears different colored tennis shoes."

"What? Why?"

"Just to get attention, I think. When he buys shoes, he gets two pairs and then switches them. It's kind of a thing. Other kids at school do it too."

JP thanked her and walked back to his truck. Embarrassment could escalate, especially with teenage boys.

JP walked over to the house. When he knocked, a shirtless teenage boy answered the door, chewing on something that smelled like burnt cheese. He fit Penny's description. JP glanced down and saw one red and one bright blue shoe.

"You must be Dylan," JP said.

"Yeah, that's me. What's up?"

"I'm here about Mateo Alvarez."

Dylan scoffed. "I didn't do anything to him."

"I'm just gathering information," JP said. "No one's in trouble here."

"What do you want to know?"

"Did anyone around here have a problem with Mateo?"

"What kind of problem?"

"Any kind," JP said.

Dylan shrugged. "He pushed me once."

"And?" JP asked.

"I laughed it off," Dylan said. "It wasn't a thing."

"You sure?" JP asked.

Dylan's eyes glanced sideways. "It was stupid."

JP waited.

"He thought I was gonna hit him," Dylan said. "I wasn't. I just messed with him."

"Enough to want payback?" JP asked.

Dylan frowned. "No. He wasn't worth that."

JP believed him. Not because Dylan was noble, but because if Dylan wanted to hurt Mateo, he would've done it close to home, not with planning and sedation.

"Do you know anyone who had it out for Mateo? Something serious?"

"Not really," Dylan said. "Is the kid okay?"

"He's in the ICU."

"I'm sorry, man. I don't know anyone who would do that to him. I probably teased him too much, but I'd never do anything like that."

JP gave him a card and asked him to call if he learned anything new. He didn't expect to hear from Dylan. JP stepped away and made a note. It's not this.

Next stop was the school. The vice principal—a woman, seemingly too young considering the job—met him in a cramped office that smelled faintly of stale coffee. JP explained his mission.

"We don't have a record of any serious problems like that," she said. "Mateo wasn't involved in conflicts."

"Anyone accuse him of something?" JP asked. "Cheating? Theft? Girl problems?"

She gave it some thought. "There was an incident with a phone."

JP's pulse ticked up. "Go on."

"A boy accused Mateo of taking it," she said. "Turned out the phone was in the boy's backpack."

"Was there any fallout?" JP asked.

"No," she said. "The boy apologized. Mateo didn't even look upset."

JP thanked her and left. He sat in his truck afterward and reviewed the list in his head:

- No gang ties
- No drugs
- No debts
- No romantic entanglements
- No online conflicts

- No retaliation-worthy incidents

There were small human frictions, but nothing that justified the kind of effort that had gone into hurting Mateo.

JP thought about the van. The sedation. The way Mateo had been left, not hidden, not finished. His abductors had been interrupted.

His phone buzzed. Sabre.

"Hi, honey," JP said. "How's it going on your end?"

"I'm not finding anything that explains Mateo as a target."

"Me either. I don't think this was about settling a score with Mateo."

"What makes you say that?"

"I don't think he's done anything to warrant it. Besides, I've seen plenty of revenge cases before. They're messy. They're emotional, and they're loud. This has been quiet, controlled, and planned. And when it went wrong, it went wrong fast, which meant the mistake was probably logistical."

"If anything, it was about saving him," Sabre said. "What else have you got?"

JP told her about the van he'd found. "Miller will take it from here. But one thing I learned is that Mendoza wasn't just covering a shift. He asked about that route specifically."

"Which means he wanted *that* juvenile pickup," Sabre said.

"Or that time window," JP countered.

"I don't want to overreach, but it feels like their plan went terribly wrong."

"I agree. But what was their plan?"

"I don't know what they intended," Sabre said. "I don't know who they were after, if anyone. But drugging a child in a van isn't opportunistic. It's premeditated."

Chapter 14

Tuesday late afternoon

Sabre didn't want a theory. Theories made chaos feel organized. They gave fear a shape you could point to. But she'd practiced law long enough, and lived long enough, to know the danger of deciding too early what something meant.

Still, she couldn't shake the feeling that Mateo Alvarez didn't belong at the center of what had happened. Not because she knew who did it, or why. But because the pieces didn't sit right when you tried to stack them.

She unlocked her office and stepped inside. The late afternoon sun slanted through the front windows. The courthouse day still hummed in her bones—voices, footsteps, paperwork, lives reshuffled by a clerk's stamp. She put her keys in her pocket and didn't bother turning on the overhead lights.

The quiet felt earned.

Sabre crossed to her desk and opened Mateo's file. She didn't read it like a lawyer would. She read it like an investigator trying to understand why a child ended up in an ICU bed with sedatives in his system.

Mateo had no pending hearing that hinged on compliance and no reason, on paper, or otherwise, for anyone to focus on him.

And yet, a transport van had gone dark, a shoe had come off with blood inside it, and he'd been drugged and left in a drainage canal. None of that lined up with the kid she'd met—or anything either she or JP had discovered.

She called Detective Miller. "Anything new on Mateo?"

"I interviewed the mother, Brandy Alvarez. I didn't get a good read on her. She's angry, but mostly at the system. I get the impression she's more concerned about a payout from the county than she is about getting her son back."

"Could it be part of her whole plan?"

"It could be. I'm not sure she's that smart. But I think she's a good liar, so I'm not ruling her out."

"What about Dad?"

"So far, I haven't found him. He's not in prison, at least not statewide."

"Thank you. I'll pass this on to JP. We'll let you know if we find anything new."

Sabre hung up and opened her laptop. Marisol's email was still in her inbox, with a secure link and a short message: I preserved the logs like you asked. Please be careful.

Sabre clicked through the transfer order, timestamp, and audit trail. She scrolled slowly, the way you did when you didn't want to miss something that mattered. There it was. A blink of an edit, another youth populating the name field, then disappearing as quickly. She paused it, trying to get the name, but couldn't. She knew it wasn't Mateo's because it wasn't the right length.

Sabre stared at the text box. The edit flash wasn't proof of anything. But it was a fact that didn't belong in a routine transfer.

She opened the audit trail and read the entries with care. The system recorded access—who opened the order, who saved it and when, but it didn't tell her why. That was the problem. Her instincts wanted to fill the space with motive, but she forced herself to stop.

A change could be a mistake. A correction could be an honest fix, but it could also be something else.

She wrote one line on a legal pad: *Name field changed → changed back. Why?* Below, she added another: *Did someone change it so Mateo would be in that van? If so, why?*

She sat back and pressed her fingers to her temples. Mateo's words had come through Marisol, and Marisol hadn't sounded dramatic. She'd sounded unsettled. There was a difference. And there was the other thing; Mateo had been watching the van. Asking about who else had ridden in it. Saying another child's name under his breath, but that hadn't panned out, unless Sabre missed something. She didn't even know if it mattered. But it supported the feeling she couldn't dismiss: Mateo had been looking for something, or recognizing something, right before everything went wrong.

She stood and paced the length of her office, the floorboards giving their familiar creak under each step. Her thoughts moved in short, punchy lines the way they did when she was trying not to panic.

According to JP, Mendoza wanted that route; he'd planned something. If it wasn't a heat-of-the-moment decision, then the sedation wasn't either.

Sabre stopped pacing. The sedation bothered her. She'd seen overdoses. Kids who had gotten into their parents' prescriptions or bought pills from someone older. Those cases had a particular chaos to them—panic, secrecy, shame. This wasn't that. This looked like control, which meant intent.

She sat again and wrote another line: *Drugging suggests intent to control Mateo. Leaving him where he could be found suggests panic or interruption.*

The idea that formed wasn't a conclusion or even a clean theory. It was more like a question that wouldn't stop pressing against the inside of her ribs. *What if Mateo wasn't the point? Was it something he saw that he shouldn't have?*

If only Mateo were awake to tell her something, anything.

Sabre looked around her office, the framed photos, the files stacked neatly, the small signs of a life that insisted on normalcy. She thought of Mateo in the ICU, unconscious, possibly robbed of ever having the chance to tell his story.

Chapter 15

Tuesday night, 7:32 p.m.

DuBois hated when his phone rang just as he was leaving work. It almost always meant he would have to stay late. Within minutes he was on his way to the crime scene.

Homicide investigations always started the same way. Too much noise. Too many people trying to be helpful. A house that no longer felt like a home because something violent had rearranged it permanently.

DuBois parked in front of Wilcox's house. It was in a middle-class neighborhood with a well-kept lawn. There were no obvious signs of a struggle outside.

Once inside the front door, he let the scene settle into his bones before he started asking questions. Unlike the calm exterior, the inside had drawers pulled open, cushions shifted, and a lamp on its side. It was messy, but not frantic.

"Robbery," one of the uniforms said from behind him. "Looks like he surprised someone."

DuBois crouched near the entry table where a set of keys lay, then straightened and walked toward the living room.

Wilcox was where the patrol report indicated. He lay on his back near the sofa, one arm angled awkwardly beneath him, with a single gunshot wound to his chest, likely from close range, with no defensive injuries visible. The assault had probably been quick.

"Who ID'd him?" DuBois asked.

"One of ours," the uniform said. "Patrol recognized him. Said he's a probation officer who works juvenile. We confirmed through dispatch. His name came back as Abram Wilcox. This is his house."

"Did you check his pockets?"

"Yes, no wallet. No ID."

DuBois looked around the room again. The television was intact. There was no laptop or other electronics. Perhaps they'd been taken. A pale band on Wilcox's wrist suggested a missing watch.

"Did you see forced entry?" DuBois asked.

"The back door," the uniform said. "Lock's broken. Possibly kicked open."

"Did the neighbors hear anything?"

"A single gunshot. Some thought it was a car backfiring," the uniform said. "No one heard any arguing or reported seeing a vehicle here. We're still canvassing."

DuBois walked through the rest of the home, tracking details without committing to meaning yet—the broken door, missing valuables, no personal papers scattered, no rage damage.

This probably hadn't been personal. At least, it didn't look that way.

A tech approached. "Ballistics will take some time, but it's a common caliber. Nothing exotic."

"Cameras?" DuBois asked.

"The neighbor across the street has one," the tech said. "He caught a figure moving through the yard. He or she was wearing a hoodie and a mask. The medium build makes the gender hard to tell."

DuBois exhaled. "Of course."

Another man approached with gloves on, calm, clinical—the medical examiner.

"Single gunshot wound to the chest," the ME said. "Close range. No stippling beyond what you'd expect at a few feet.

No defensive wounds. The time of death is consistent with what your neighbors reported. It happened within the last couple of hours."

"No signs of a struggle?" DuBois asked.

"Not beyond displacement," the ME said, gesturing to the room. "He likely didn't see it coming."

"Cause of death?"

"Preliminarily? Gunshot wound. I'll confirm after the autopsy."

DuBois nodded. That was all he'd get tonight.

He stepped outside and scanned the street. It was quiet, normal, a place where people went to work and came home believing bad things happened somewhere else.

Another detective, Asa Perkins, a tall thin man in his late thirties, walked up from his perimeter search.

"What's the victim's background?" DuBois asked.

"He's a youth probation officer," Perkins said. "He doesn't seem to have any enemies or threats on file, but I'm sure a closer look will give us something."

Probation officers got yelled at, blamed, and hated, but rarely targeted like this. Not unless something else was in play. The missing items fit a robbery. The smash-style entry pointed to a stranger. Almost everything fit. That bothered him.

"Any family?" DuBois asked.

"His teenage son died in a car accident last year, and the victim's recently divorced."

DuBois nodded. "Let's check out coworkers and other family members, but keep the focus where the evidence points."

"Which is?" Perkins asked.

"Random," DuBois said. "At least for now."

He hated saying it. *Random* was a word people used when the story was incomplete. But right now, the story was coherent. A stranger enters through the back. Wilcox surprises him or her. One shot. Grab what you can. Leave clean.

DuBois went back inside and snapped a few photos for his own reference, not evidence, just memory aids. The way the back door hung crookedly. The absence of blood spatter beyond the immediate area. The lack of anything that looked like fury. No overturned photos. No broken frames. No messages written in anger.

In the living room, he looked once more at Wilcox's face. He looked neutral in death, almost calm.

"This looks textbook," DuBois said quietly, and textbook bothered him.

"Sir?" a uniform asked.

"Nothing," DuBois said. "Talking to myself."

He stepped away from the body and began issuing instructions. Canvas the block again, check pawn shops for the valuables, run similar robberies in the area. Keep it moving. That was how you caught strangers.

He went out to his car and slid into the driver's seat.

The evidence almost lined up too well. DuBois had learned the hard way that when a case behaved perfectly at the start, it usually meant the crime was hiding something deeper. But for now, he had no reason to justify pulling other threads.

Abram Wilcox was dead, the scene said stranger, and until the evidence argued otherwise, that was the story.

Chapter 16

Wednesday morning

Wednesday mornings in juvenile court always carried the same illusion, order imposed just tightly enough to hold things together until noon. Sabre sat on the bench outside of Department One, reviewing a file. Bob, her coworker and best friend, nudged her. She looked up and saw someone moving toward her with purpose.

"Who's that?" Bob asked.

"Officer Reyes," Sabre said. "He's juvenile probation."

"Friend or problem?"

"That depends on the case. He's been both."

The man stopped in front of her, his expression careful, practiced. "Sabre," he said quietly. "Can I pull you aside for a minute?"

She glanced at her phone. Eight minutes until the first case was called. "Sure."

Reyes led her toward the side hallway near Department Two, where the traffic thinned, giving them more privacy.

Reyes didn't speak right away. That alone told her this wasn't routine. They'd been working the same courthouse long enough for Sabre to read the difference. Reyes wasn't someone who chased attorneys down unless there was a reason. And he wasn't someone who shared more than he had to.

"There was a homicide last night," he said.

Sabre's first instinct was procedural. "And?"

"The victim was Abram Wilcox," Reyes continued. "A youth probation officer."

Sabre frowned. "I'm sorry he's dead. But why are you telling me?"

Reyes waited until they were fully out of anyone's earshot. "He was the father of Liam Wilcox."

Sabre felt the shift internally, the way certain names never fully left her once they entered her case files.

"Liam Wilcox," she repeated. "The kid who died in the car accident."

"Yes," Reyes said. "About eight months ago."

She took a moment to recall the case. Her client was Giovanni Taber. He'd been sixteen at the time and a new driver, with two friends in the car. He'd hit a curve that tightened unexpectedly, along with loose sand on the road. He'd lost control and couldn't regain it.

One of his passengers had survived. She'd argued that Giovanni hadn't been speeding, nor had he been reckless. She'd also asserted that Liam had been told, more than once, to put on his seat belt and refused.

The judge had split the difference. He'd ruled not guilty of manslaughter, but guilty of a lesser offense. The charge was enough to follow Giovanni everywhere, but not as bad as the sorrow he'd felt for killing his friend.

"How was Mr. Wilcox killed?" Sabre asked.

"A home invasion robbery," Reyes said. "That's how it's being classified right now. Forced entry. Shot inside the house."

Sabre absorbed that. "Anything taken?"

"Wallet. Electronics. Nothing unusual."

"And you're telling me because of Giovanni?"

"Yes," Reyes said. "Because you represent him, and because I'd rather you hear it from me before this turns into something it's not."

That landed. Not a leak. A choice. Sabre leaned back against the wall.

"I don't see a motive," she said after a moment. "Why would Giovanni want to kill Liam's father? Giovanni didn't walk away from that incident without paying a price. He served time and is still under supervision. He's been in dependency since his placement fell apart after the adjudication. He never blamed Mr. Wilcox for that. He blames himself."

Reyes nodded. "I know. I remember."

And he did. He'd been in the courtroom for most of the trial. He wasn't assigned to the case. He was there supporting his friend, Abram Wilcox.

Sabre was skeptical. "You were Abram's friend. Why would you want to help me or my client?"

"Because I sat through that trial. I think Giovanni Taber suffered enough. It was clearly an accident."

Sabre wasn't sure what to say to that. She hesitated, then said, "Killing Mr. Wilcox would only hurt Giovanni. It would put him right back under a microscope."

"That was my read too," Reyes said. "But homicide doesn't start with reads. They start with names."

Sabre exhaled slowly. "Has anyone suggested Giovanni is a suspect?"

"No," Reyes said quickly. "Not at this point. It's all preliminary, but his name will come up."

"It always does," Sabre said.

Reyes grimaced. "I wanted you to hear it from me before the news made its way through the building."

Sabre studied him. That was Reyes. He wouldn't cross a line, but he'd walk right up to it if it meant things didn't spin out of control.

"I appreciate that."

They stood in silence for a moment, the muffled sounds of court filtering in around them.

"I'll talk to Giovanni," Sabre said finally. "He needs to know what's happened."

"That's probably wise." Reyes turned to go, then paused. "I'm sorry," he said. "I know that case was difficult."

Reyes walked back toward the courtroom, leaving her alone in the hallway.

Abram Wilcox was dead, a probation officer and the father of a boy whose death still echoed through her files.

Giovanni Taber, still a kid himself in so many ways, was about to have that weight added back onto his shoulders.

As she walked back toward Bob, he approached. "Are you okay?"

She shook her head. "I just found out the father of one of my client's victims was killed."

"That can't be good. What happened?"

Sabre gave him a short description, then headed into the courtroom as the clerk called the first case. For now, this was a different matter, a different tragedy, a different file.

Chapter 17

Wednesday afternoon

The apartment complex where Brandy Alvarez lived looked tired in the late afternoon heat. Faded paint. Iron railings that had been repainted too many times. The kind of place where people kept their doors locked but their windows open.

JP sat in his truck across the street for a minute, watching.

Brandy came out once, lit a cigarette, smoked half of it, then crushed it under her heel like she was mad at it.

JP stepped out. She spotted him before he got halfway across the lot.

"Are you lost?" she asked.

"That depends," JP said. "Are you Brandy Alvarez?"

"Maybe. Who are you?"

"I'm JP Torn. I'm a private investigator. I work with Sabre Brown, your son's attorney."

That changed things. Not softer. Not friendlier. But she didn't walk away.

"What do you want?" she asked.

"I want to find out what happened to Mateo."

"Me too. I just found out he is in the hospital."

"That's right, ma'am." JP glanced around. "Have you been here long?"

"Since I got out three weeks ago." She folded her arms. "So, why are you here?"

"Your son was intercepted during transport," he said. "Whoever took him didn't do it randomly. They knew enough to be in the right place at the right time."

She didn't respond, but her eyes stayed on him.

"I'm trying to figure out who that might be," JP continued. "So, I'm going to ask you some direct questions."

"Ask."

"Did you have anything to do with it?"

"No." No hesitation.

JP nodded once. "I believe you."

She blinked, just slightly. "That easy?"

"Most people lie a little before they say no," JP said. "You didn't."

That didn't make her comfortable. It just made her quieter.

JP shifted. "Let's talk about his father."

"He's dead," she said.

"Maybe."

She shook her head. "He's gone."

"That's not the same thing."

She looked away.

"Did he ever threaten to take the boy?" JP asked.

She exhaled through her nose. "Yeah," she said. "He said it."

"Do you think he meant it?"

"Yes."

JP nodded. "Tell me about him."

She laughed once, low and tired. "What do you want to know?"

"Why the court wouldn't give him the kid."

"That part's easy," she said. "He was a gangster who didn't think rules applied to him."

"Was he violent?"

"When he needed to be."

"With you?"

She didn't answer.

JP let it go. "I know he tried to get custody and was denied. Did he take that hard?"

"He went off on everyone around him."

JP studied her. "Why'd he disappear?"

She looked back at him, something different in her eyes now. "You ever know someone," she said slowly, "who lives like there's no tomorrow?"

"Yes, ma'am."

"They don't usually get one," she said.

"That's not an answer."

"It's the only one I got," she replied.

JP nodded. "You told Mateo he was dead."

"I needed him to stop waiting," she said, quieter now. "You don't know what that does to a kid."

JP didn't argue that. "Did you ever hear from him after he disappeared?"

"No."

"If he's alive," JP said, "and he knew your son was being moved–"

"He didn't," she cut in.

"You don't know that."

"I do."

"How?"

"Because he wouldn't do it like this," she said.

JP stilled. "Like what?"

She shook her head.

"He wouldn't sneak around," she said. "He wouldn't use other people. He'd just take him."

Direct. Personal. Messy. JP filed that away. "That don't mean he ain't involved," JP said.

She looked at him. "You think he's behind it."

"I think he's not off the table."

She leaned back against the wall.

"If you find him," she said, "you'll wish you didn't."

JP didn't react. He stepped back. "I'll take that risk."

He paused. "Do you want to help your boy?"

"Of course."

"Then stay where I can find you," JP said. "And if anything comes back to you, anything at all, you call me." He handed her his card.

She didn't answer, but she took the card and put it in her pocket.

Chapter 18

Wednesday afternoon

Giovanni sat on the edge of the couch in the group home's visiting room, elbows on his knees, hands clasped together like he was trying to keep them from shaking. The air smelled faintly of a boy's locker room.

He was seventeen but looked younger. He was lean, with long limbs and unfinished angles, as if he hadn't quite caught up to his own height yet. His dark hair fell forward over his forehead and was cut too short on the sides by someone with clippers and no patience. A fading bruise shadowed one cheekbone, and the faint acne scars along his jaw gave him a look of trying too hard to be older than he was. His shoulders were broader than they'd been six months ago, but he still carried himself like someone bracing for impact.

He looked up when Sabre walked in.

"Hey." She took the chair across from him.

"Hey." His voice was steady, but his eyes weren't. They darted once to the door, then back to her.

Sabre set her file on the low table and waited until the staff member glanced at her watch and walked away.

"How's it going here?" Sabre asked.

Giovanni shrugged. "It's okay. Same stuff. Curfew. Chores. They don't trust anybody."

"That's not personal."

He gave a humorless smile. "Feels like it is."

Sabre took a breath. "I need to tell you something," she said. "And I need you to listen all the way through before you react."

Giovanni's shoulders tightened. "Okay."

"Abram Wilcox, the father of Liam Wilcox, was killed last night."

Giovanni's head came up fast. "Liam's dad is dead?"

"Yes."

His face drained of color. "How?"

"The police think it was a robbery," Sabre said carefully. "He was shot in his home."

Giovanni leaned back against the couch, staring at the far wall. "Geez."

Sabre watched him closely. Shock came first, then something heavier.

"I know you knew him."

Giovanni nodded slowly. "Yeah. I mean... yeah. I'd been to his house. Liam and I hung out there. His dad was around a lot."

"Did you have contact with him recently?" Sabre asked.

"No," Giovanni said. "Not since... everything."

"Have you been to his house since the accident?"

"Why would I? Liam is gone." The boy sighed. "Actually, I thought about going there sometimes to tell him how sorry I am. But I didn't."

"I need to ask you directly," Sabre said. "Were you involved in what happened to Mr. Wilcox in any way?"

Giovanni's eyes snapped back to hers. "No."

"Did you go anywhere near his house last night?" she asked.

"No."

"Were you here all evening?"

"Yes. I went to my room right after dinner. I stayed there until bedtime."

"Was anyone in your room during the evening?"

"No. I was alone, playing video games, until Jeremiah came to bed."

"What time was that?"

"About nine or so."

"Did you ever tell anyone that you'd like to hurt Liam's dad?" Sabre asked.

"No!" The boy seemed stunned by the question. "I wouldn't do that. I didn't hate him."

"You didn't?" Sabre asked gently.

Giovanni shook his head. "He hated me. That's different."

Sabre let that sit.

"He blamed me," Giovanni continued. "I get that. Liam was his kid. But I didn't mean for it to happen. I tried to get Liam to wear his seat belt, but he just laughed at me." His jaw clenched. "I already live with that."

"Did Abram Wilcox ever threaten you?"

Giovanni thought about it. "Not straight out. But he'd look at me like he wanted me to remember that *he* hadn't forgotten."

"In court?" she asked.

"Yeah. And once after," Giovanni said. "I ran into him outside a store. He didn't say anything. Just stood there. But..."

"What?"

"He pointed his finger at me like this." Giovanni shaped his hand into a gun.

"Did that scare you?" Sabre asked.

"Everything scared me back then."

"Did you ever think about going after him?"

"No! Why would I? That would just ruin everything more."

Sabre watched his hands. They were steady now. "Giovanni," she said, "because of the history, the police may want to talk to you."

His shoulders slumped. "I figured."

"If they do," Sabre continued, "you don't say a word without me there. Do you understand?"

"Yes."

"And if anyone else asks you questions about Abram Wilcox, or offers you help, or even just wants to talk about it," Sabre said, "you don't talk, and you call me."

Giovanni nodded. "Nobody's talked to me."

"Good," Sabre said. "Let's keep it that way."

She stood and gathered her file.

"You believe me, right?" Giovanni asked quietly.

"Yes."

He let out a breath he'd clearly been holding. "Thank you."

Sabre paused at the door. "I'm sorry you're dealing with this again," she said. "None of it should be on you."

Giovanni gave a small nod. "It's always there."

Sabre stepped into the hall, the door closing softly behind her. Giovanni Taber hadn't killed Abram Wilcox. She was almost certain of that.

Chapter 19

Wednesday late afternoon

JP had gotten an update from Sabre about the Wilcox situation, but he wanted to talk to others at the group home to make sure they hadn't missed anything.

The home sat back from the street, a squat building with a chain-link fence and a basketball hoop missing half its net. It was the kind of place where time moved in blocks: dinner, meds, lights out, and nobody bothered pretending the gaps in between were closely watched.

The staff member on duty introduced himself as Iverson. He was in his forties and carried a coffee-stained clipboard. His tired eyes suggested he'd answered the same questions too many times already.

"You're asking about Giovanni Taber." Iverson flipped a page without looking up.

"That's right," JP said. "I'm a private investigator who works for his attorney."

"He came in for dinner around five-thirty," Iverson said. "Signed in like he's supposed to. He ate, then hung around the common room for a bit."

"Anyone walk him in?" JP asked.

"No," Iverson said. "He came back on his own."

"Did he leave again?" JP asked.

"Not officially."

JP let that word hang. "Meaning?"

"This isn't a locked facility," Iverson said. "Kids are supposed to check out if they leave, they're not supposed to leave without permission, and they have curfews. Not all of them follow the rules."

"But Giovanni didn't check out," JP said.

"No. And I didn't see him leave."

"Did you see him later?" JP asked.

Iverson nodded. "Around nine. He was back in the common room before quiet hours, watching TV with the others."

"So, between five-thirty and nine, you didn't have eyes on him the whole time."

Iverson gave a wry smile. "I don't have eyes on anybody the whole time."

JP thanked him and stepped into the hall, where the building's low hum filled the silence.

Next stop was Giovanni's roommate. A kid named Jeremiah, seventeen, sharp-eyed and wary in the way kids learned when adults kept notes about them.

"You asking if Gio bounced?" Jeremiah said.

"I'm asking what you saw," JP replied.

The teenager shrugged. "I saw him at dinner, then I saw him later around bedtime, but I didn't see him in between."

"Did he mention going anywhere?" JP asked.

"No," Jeremiah said. "And he mostly kept to himself."

"Was that normal?" JP asked.

Jeremiah shrugged again. "Yeah."

JP talked to two more boys who had the same story. They saw him at dinner, then later, but nothing in between. Nobody saw Giovanni leave, but nobody saw him stay either.

JP stepped outside and used his phone to check the distance between the group home and the Wilcox residence. Three miles. Walkable, if you were motivated, but impossible without enough time.

Could Giovanni have walked three miles, done something terrible, and walked back before nine? Maybe. Was it likely? No.

The kid didn't have a car or access to one that JP was aware of, but he could've gotten a ride with someone. JP leaned against his truck and exhaled slowly. The alibi wasn't airtight, but didn't smell like a lie, either. It smelled like a kid living in a place where no one was counting minutes because no one expected anything to happen in them.

Giovanni's story held. The adults confirmed it. The gaps were structural, not suspicious. JP was pretty confident Giovanni hadn't killed Wilcox, but he needed to know what law enforcement had.

DuBois picked up on the third ring. "Let me guess, you're calling about the Wilcox murder."

"Tell me it's boring," JP said.

"So far," DuBois replied. "It looks like a robbery."

JP exhaled, slow and quiet. "Good."

"The back door was kicked, and the cause of death was a single shot to the chest. The perp took electronics and his wallet. No personal items were disturbed. I mean, they looked through some drawers, but no damage beyond what you'd expect."

"As you know," JP said, "Sabre represents the kid who was driving the car when Wilcox's son was killed."

"Taber's not a suspect," DuBois said. "At least not yet. Of course, I'll talk to him just to clear the air."

"What's the neighborhood like?" JP asked.

"Quiet," DuBois said. "We've had similar burglaries nearby with the same general timing, early evening, but there is one thing."

"There always is."

"The neighbor's camera across the street caught someone moving through Wilcox's yard."

"Got a face?"

"No. Just a hoodie pulled over his face. Average build."

"That's normal."

"The timing's a little off," DuBois said.

That seemed unusual. "How off?"

"The intruder shows up almost twenty minutes before the estimated time of death," DuBois said. "He or she moves around the side yard, disappears, and comes back later."

JP frowned. "They could've been casing the place."

"Maybe," DuBois said.

"Or waiting for the house to empty," JP added.

"Wilcox was home."

"Did they know that?"

"No way to tell," DuBois said. "They could've thought he'd left, or they could've been watching."

JP rolled that around without biting into it. "Did the camera catch a vehicle?" JP asked.

"No," DuBois said. "No obvious arrival."

"So, they parked out of view," JP said.

"Or walked," DuBois countered.

That theory didn't look good for Giovanni. "Anything else?" JP asked.

"The lock damage on the back door suggests it may not have been the first attempt," DuBois said. "Like someone tested it earlier."

JP grimaced. "That happens too."

"I'll call you after I talk to Taber," DuBois said.

"Please do," JP replied.

"Also, if this stays a robbery, I won't argue with you."

DuBois gave a short laugh. "That might be a first."

"Don't get used to it," JP said.

Chapter 20

Wednesday night

Sabre had just set the last plate on the table when JP came through the front door, keys in hand. The house was quiet in that brief way it only was right before dinner, too still to last.

He caught her eye. Now, the look said. They stepped into the kitchen, lowering their voices.

"I checked Giovanni's alibi," JP said. "It's not airtight, but DuBois says he's not a suspect."

Sabre leaned against the counter. "Good. I really don't think he's capable."

"Dubois is running with the robbery theory, and so far, it's holding," JP said.

Footsteps thudded down the hall. Conner, JP's nephew and ward, appeared first, already reaching for a dinner roll. Morgan, his younger sister, followed, earbuds dangling around her neck. Dené came last, quieter than the other two, with JP's brother, Gene, close behind her.

This was their family now. Not the one she'd imagined, but the one they'd built. Gene's kids, Conner and Morgan, moved in when their father went to prison. Dené came next, after losing her mother. Gene moved in last, after the earthquake left him seriously injured. It wasn't the life Sabre had pictured, but she wouldn't trade it.

"Smells good," Gene said, settling into his chair.

"Everybody sit," Sabre said. "Before this dinner gets cold."

They took their places around the table, with Conner and Morgan bickering playfully, their father watching with a half-smile, and JP pouring water into their glasses.

For a few minutes, it was just a family dinner, ordinary and grounding. It felt good. It had been a while since they all sat down together.

JP turned to Sabre. "I talked to Miller today. He thinks Mateo's case is more personal."

Dené cut in. "You mean Mateo Alvarez?"

The table went quiet. Sabre looked at her. "You know Mateo?"

Dené frowned. "Yeah. He hasn't been at school all week. People are asking about him."

JP touched her arm. "How do you know him?"

"He's my friend," Dené said, sounding like that should've been obvious. "We hang out at school and sometimes after."

Sabre felt her chest tighten. "How close of a friend?"

"Pretty close," Dené said. "He walks me home when we stay late. We study together, and he helps me with math."

Morgan looked between them. "Wait, that Mateo?"

Dené nodded.

Sabre kept her voice even. "Mateo's in the hospital. He's sick."

Dené's eyes widened. "Is he gonna be okay?"

"Yes," Sabre said. "He's being taken care of."

Dené nodded, then frowned. "That's weird."

JP tilted his head. "What is?"

"He was nervous last time I saw him," Dené explained. "More than usual."

"When was that?" Sabre asked.

"Monday," Dené said. "After lunch, he told me he had to leave because he was moving again."

Sabre tensed. "Did he say where?"

"No. Just that no one told him until the last minute, and that he hated packing."

Gene spoke up gently. "A lot of kids hate that."

"Yeah," Dené said. "He wants to go to a foster home, but he's afraid he'll have to change schools again."

Sabre and JP exchanged a glance across the table. No one spoke for a moment.

Conner shifted uncomfortably. "Is he in trouble?"

"No," Sabre quickly countered. "He didn't do anything wrong."

Dené let out a breath. "Good. Because he's not like that."

Sabre believed her.

Dinner continued, but the energy had changed. The chatter never quite came back. After plates were cleared and Conner and Morgan drifted off, Gene lingered long enough to give Sabre a quiet look, one that said he'd noticed the interest Dené had in Mateo.

Sabre stood at the sink, staring out the window.

"Dené didn't know she knew something," JP said quietly behind her.

"No," Sabre said. "But I wonder if she knows more than she's saying. I'll talk to her later."

"Mateo isn't just another kid to her," JP said.

Sabre turned off the light over the sink and leaned back against the counter, her mind already replaying Dené's words.

Mateo hadn't just vanished from the system. He'd vanished from a full life, and the people around him had noticed. That made everything feel heavier.

~~~

It was 9:52 p.m. when JP's phone rang. He glanced at the number and almost let it go. Unknown. Late enough to matter. He answered anyway.

"JP." A breath on the other end. "This is Brandy. You said to call if I remembered anything."

"Go ahead."
~~~

There was a pause. "You asked about Mateo's father," she said. "About who he knew."

"I did."

"I didn't tell you everything."

That didn't surprise him. "What didn't you tell me?"

"He had people," she said. "Not just gang guys. People who handled things."

"Handled what?"

"Problems."

"Does that include taking a kid out of a transport van?" he asked.

"I don't know," she said quickly. "I'm just saying, if Mateo's father isn't dead—"

"You don't think he is?" JP cut in.

"I think men like him don't just disappear," she said. "They lay low. They wait."

JP studied the wall across from him, letting her keep talking.

"And if he came back," she continued, "he wouldn't go through the system. He'd take what's his."

There it was. A theory that almost made sense.

"Why are you telling me this now?" JP asked.

"I didn't think it mattered before," she said. "Now I do."

"Do you have a name?" he asked.

"No," she said. "But I might be able to find one."

JP's eyes sharpened slightly. "How?"

"I still know people," she said. "People who know people."

"Uh-huh."

"I can ask questions you can't," she added.

That part was true. "And why would you do that?"

"Because that's my son."

"Call me if you get something real," he said.

"I will."

The line went dead.

Chapter 21

Thursday morning

Luis Mendoza's previous address sat above a tire shop that looked closed. JP knew it was good information because it came from Frank. He parked across the street and watched for a full minute before getting out. The smell of rubber and oil hung in the warm summer air. There were no lights upstairs, no movement, and no sounds except for the traffic and a radio playing somewhere down the street.

He climbed the exterior stairs and knocked anyway. No response. JP checked the mailbox by the door. It was stuffed with flyers, but no recent deliveries. He stepped back and scanned the street below. Mendoza wasn't here. JP didn't expect him to be, but sometimes people returned to old addresses. It was worth a check. JP made a note and moved on.

The second address came from a DMV record that hadn't been updated in years. A shared house near the edge of Barrio Logan, with paint peeling and three junk cars parked on the dead lawn.

A woman answered the door. She was in her late thirties and wary.

"I'm looking for Luis Mendoza," JP said.

She shook her head. "He doesn't live here."

"When did he leave?" JP asked.

"Months ago. He didn't say where he was going."

"Did he leave in a hurry?" JP asked.

She snorted. "Everyone leaves in a hurry."

That tracked.

JP drove for another twenty minutes, checking places where drivers rotated through couches and spare rooms. Nothing stuck. Mendoza had done what people like him often did when things got uncomfortable, he'd gone quiet.

JP pulled into a gas station parking area and sat for a minute, engine off, phone glowing in his hand. He scrolled through his contacts and stopped on Frank.

The call connected on the second ring. "JP," Frank said. "You don't call unless you want something."

"Still hurts my feelings," JP said.

Frank laughed. "So, what is it?"

"I'm calling about the woman connected to Luis Mendoza. Did you find anything?"

"I just got it. The name is Nadine. I don't have a last name."

"Where do I find her?"

"She works at a taco shop in a strip mall in National City."

"How will I recognize her?"

"She'll be the one with the bright pink hair." That must be the same woman Mendoza's neighbor talked about picking him up.

"How old is she?" JP asked.

"Too old for bright pink hair."

"Everyone's too old for bright pink hair."

Frank paused. "By the way, you didn't hear any of this from me."

"I never do."

~~~

JP pulled into the strip mall Frank had mentioned and sat long enough to watch the rhythm. The mall had a taco shop that did steady business, a check cashing place with a line, and a pawn shop with barred windows and a door that buzzed before it opened.
~~~

JP went into the taco shop and spotted Nadine right away. Frank was right. She was hard to miss.

He approached the counter. "Hi Nadine."

"How do you know my name?"

"Everyone knows your name," JP smiled. "We have a mutual friend."

"Who?"

"Luis Mendoza."

She guffawed. "What makes you think we're friends?"

"Because you have a lot of contact with him when he's on the road."

"Who *are* you?"

"The name's JP, ma'am."

Nadine stared at him. "I don't know where you're getting your information, cowboy, but I don't know Luis that well. He comes in here sometimes, but he hasn't been in today."

"When was he here last?" JP asked.

She seemed to think about it. "He came in a couple of days ago, looking tired."

"What was he driving?"

"I don't know. I didn't see."

"Do you know where he's living?"

"Nope." She frowned. "I have customers waiting. Are you ordering something?"

JP looked behind him. No one was in line, but she was obviously done giving information. He thanked her and moved on.

Mendoza was a contract driver, the kind of job that didn't pay enough to build savings but paid just enough to create dependency. Guys like him didn't have exit strategies. They had habits, obligations, and loose ends that tugged whether they wanted them to or not.

He walked over to the check-cashing business. The clerk didn't know Mendoza's name, but she recognized his face once JP showed her the photo.

"He was here Monday," she said. "He cashed a check."

"Big?" JP asked.

"No. Just regular."

That mattered. People planning to disappear needed all the cash they could get their hands on.

JP stepped back outside and called Eddie. "Have you heard anything new on Luis Mendoza?"

"He's been seen at the downtown library," Eddie said. "He was using a public computer."

That tracked. A man who didn't want to be found but didn't want to be offline either.

"Thanks," JP said.

He hung up and drove to the library in downtown San Diego. It was quiet on the surface, but restless underneath. Keyboards clicked. Chairs scraped softly against tile. Someone sneezed and apologized to no one in particular.

JP paused just inside the doors and let his eyes adjust.

If Mendoza was here, he wouldn't be obvious about it. He'd keep his head down and stay just long enough to get something done, but not long enough to be remembered.

JP moved slowly through the first floor, pretending to read bulletin boards and flyers while he watched the people instead. He observed a man asleep over a newspaper, two teenagers sharing earbuds, and a woman muttering at a phone screen like it had personally wronged her—but no Mendoza.

He took the stairs to the computer level and made a slow circuit between rows of terminals. The soft hum of machines filled the space, broken only by the occasional cough or paper rattle. A security guard stood against the far wall, bored but observant. Still nothing.

After a full sweep, he approached the reference desk. The librarian looked up with practiced neutrality. She was in her late fifties with sharp eyes that noticed everything.

"May I help you?" she asked.

"Maybe," JP said. He took out his phone and pulled up the photo. "I'm looking for this man. Has he been in today?"

She glanced at the screen and nodded immediately. "Yes," she said. "Earlier this afternoon."

"Was he here long?"

"Not really," she said. "Long enough to use a computer. But he seemed anxious."

"How?" JP asked.

"Why do you want to know?"

"I'm a private investigator. I work for a juvenile court attorney. A child went missing, and I'm following up."

"He sat right there, using that computer." She nodded to a computer very close to her desk.

"Could you see what he was looking at?"

She tilted her head, stalling as if she was deciding whether to talk or not.

"It's really important that we find this guy for the kid's sake and maybe his own."

"The guy kept refreshing pages, different local news sites."

"What kind of news?" JP asked.

She lowered her voice, even though no one was listening. "Something about a missing person. It appeared to be a minor. He also checked hospital notices and police updates."

JP kept his expression neutral, but something tightened in his chest.

"He wasn't doing research," the librarian continued. "He was checking, like he was looking for something in particular."

"How do you know? Could you see what he was doing?"

"I could see most of what he was doing. It made me curious. So, when he left in a hurry and didn't shut down the computer all the way, I checked to see what he was looking at. I always check so someone else doesn't use an open login."

"Did he say anything when he left?"

"No. But a couple of policemen came in, and he hightailed it."

"Which would explain why he didn't get the computer shut down correctly," JP said. "Did he seem like a regular?"

She shook her head. "I've never seen him in here before." She paused. "Do you really think this guy has something to do with the missing child?"

"I know he has information that can help us. He's also evading the police, which means he's afraid of something."

"Then I hope you find him."

"So do I."

JP thanked her, stepped away from the desk, and stopped near the windows that looked out onto the street. Traffic moved past in steady lines. People walked with purpose. No one looked like they were running from anything.

Mendoza hadn't come here to hide. He'd come to check the damage. To see if the child had been found or if the story had broken. To see if the worst part was already public.

JP mulled that over. Mendoza didn't know who the kid was or where he'd ended up. And he didn't know how badly things had gone wrong, but he knew enough to be afraid.

JP headed back downstairs and into the daylight, the noise of the city rushing in around him.

What happened to Mateo hadn't gone the way Mendoza was told it would. And people who realized they were in over their heads often just waited and watched. Until eventually they broke.

Chapter 22

Thursday afternoon

DuBois sat in his office with a stack of reports spread across his desk.

He picked up the phone and dialed Perkins, the detective he'd assigned to call pawn shops. "Anything from Wilcox yet?" he asked.

He heard some paper shuffling.

"Nothing," the detective said. "No hits on serial numbers, no electronics flagged, and no quick flips. If this was a grab-and-go, something should've surfaced."

DuBois hung up and leaned back. Stolen goods didn't always show up immediately, but nothing surfacing started to thin the air around a robbery.

He pulled the neighborhood map closer and marked off recent burglaries with similar entry points, similar timing, and similar missing items. None had ended with a dead body.

He replayed the neighbor's camera footage again, slowing it frame by frame. The intruder appeared at the edge of the yard, lingered, disappeared, then reappeared later. Not frantic or rushed. Just waiting.

"Who waits?" DuBois muttered.

He flipped through the ME's report. Single shot. Clean trajectory. No struggle marks beyond the door. The kind of efficiency that suggested either luck or intention.

DuBois stood and walked to the whiteboard, erasing what didn't seem to fit anymore. He rewrote the heading:

ROBBERY and beneath it *WITH INTENT*

It wasn't a declaration. It was a placeholder.

He checked the time and grabbed his jacket. He needed to see the house again, not the scene, but the street. He needed to see the context, the places where assumptions hid.

~~~

The neighborhood looked the same as it had the night before. Lawns trimmed. Cars parked evenly. A place where violence didn't announce itself.

DuBois knocked on the door across the street.

The man answered, cautious. "I already talked to the police," the neighbor said.

"I know," DuBois replied. "I just have one more question. Did you see anyone leave after the gunshot?"

The man thought about it. "No," he said. "I heard the shot, then sirens later. That's it."

"No running?" DuBois asked. "No car starting?"

"No. That's what I thought was weird."

That word again. Back in his car, DuBois sat for a moment before turning the key.

A robbery that didn't rush. Stolen items that didn't move. A killer who waited. None of it disproved the theory, but none of it supported it either.

DuBois drove back toward the station. He would keep working the robbery angle, because that's where the evidence pointed. But he would also start quietly asking a different question: *Who needed Abram Wilcox out of the way?*

~~~

DuBois drove back to his office and watched the footage without sound this time. He'd learned long ago that audio often lied. Sirens, shouting, neighbors narrating their own fear—it could all keep you from seeing what people actually did, what movement, timing, and pauses did.

The intruder appeared again on the screen, grainy but steady, crossing the edge of the frame near Wilcox's side yard. DuBois leaned forward, elbows on his desk, and slowed the playback.

The man stopped. He didn't hesitate or appear startled. He just stopped and stood there, half in shadow, as if listening. As if waiting for something to line up. Then he moved again, purposefully, toward the house.

DuBois scrubbed back and replayed it. "Robbers don't do that," he whispered.

He printed the still frames and spread them across the desk. The intruder didn't bolt after the shot. There was no burst of motion, no frantic sprint. He had waited again after.

DuBois picked up the phone and called the responding patrol officer. "Do you remember anything about the timeline after the gunshot?" he asked.

"Nothing unusual," the officer said. "The neighbors didn't report anyone fleeing."

"No sound of car doors?" DuBois asked.

"Nope. And no engines or yelling."

DuBois thanked him and hung up.

He walked to the whiteboard and added times beneath the robbery heading. The math didn't lie. Whoever killed Abram Wilcox had time, more than he needed. That meant confidence or familiarity.

He circled the word *WAITED* and stepped back.

DuBois wasn't ready to blow up the robbery theory yet. He'd learned the hard way that premature certainty killed cases faster than bad facts. But this one wasn't sitting right, and it wasn't going to improve on its own.

He flipped through Wilcox's personnel file again. He was a probation officer with a clean record. There were no disciplinary notes, and nothing that screamed danger, except the job itself.

You don't make friends doing that job, DuBois thought.

He closed the file. There were still pawn shops to check, forms to file, and boxes to tick. On paper, the case stayed a robbery. But in his head, it had shifted.

The crime wasn't about what was taken. It was now about timing, access, and the patience of someone who'd planned to be there long before the door ever opened.

With the new theory, he had other avenues to check. He wanted to talk to Giovanni Taber, and he decided to take another hard look at who Wilcox had ticked off in his line of work. Probation officers always upset people, even juvenile ones.

He picked up his cell and called Sabre to set up an appointment. Then he dug into Wilcox's caseload. Probation files weren't written to tell stories. They were written to document behavior, violations, missed meetings, and failed tests. But if you read enough of them, you could still hear the people inside.

DuBois sat at his desk, coffee going cold, scrolling through Wilcox's active and recently closed cases. Not looking for the worst kid. Those were obvious. He was looking for the one who didn't quite line up. The one who lingered. The one Wilcox might've pushed just a little too far.

It took longer than he liked. An hour. Then two. He was halfway through another file when something small caught his eye. Not the offense. Not the kid. The frequency.

He scrolled back up. The client was seventeen-year-old Thomas Camden, with a record of auto theft, possession, and a couple of probation violations. Nothing unusual.

But the contact log, that was different. Wilcox had logged more face-to-face contacts with Camden than any other kid on his caseload. By a lot. Weekly. Sometimes twice a week. Unscheduled drop-ins. Home visits that weren't required. Even a couple of late-night field contacts. That wasn't standard supervision. That was pressure.

DuBois opened the narrative notes. Wilcox's tone was tighter here. Less clinical. *Subject displays defiance. Minimizes responsibility. Requires increased monitoring.*

DuBois scrolled further. Then found it. A supplemental note. It was short, buried, and easy to miss. *Subject made verbal threat during home contact. Statement: "You keep pushing me, I'll push back."*

DuBois sat back. There it was. Not loud. Not dramatic. But real. And it hadn't gone anywhere. There was no follow-up escalation. No incident report. Just logged and left.

He pulled the arrest history. Camden had picked up a new charge two days ago for resisting. It wasn't much, but it had landed him in juvenile hall. Which meant he was accessible.

DuBois went to see him.

Camden didn't look like someone who planned murders. He struck him like someone who made bad decisions quickly. He was lean, restless, and had eyes that didn't stay still long.

He sat across from DuBois with a kind of loose tension, like he was always ready to bolt even when there was nowhere to go.

"Are you Thomas Camden?" DuBois asked.

"You know I am."

"Humor me."

"Yeah," Camden said.

DuBois nodded. "I'm looking into Abram Wilcox."

"What about him?"

"He's dead."

Camden leaned back. "So I heard."

"Did you have contact with him recently?"

"Yeah. He was my PO."

"More contact than most?"

Camden shrugged. "He didn't like me."

"Why?"

"Because I didn't pretend," Camden said. "All those other kids, they nod, say 'yes, sir, and no, sir.' I don't do that."

DuBois watched him. "Did you threaten him?"

Camden's eyes flicked. Then back. "People say stuff."

"You said you'd push back."

"He came at me first," Camden said. "Showing up at my house like he owned the place. Talking to my mom like I wasn't even there."

"Did that make you angry?"

"Yeah," Camden said. "It made me angry."

"Angry enough to go to his house?"

Camden let out a short laugh. "I'm not stupid. Look at me. Do you think I'm planning break-ins now? Wearing a mask? Kicking doors?"

"You tell me."

"You're looking at the wrong guy."

"Did you go to his house the night he died?"

"No."

"Where were you?"

"At home," Thomas said. "Ask my mom."

"Anyone else with you?"

"No."

Not a great alibi. Not a terrible one either.

"Did you hate him?" DuBois asked.

Thomas didn't hesitate. "Yeah," he said.

"Enough to kill him?"

Thomas leaned forward slightly. "If I wanted him dead," he said, "I wouldn't do it like that."

"How would you do it?"

Thomas gave a thin smile. "Not your problem."

DuBois let that go. "Did you ever talk to anybody about him? About what he was doing?"

Thomas hesitated. "Just my mom."

Outside, DuBois stood by his vehicle for a moment before getting in. Thomas Camden had motive. Wilcox had been pushing him hard enough to make him a real possibility.

Chapter 23

Friday morning

The last case on Sabre's calendar collapsed the way so many of them did, quietly, with a shrug and a continuance.

She stood at the counsel table while the clerk called the next hearing, knowing she wouldn't be staying for it. The courtroom hummed with low conversation, deputies shifting, and parents whispering to attorneys. Sabre gathered her files, slid them into her bag, and nodded to the bailiff on her way out.

Another morning in Department One. Another set of lives paused, not resolved.

In the hall, she checked her phone. No missed calls. That too felt temporary. She found Bob and told him she was leaving and couldn't make lunch.

Sabre stopped at her nearby office long enough to drop off files and tell Elaine she'd be out the rest of the afternoon. "If anyone calls, tell them I'm with a client."

She drove east, letting the familiar route settle her nerves. Work didn't stop just because one case turned sideways.

Giovanni didn't look surprised when she walked into the home's front office. Instead, he looked wary. He sat on the edge of a molded plastic chair, hands clasped between his knees, eyes fixed on a point just beyond her shoulder. The television in the corner murmured to itself, some afternoon show none of them were listening to.

"They said you were coming."

Sabre nodded and took the chair across from him. "I didn't want you to hear this from anyone else."

He swallowed. "Is this about Mr. Wilcox?"

"Yes."

Giovanni's jaw tightened, but he didn't look away. "The cops think I did it, don't they?"

"No," Sabre countered. "At least not yet."

That earned her a glance.

"But Detective DuBois needs to ask some questions, and I'll be here with you."

The teenager leaned back, his chair creaking under him. "I already told you what happened. I was here all night."

"I know," Sabre said. "And nothing about your story has changed."

"That doesn't matter," he said quietly. "It never does."

Sabre grimaced. Juvenile clients learned early that consistency didn't always protect them.

"Just answer what's asked," she coached. "Don't guess or fill in the silence. If you don't remember something, you say that."

He nodded.

"They're still calling it a robbery," Sabre added. "This isn't personal."

Giovanni let out a breath that sounded like it had been trapped in his chest for days. "He hated me," he said suddenly.

Sabre let him talk.

"Liam's dad," Giovanni went on. "He blamed me. He didn't care what the court said. Or what anyone said. He looked at me like I was already dead."

"That doesn't make you responsible for what happened to him," Sabre said.

Giovanni stared at the floor. "It feels like it does."

Sabre leaned forward. "Did Mr. Wilcox ever threaten you?"

"No." Giovanni shook his head. "Not like that. He just showed up places and stared. Once he told me, 'Accidents don't end anything.'"

Sabre filed that away, her expression neutral. "Anyone else ever bother you?" she asked. "Did any of his friends or family ever blame you?"

"Just him, that I know of."

Sabre stood. "DuBois will be here in a few minutes. We'll handle it together. In the meantime, I'll wait outside for him to arrive."

Giovanni stood too. "I didn't do this."

"I know." Sabre meant it.

Sabre walked to her car and made a call, engine off, files in the passenger seat.

"Rady Children's." A woman answered.

"This is Sabre Brown. I'm calling about Mateo Alvarez."

"One moment."

It was a different voice this time. "Nurses' station."

"He's out of ICU?"

"Yes," the nurse said. "He was moved this morning."

"Is he awake?"

"Intermittently," the nurse said. "He's opened his eyes, responded to simple prompts. Still groggy."

"Has he spoken?"

"Not really," the nurse said. "And he's not awake for very long at a time. Nothing consistent."

"I understand," she said. "Thank you."

She ended the call and sat there for a bit, then went inside to wait for DuBois to arrive.

Chapter 24

Friday afternoon

DuBois didn't like interviewing kids in general, and the group home smelled like teenage boys, so he hoped to make this quick. He signed in at the front desk, flashed his badge out of habit more than necessity, and was led to a small room with a round table and three chairs.

Taber was already there, with Sabre beside him, close enough to be present, but not touching. DuBois noted that she was good at her job.

He took the seat across from them and focused on the teenager. "I'm Detective DuBois. We've met before. Do you remember me?"

"Yes, sir."

"This isn't an arrest." DuBois kept his tone conversational. "And you're not in trouble. I just need to ask some questions about Tuesday night."

Taber glanced at Sabre. She gave a small nod.

"Okay." The kid seemed to relax a little.

DuBois opened his notebook but didn't look at it. "Tell me where you were between five-thirty and nine p.m."

"Right here, at the house," Taber said. "Dinner was around six. I stayed in after."

"Anyone see you?" DuBois asked.

"The staff was around. The other guys were in and out."

"Was anyone with you the whole time?" DuBois pressed.

"No," Taber said quietly. "Not the whole time. I was mostly in my room."

That answer made sense. "Did you leave at any point?" DuBois asked.

"No. I don't have a car."

"Could you have walked to the Wilcox home?" DuBois asked.

The kid looked up, startled. "It's far."

"How far?" DuBois asked.

"Like three miles. Maybe more."

DuBois made a note. *A long walk, but doable.*

"So, you know where Mr. Wilcox lived?"

Taber stiffened.

Sabre leaned in slightly. "You can answer."

The boy choked up a little. "He lived near the park. I'd been there many times when Liam was alive."

"Did you go there Tuesday night?" DuBois asked.

"No." Taber shook his head vigorously. "I swear."

DuBois believed him, not because of the speed of the answer, but because of what came with it. Fear, yes. Anger, maybe. But not calculation.

"When was the last time you saw Abram Wilcox?"

"A few weeks ago. At a store."

"Did you talk to him?"

"I wanted to. I wanted to tell him how sorry I was about Liam."

"Why didn't you?"

"Because he looked so angry. Then he made a gesture like he was going to shoot me. So, I walked away."

"Were there any other incidents between the two of you?"

"Just one time months ago," Taber said. "After court. He waited outside, but he didn't say anything."

"Other than that, did he ever threaten?" DuBois asked.

"He didn't have to. And I only saw him at court after Liam..."

DuBois closed his notebook.

"Taber," he said, "I'm going to be straight with you. Right now, the evidence points to a robbery. But," DuBois continued, "I need to ask these questions because sometimes people see things they don't think matter."

Taber frowned. "Like what?"

"Has anyone asked you about Mr. Wilcox recently? Maybe, about where he lived? Anything like that?"

Taber thought for a moment. "No."

DuBois studied him for a bit, then stood. "That's all I have for now."

He paused at the door. "If you remember anything later, even something that feels stupid, tell Ms. Brown. We'll follow up."

The kid nodded.

Outside, DuBois stood for a moment, breathing in air that felt great after the small room.

Giovanni Taber had motive, proximity, and opportunity, but just barely. But DuBois couldn't shake the feeling that if the teenager had done this, the scene would've looked very different.

The perp had been patient. Teenage boys were rarely patient, especially those who were barely holding themselves together.

DuBois drove back to his office and started checking Wilcox's phone records. He didn't expect them to tell him much. They rarely did. Most of the time, it was just a collection of calls to family or coworkers, a predictable orbit that confirmed what they already knew.

He scanned the call log again, slower this time, pen hovering over the pages. One number caught his eye, not because it was unfamiliar, but because it didn't belong. It was a short outgoing call, less than a minute, to Child Protective Services.

DuBois frowned. Wilcox hadn't worked with social services, except maybe peripherally. He worked delinquency. It was possible he had followed up on a minor who had been in the dependency system and moved over to delinquency. But DuBois had reviewed Wilcox's caseload and hadn't seen anything that tied to social services.

DuBois circled the number, then picked up the phone and called it. After two transfers and a brief hold, a woman answered, her voice tired. "Child Protective Services."

"This is Homicide Detective DuBois with San Diego Police," he said. "I'm following up on a call made to your office a few days ago by a probation officer, Abram Wilcox."

There was a pause, followed by keyboard clicks.

"Do you have a case number?" she asked.

"I don't," DuBois said. "That's kind of the point."

"Do you have the exact time, or maybe the phone number that generated the call?"

DuBois gave her the information she asked for.

Another pause. Longer this time.

"I see the call," she said. "It didn't generate a case."

"Why not?"

"Because it wasn't a formal inquiry," she explained. "It was a quick verification question."

"About what?" DuBois asked.

She hesitated. "About a juvenile's status."

"Who?"

"Giovanni Taber."

He hadn't wanted to hear that. "What exactly was asked?" he said.

"He wanted to know if the juvenile was scheduled for a placement change," she replied. "Or if he'd already been moved."

"And?" DuBois asked.

"There was no transfer scheduled," she said. "I told him that. He said 'okay' and ended the call."

"That was it?"

"Yes. It lasted maybe forty seconds."

DuBois thanked her and hung up.

He sat back in his chair and mulled it over. Wilcox had called simply to check where Giovanni Taber was.

DuBois opened the kid's file and flipped through it again. The accident. The court ruling. The lesser conviction. The anger that never quite found a place to land. Parents didn't stop grieving just because a judge said the law had been satisfied.

Wilcox had been worried, or angry, or both. DuBois decided to revisit Taber's alibi. Not because he thought the boy was lying. He had to because the robbery theory didn't explain why a probation officer would be checking on the whereabouts of the boy who'd killed his son—right before someone came through his back door with a gun.

Chapter 25

Friday afternoon

At his home desk, JP thought about the things people forgot to change when they panicked. They often still ran their routines because they didn't know what else to do.

Luis Mendoza had gone dark fast, no phone, no cards, no digital residue worth chasing. That meant he was leaning on something old-school. People did that when they were scared and out of options. JP stood and headed out. It was time to go back to Rosalia's.

He parked around the corner and walked back to the home, head down, just another man cutting through a neighborhood on a Friday afternoon. He crossed the street and leaned against a light pole where he could see the front door clearly. This wasn't where someone hid. This was where someone tried to stay normal.

JP waited. At 3:12 p.m., the door opened. Rosalia Mendoza stepped out, locking up behind her. She wore jeans, a sweatshirt, and her hair pulled back tight. She didn't look over her shoulder or scan the street. She just stood there for a moment, as if steadying herself, then walked to her car.

JP hurried back to his car, waited until she drove off, then followed, never close, never obvious.

She went to the grocery store, then made a quick stop at a pharmacy, ordinary stops that didn't mean anything on their own. Then she turned onto a narrower street lined with small storefronts and parked near a panadería wedged between a travel agency and a barber shop.

JP circled the block, parked across the street, and got out. Not ready to go inside, he crossed to the opposite sidewalk and took a position beside a bus stop bench, close enough to see through the large front window.

Rosalia stood near the counter, not ordering, not browsing. She just waited.

JP crossed the street and stepped inside. The smell of sugar and yeast hit him immediately. He bought a coffee he didn't want and waited near the back wall, pretending to look at the bread on the shelf.

Rosalia moved toward a corkboard mounted on the wall near the back, half hidden behind a rack of bread baskets. The board was covered with flyers, handwritten notices for lost dogs, and room rentals.

She scanned it quickly, then reached up and removed a small, folded piece of paper pinned behind a larger flyer in the corner.

JP felt the quiet click of recognition.

She slipped the note into her pocket, glanced toward the counter, and walked out. Without buying anything or talking to anyone, Rosalia got back into her car and drove away.

JP stayed inside for another minute, watching the shop. People came and went. A woman balanced two pastry boxes, and a man argued gently with a child about which concha to pick.

JP moved toward the board. Up close, it was exactly what he'd expected, a community communication center. Notes were layered on notes, some fresh, some yellowed, and in no order.

JP took his coffee and stepped back outside. He hadn't found Mendoza, but he'd found the route Mendoza was using. And routes like that only worked until someone patient enough learned how to follow them without being seen.

More importantly, he knew that Mendoza was still local. The man was stalling because he didn't know what his next move was.

~~~

JP parked three blocks from Rosalia Mendoza's duplex. He knew from experience that people in hiding liked places that let you sit, watch, think, and leave without being remembered.

So, JP began at a public library two blocks from Rosalia's house. He walked through slowly, scanning faces instead of screens. A security guard nodded at him, bored. A librarian looked up briefly, then back down.

He showed the librarian Mendoza's photo.

"He looks familiar, but I can't be certain."

"He would likely be using the computers."

She shook her head. "I just can't say for certain."

He asked a better question. "Anybody been using the computers just to charge a phone?"

She frowned, thinking. "That happens."

"Anybody nervous about it?" JP asked.

That gave her pause. She shook her head. "Not lately."

JP thanked her and left.

Next stop was a bus terminal, a small transfer hub where routes overlapped, and people waited too long because they didn't know which way they were going. JP walked the perimeter, eyes up, ears open, but learned nothing new.

He drove farther south, stopping at a park tucked between apartment buildings. He walked the paths, watched the benches, and paid attention to who stayed longer than they needed to. It led him nowhere.

By the time he reached the Wash-and-Go, he was frustrated, but still hopeful. Laundromats were where people went when they needed electricity, warmth, and anonymity all at once.

JP parked and went inside.
~~~

The sound hit him first, washers pounding, dryers rattling, voices bouncing off the tile. The hum of machines was loud enough to swallow conversation. A man could sit there for hours and disappear without ever leaving town.

JP fed the change machine, letting the attendant clock him as harmless. He sat on a bench and waited, watching who came and went.

After ten minutes, he approached the attendant, a young man, only half alert.

"Has there been a guy in here lately," JP asked casually, "who doesn't do laundry?"

The attendant smirked. "That narrows it down to about forty people."

JP pulled his phone and showed him Mendoza's photo without comment.

The smirk vanished. "Yeah," the attendant said. "That guy."

"When?" JP asked.

"A couple of days ago. Late morning."

"What did he do?" JP asked.

"He charged his phone and didn't stay long."

JP waited.

The attendant lowered his voice. "He kept checking the door like someone was looking for him."

"Watching for cops?" JP asked.

The attendant shook his head. "It's hard to say. Maybe."

"Did anyone meet him?"

"No. And he didn't stay very long."

JP pocketed his phone and stepped outside.

Now it made sense. Mendoza wasn't moving in straight lines. He was bouncing between neutral zones where he could accomplish small tasks without being seen.

JP leaned against his truck and analyzed the pattern. Mendoza was still around and still afraid, but maybe not of law enforcement. If the driver thought the police were closing in, he would have fled to another city with a new name or crossed the border. *Unless he had an important reason to stay here.*

JP just had to figure out what that was. It could be money. In fact, it was usually money.

Chapter 26

Friday afternoon

DuBois didn't believe in coincidences, especially if they repeated themselves.

He sat at his desk with Abram Wilcox's financials spread out, the hum of the bullpen fading into background noise. He had bank statements with the withdrawal entries and dates circled in red pen.

Robbery victims had patterns. They lost wallets, electronics, and sometimes cash they'd just withdrawn for a purchase or a night out. What they didn't usually have was a quiet trail of withdrawals spaced just far enough apart to avoid attention. Wilcox did.

DuBois tapped the top page with his pen. Five withdrawals, all five grand in cash over a six-week period. Significant sums, but not enough to trigger an automatic alert. He'd been careful.

He pulled the timestamps closer. The withdrawals took place late afternoons and early evenings, but never on weekends.

DuBois leaned back and exhaled. If Wilcox had been randomly robbed, the withdrawal pattern didn't fit. Robbery was impulsive. It didn't leave tidy financial footprints leading up to it.

People who planned something and weren't sure how it would end, moved money first. They did it quietly, and in pieces, so they would have cash on hand without leaving a trail.

DuBois stood at the window, watching traffic slide past below. Commuters. Delivery trucks. Everyone moving like the day had meaning beyond itself.

As a probation officer, Wilcox had made enemies just by doing his job. That part still fit. But enemies didn't usually get paid.

DuBois turned back to his desk and grabbed Wilcox's phone records, flipping past the work numbers and family contacts. Something was missing. Not a number, but a reason.

He picked up his phone and made a note for later. *Re-check financials. Re-check timeline. Ask who Wilcox was worried about, not who was mad at him.*

DuBois capped his pen. The robbery theory was getting crowded out by something quieter, something that required planning. And planning meant motive lived before the night Wilcox died, not after.

DuBois couldn't shake the feeling he was seeing something totally unrelated to the robbery.

Chapter 27

Friday evening

JP let the call go to voicemail the first time. It was an unknown number, and he was in the middle of something.

He listened to the message a minute later. "JP, it's Brandy. I... I think I've got something. Not over the phone. Call me, and we can meet."

He finished what he was doing, and when he dialed back, she picked up on the first ring.

"Where?" he asked.

She gave him the location. A taco stand in an hour.

JP almost said no. Instead, he said, "I'll be there."

The taco stand was closed when he arrived, metal shutters pulled halfway down, the neon sign still buzzing faintly like it hadn't gotten the message. A single light hung over the side of the building.

Brandy stood just outside it, arms folded, shifting her weight from one foot to the other.

He stepped out, closed the door, and took a second to take her in before he said anything. She seemed a little edgier than before. He wondered if she was using.

"You said you had something," JP said.

"I do," she answered.

JP stayed where he was for a moment, then walked closer, stopping a few feet short of her. Not crowding. Not casual either. "Let's hear it."

Brandy glanced once toward the street, then back at him. “Mateo's father wasn't working alone before he disappeared.”

“You said that already.”

“This is different,” she said. “I know who he was tied to.”

JP watched her carefully. “How do you know that?”

“I asked,” she said. “People remember things when you remind them why they should.”

That wasn't an answer. “What's the name?” JP asked.

She hesitated.

“You don't have it,” he said.

“I can get it,” she snapped.

There it was again. Potential. Not product.

JP didn't move. “Then get it,” he said.

“It doesn't work like that,” she said, her voice tightening. “You don't just walk in and ask. You have to grease things. Make it worth their time.”

JP let out a slow breath through his nose.

“How much?”

Her eyes blinked. She apparently hadn't expected him to ask that fast. “A few thousand,” she said. “Not a lot. Just enough.”

JP almost smiled. “Not a lot,” he repeated.

“It's not,” she said quickly. “Not for what this will lead to.”

JP took a step closer now, just enough to change the angle.

“For what it *might* lead to,” he corrected.

Brandy's jaw tightened.

“This is about your son,” JP said. “Or it's about money. You need to decide which one you want me to believe.”

Her eyes flashed. “You think I'm playing you?”

“I think you're trying to sell me something you don't have,” JP said.

“That's not fair.”

“It's accurate.”

Brandy uncrossed her arms, then crossed them again, like she couldn't decide where to put them.

"You don't understand how this works," she said. "People don't just talk. You have to give them a reason."

"I already have one," JP said.

She shook her head. "Not the kind they care about."

JP studied her for a moment. "You already talked to someone," he said. It wasn't a question.

Brandy froze, just for a fraction. "I always talk to people."

"Yeah," JP said. "And they didn't give you anything you could use. So, now you're trying to turn it into something you can get paid for."

Her eyes narrowed. "That's not what this is."

"Then give me the name," JP said.

Silence. A car passed at the end of the block, headlights sweeping briefly across them before disappearing.

Brandy looked away first. "I can get it," she said again. "But I'm not doing it for free."

JP nodded once. "Then don't."

Her head snapped back toward him. "What?"

"I don't pay for guesses," JP said. "You bring me something real, I'll listen. Until then, we're done."

"You're making a mistake."

"Maybe," JP said. "But it won't be that one."

Brandy stepped closer now, closing the gap he'd left. "If you find Rafael, you let me know."

"That's not how this works."

"It is if you want me on your side."

"I don't know what side you're on yet," he said. "I'm not convinced you're not the one who set this whole thing up."

Brandy didn't respond. She didn't move. For a second, she looked like she might say something else. Then she stepped back.

JP turned, walked back to his car, and didn't look back.

Chapter 28

Saturday morning

JP signed in at the front desk of the precinct and waited, watching officers move through the space with controlled urgency. Phones rang. A printer jammed. Somewhere down the hall, someone laughed loudly. Miller had called him that morning and asked him to come in for a meeting. He assumed it was about Mateo's abduction.

A few minutes later, a uniformed officer waved him through security. JP followed the familiar route past open cubicles and closed doors, stopping when Miller stepped out of an office and motioned him inside.

"Thanks for coming." Miller closed the door behind them and gestured toward a chair.

"No problem. I wanted to tell you about Mateo's mom anyway." JP told him exactly what went down.

"So, you think it was just a shake down?"

"I think she knows more ways to get money than a roomful of lawyers."

Miller laughed. "You better not let Sabre hear you say that."

"Yer right."

"I checked out the mother's alibi. She said she was with her friend and neighbor, Franny Kirk."

"How'd that go?"

"Franny said all the right things, but they sounded rehearsed. You might want to take a crack at her. She might succumb to your down-home charm."

"I'll give it a shot."

"I've been trying to get information on Mateo's father, Rafael, but so far, no luck. He seems to have just disappeared. I've got Perkins checking the entire prison system. I'll let you know what he comes up with."

"And we still haven't found Mendoza," Miller said. "Whatever he's doing, he's being careful."

JP took a seat. "I haven't either, but I've found evidence that he's still local, and I believe he's scared."

Miller studied him for a second. "Yeah. That tracks."

He opened a folder but didn't slide it across right away. Instead, he said, "You were a cop."

"A long time ago."

"Not that long," Miller said. "Long enough to know I don't do this lightly."

JP said nothing.

Miller tapped the folder once. "I'm certain if I show up, Mendoza will run from me, but he might talk to you."

JP met his eyes. "And you don't want me stepping in the wrong place."

"Exactly. Or tipping him off," Miller added.

"That's fair."

He slid the file across the desk to display photographs from the transport van's dash cam, all at ground-level.

"Don't take copies," he said. "Don't share it. And if you find him, you call me before you do anything else."

JP looked down at the photos. "Understood."

"Can you walk me through these, from the stop forward?" JP asked.

"The van stops where we thought it did," Miller explained. "That hasn't changed. What has changed is what we're seeing after."

JP pointed. "Footprints."

"Two sets, in addition to Mateo's," Miller said. "They're both adult, different sizes and different tread patterns."

"Do they overlap?" JP asked.

"Yes. Which means two adults were present during at least part of the event."

JP studied the photos. "One stays close to the van and only on the driver's side, which is probably the driver."

"And the other moves farther away," Miller said. "Toward where we found the kid."

JP nodded. "Escalation."

"That's our read," Miller said. "Near the van, disturbance is minimal and controlled. Past that point, it's not."

Miller flipped to the next photo. "Here you see broken brush and irregular stride length. But no drag marks. And only two sets of prints."

"Which means Mateo was moving under his own power," JP said. "And only one adult was with him."

"At least for a while," Miller agreed. "But the footprints are not even or steady."

"Like he was staggering."

"Exactly. Which means he may have been drunk, sick, or drugged."

JP pointed to the next image. "Is that blood?"

Miller's expression tightened. "That's what changed things. It's not the victim's."

"How do you know?" JP asked.

"The hospital intake gave us his blood type," Miller said. "This doesn't match."

"But you don't know whose."

"No," Miller said firmly. "And we're not assuming. But the phone data is interesting."

JP looked up. "How so?"

"Mendoza's phone goes dark when the van stops," Miller said. "Then it comes back online later, closer to where the van was dumped. So, it's likely not a dead battery."

"It could've been a meeting or a confrontation."

"Or someone telling him to shut it off," Miller said.

JP closed the folder. "But you're confident this wasn't a single uninterrupted event."

"Yes," Miller said. "Something changes after the stop. Someone else is present, and it appears the control shifts."

"And after that," JP said, "Mendoza panics."

"That's consistent with how we interpret the evidence," Miller replied.

"Are you still treating Mendoza as a suspect in the abduction and assault?"

"Yes," Miller said. "But not as the sole actor. And I don't think he was the person who escalated things." The detective locked eyes on him. "Whoever stepped in when the van stopped is the one who worries me."

JP stood. "I bet that's who Mendoza is hiding from. That and the cops."

Miller didn't disagree. "Then if and when you find him, you need to get him in to talk to me."

JP stepped out into the hallway determined to find Mendoza. He still had a couple of places to check.

Chapter 29

Saturday afternoon

JP stopped at Rosalia Mendoza's again and was relieved to see that someone was there. He decided it was time to play his hand, so he knocked on the door.

Rosalia reluctantly opened the door. The chain stayed latched, the gap just wide enough for her to see him clearly and for him to see the worry in her haggard expression. "Yes?"

JP held up his hands, palms out. "I'm not the police."

"Then who are you? And what do you want?"

"JP Torn," he said. "I work for a juvenile court attorney. A kid got hurt recently, and your brother was there when it happened."

Her jaw tightened. "Luis didn't hurt anyone."

"I know," JP said calmly.

That made her look at him again, this time sizing him up and down.

JP waited. Silence was one of the few things people didn't know how to fight.

Finally, Rosalia slid the chain free and opened the door, but kept the entry blocked.

"I don't know where he is."

"I didn't ask," JP replied. He stayed where he was. People noticed when you respected them. "You're scared for him."

Rosalia let out a short, humorless laugh. "Wouldn't you be?"

"Yes, ma'am. Especially if the wrong people were looking for me."

That did it. Her shoulders sagged, and she let out a sigh. "He didn't plan any of this," she said. "Luis took the job because it was steady, and he needed the money. He never wanted trouble."

"I believe you," JP said. "That's why I'm here."

She folded her arms. "Then why does everyone keep acting like he's the problem?"

"Who is everyone?"

"The cops."

"Because he didn't disappear cleanly," JP said. "That makes him easy."

Rosalia looked away, blinking hard. "Luis called me after it happened. He said something went wrong. That that particular kid wasn't supposed to be there."

That was new information. "What else did he say?"

"Nothing that makes sense," she said. "Just that he was scared. That someone else lost control and that he tried to stop it."

"Did he say who?" JP asked.

She shook her head. "No. And I didn't ask."

That told JP plenty. "Did you help him?"

"Yes," she replied without hesitation. "And I would do it again."

"I know," JP said. "But you didn't hide him here."

Her eyes flicked up, sharp, quick.

And just as quickly, JP heard a soft thud from inside. It came from the back of the house.

Rosalia didn't move. She didn't breathe. That told him everything he needed to know.

JP stepped sideways, just enough to see past her shoulder. "Luis," he called. "You don't want to run from me."

Rosalia grabbed the door instinctively. "There's no one—"

JP heard a door at the back of the house open. He moved, not fast enough to spook, but fast enough to matter. He slipped past Rosalia before she could stop him.

"Hey!" Rosalia yelled.

JP was already through the house. The back door slammed open just as JP hit the kitchen. A man bolted through it.

"Luis!" JP called.

Mendoza didn't look back.

JP hit the doorway and pushed outside. The yard was tight, fenced, cluttered with old patio furniture and a narrow path along the side.

Mendoza was already halfway down it. He was fast, desperate.

JP went after him in a full sprint, dodging obstacles in his way.

Mendoza vaulted the side gate, barely clearing it.

JP reached it seconds later, shoved it open, and pushed through. They hit the alley, stumbled over trash cans and loose gravel. A stray dog was barking somewhere behind a fence.

Mendoza cut left.

JP followed. "Luis!" He called again. "I'm not your problem!"

That got a glance. Just one. Over Mendoza's shoulder.

JP saw him clearly now. Mid-thirties. Lean. Worn down. Eyes wired with fear, not anger.

"Stop running!" JP shouted.

Mendoza didn't. He cut between two buildings, squeezing through a narrow gap.

JP followed, slower now. Careful. Not a place where you rushed blind. By the time JP cleared it, Mendoza was gone. Just like that.

JP slowed to a stop in the open lot beyond. He listened, but there was nothing but distant traffic and the echo of that dog still barking.

He exhaled, then turned back, retracing his steps to the house. Rosalia stood just inside the back door now, pale.

"You shouldn't have done that," she said.

"He's alive," JP replied.

She didn't answer.

"He's scared of the wrong people," JP said. "Not me."

"They'll kill him," she said again, quieter this time.

JP believed that.

Rosalia's voice dropped. "They'll kill him if they find him."

JP took her word for it. "Who are they?"

"I don't know. But Luis didn't beat that kid," Rosalia said firmly. "He wouldn't. He couldn't."

JP met her gaze. "I believe that too."

She studied him for a long moment. "Then why are you really here?"

JP answered honestly. "Because your brother's fear tells me who the real danger is."

Rosalia swallowed. "I don't know who hired them. Luis didn't trust anyone enough to say any names out loud. He wanted to keep me out of it."

"That's okay," JP said. "You've already told me what's important."

"And what's that?" she asked.

JP stepped back from the doorway. "That your brother's not running from the law. He's running from the person who is the wrong kind of help."

Rosalia closed her eyes briefly.

"If Luis reaches out again, tell him that the worst thing he can do now is stay silent," JP said. "And the safest thing he can do is tell the truth."

Rosalia swallowed hard. "He doesn't know who to trust."

JP nodded once. "That makes two of us."

JP stepped back toward the front of the house. Mendoza wasn't innocent, but he wasn't the one driving this.

JP got into his truck and drove away. He had one more stop to make. He hadn't thought about Nadine in days. That bothered him. He didn't like threads that disappeared.

Twenty minutes later, he was parked outside the taco stand where she worked. It was almost closing time, and the metal shutter was halfway down, but the lights were still on.

JP stepped out and hurried to the entry. The bell over the side window jingled as he ducked under the half-lowered gate.

Pink-haired Nadine looked up. "You again." There was no warmth in her voice, but no hostility either.

"I'm still looking for Mendoza," JP said.

She stiffened. "So?"

"He didn't just disappear," JP said. "Someone scared him."

She didn't answer.

JP leaned against the counter. "I'm not here to jam you up. I want to help."

Her jaw tightened. "I don't talk to cops."

"I'm not one."

"You carry like one."

JP shrugged. "Mendoza ran because someone is after him. If you know anything, now would be a good time to tell."

Nadine looked toward the rear of the stand, then back at JP. "There was a guy who dressed clean, like office-clean. He came by twice, asking if Luis had been around."

JP went still. "When?"

"Three or four days before Luis disappeared."

"What'd he want?"

"He just said he had 'work.'"

"Describe him."

"He was in his forties, maybe, and wore a dark jacket. I didn't see any tattoos and no gang vibe. He wasn't slumming it, instead, he looked annoyed to be here."

"Did he give a name?"

She shook her head. "But he had a car."

"You saw him in the car?"

"Yes. He parked right in front."

"What kind?"

"I don't know the make, but it was gray, not new-new, but clean. I didn't see any dents or anything that made it stand out. It had a dealer plate frame from a place out in Mission Valley."

JP filed that. "Anything else?"

Nadine hesitated. "He paid for three tacos, but he didn't eat them. He just sat there with the tacos, then threw them away when he left."

JP looked at her. "Did he seem nervous?"

"Not really," she said. "He was watching."

"Watching what?"

"Luis."

"Did he ever talk to him?" JP asked.

"No, and the guy never came back. That's the last time I saw Luis."

JP nodded. This operation hadn't been random or impulsive.

Chapter 30

Saturday afternoon

DuBois stood at the whiteboard in the small conference room, sleeves rolled up, marker uncapped but idle. Abram Wilcox's name displayed at the top, written in block letters. Under it were dates, times, and bank withdrawals. Victims who planned ahead were complicated. And sometimes also accomplices. The truth usually hid in the middle somewhere. DuBois tapped the board with the marker. People didn't pull out money in measured amounts weeks before they were killed... unless they expected to hand it to someone or already had.

DuBois stared at Wilcox's photo on the file cover. He was a middle-aged man with tired eyes. The kind of man who'd seen too much and thought he could still control the outcomes. *Control.* That was the word that kept circling back.

He pulled Wilcox's phone records again, not looking for numbers this time, but patterns. He searched for short calls, calls with no messages, and contacts that appeared briefly, then vanished from the log.

Wilcox had enemies. Every probation officer did. But enemies didn't usually get paid in advance. And they didn't usually stand in the yard and wait.

DuBois circled a date on the board. Six weeks before Wilcox died. That was when the withdrawals started. Whatever Wilcox had been up to, it hadn't begun the night he was killed.

DuBois capped the marker and stepped back. Abram Wilcox wasn't a man who'd been in the wrong place at the wrong time. He'd been preparing for something and hadn't survived it.

DuBois was done treating him like a passive victim. Whatever Wilcox had set in motion was still out there. And now DuBois intended to find out who'd been on the receiving end of those cash withdrawals.

He pulled out his cell phone and called Detective Perkins. "Pull the info you have on Abram Wilcox and join me in the conference room."

A few minutes later, Detective Perkins joined DuBois.

"Thanks," DuBois said when he sat down. "I need you to walk me through Wilcox's last month again, but slow it down this time. I want it step by step."

"The first withdrawal was on a Wednesday at 4:37 p.m. at a bank on University."

"Amount?"

"Five thousand."

"Next?"

"The following week. Thursday. Different bank. Same general time. Same amount."

DuBois finally turned, leaning back against the board. "Was it the same amount every time?"

"Yes," Perkins said.

"Keep going."

Perkins flipped a page. "Five total withdrawals. Always midweek. Always late afternoon or early evening."

"Routine," DuBois said.

"Yeah," Perkins agreed. "But not his normal routine."

DuBois pointed the marker at him.

"Explain."

"Wilcox logs everything," Perkins said. "He's consistent. Predictable. Overtime on most days. Paper trail's tight."

DuBois nodded. "And on these days?"

Perkins looked down again. "Three nights, he stays late like usual," Perkins said. "Two nights, he leaves early."

"How early?"

"Before five," Perkins said. "No overtime logged. No notes. No explanation."

DuBois walked the length of the room once, then back. "Where are the banks?" he asked. "Map them for me."

Perkins frowned, flipping pages, then pulling his phone. "Give me a second." He looked up a moment later. "They're spread out," he said. "Not clustered."

"Random?"

"No," he said slowly. "Not random. They're all along the same general corridor." Perkins turned the phone toward him. "Within a few miles of each other, but different banks, different corners."

DuBois stepped closer. "Show me."

Perkins zoomed out. Five pins. Loose pattern. But not scattered. A path.

DuBois took the marker and drew a rough line across the board.

"Is it a commute?" Perkins asked.

DuBois shook his head. "Not home to work. The angle's wrong."

He tapped one of the dates. "Now overlay the early days."

Perkins checked. "Two of these are the same zone. Within a mile."

"There it is," DuBois said.

Perkins leaned forward. "What am I seeing?"

DuBois circled the two early-leave dates. "Those are the only days he changes his behavior. He leaves early. No record. No explanation. And both of those days," DuBois continued, tapping the board, "he pulls cash in the same area."

Perkins sat back slightly. "Do you think he was meeting someone?"

"That's what I'm thinking."

"Then why the other three withdrawals?" he asked. "He stays late those nights."

DuBois turned back to the board.

"Because whatever this is," he said, "it doesn't start clean." DuBois pointed to the first date. "He tests it. Withdraws. Maybe no meeting. Maybe wrong timing."

"The next date, he adjusts. The next, he gets closer. Then, the two early days he commits."

Perkins nodded slowly. "That doesn't sound like robbery."

"No," he said. "Robbery doesn't come in installments."

The younger detective looked back at the map. "So, what is it?"

DuBois capped the marker, then uncapped it again. "Pressure," he said.

"Blackmail?"

"Maybe," DuBois said.

DuBois pointed to the two early-leave locations.

"Start here," he said. "Pull cameras from anything facing these intersections. Businesses, traffic, whatever we can get."

"Six weeks back?" Perkins said.

"Yeah."

"That's a long shot."

"So, is everything else right now," DuBois replied.

Perkins stood. "I'll start pulling requests."

"Don't just look for Wilcox," DuBois added. "Look for consistency."

"Meaning?"

"Same car," DuBois said. "Same person. Someone who shows up more than once."

Perkins nodded and headed for the door, then stopped. "Do you have any idea what he might have been blackmailed for?"

"No, but I know someone who might be able to weigh in on that." DuBois looked back at the board. "I think whatever he was doing, he thought it would solve a problem. And it didn't."

Chapter 31

Saturday late afternoon

The address sat in a quiet neighborhood that looked like it had decided, collectively, not to draw attention to itself. The lawns were neat, the garage doors closed, and the curtains pulled just enough to suggest privacy without inviting questions.

DuBois parked at the curb and sat for a moment, reviewing what little they had. Evelyn Wilcox. Divorced two years. One son, deceased.

He stepped out of the car and walked up the path, noticing the small details automatically—the camera mounted above the garage, the trimmed hedges, the absence of anything out of place.

He knocked. It took longer than it should have. Then the door opened. Evelyn Wilcox stood there, in her forties, composed in a way that didn't read as natural. Her hair was pulled back tightly, not a strand out of place. Her eyes, though, told the truth. They were tired in a way sleep couldn't fix.

"Yes?" she said. No warmth. No curiosity.

DuBois held up his badge. "I'm Detective DuBois. I'm sorry for your loss."

She looked at the badge, then at him. "Which one?"

"Your ex-husband," he said.

"You should come in."

The house matched the outside, clean, ordered, nothing unnecessary.

DuBois sat where she indicated, taking in the room without making it obvious. There were no visible photos of Wilcox and only one of Liam. It was front and center.

"I assume you're here because someone finally realized Abram wasn't as clean as he looked," she said.

DuBois appreciated her directness. "I'm here because he was murdered. And you were someone who knew him well."

A faint smile touched her mouth. "I used to."

DuBois opened his notebook, though he didn't look at it yet. "When was the last time you spoke to him?"

"About a week before he died."

"And how did that conversation go?"

She didn't hesitate. "Poorly."

"Can you be more specific?"

Evelyn leaned back slightly, studying him. "He wanted to talk about Liam. About 'moving forward.'"

DuBois said nothing.

"He liked that phrase," she continued. "Moving forward. Like grief was a schedule you could manage if you just applied enough structure."

"And you disagreed?"

Her eyes sharpened. "My son is dead. There's no forward from that."

"Did you blame Abram?" he asked.

She held his gaze. "I still do." No hesitation. No apology.

"For what?" DuBois asked.

"For pushing that boy too hard," she said. "For making everything about rules and consequences and pressure."

"And for letting him ride with Giovanni Taber?"

"Yes."

"You think Abram caused the accident."

"I think he created the conditions for it," she said. "And then he spent the rest of his time pretending he didn't."

DuBois wrote that down. Not because he needed it. Because she needed to see that it mattered.

"Where were you the night Abram died?" DuBois asked.

"At home."

"Alone?"

"Yes."

"Is there anyone who can confirm that?"

"No." She didn't flinch or try to fix it.

DuBois nodded slightly. "Did you ever threaten your ex?"

Her eyes narrowed. "Are you asking if I said I wanted him dead?"

"I'm asking what you said."

Another pause. Longer this time. "I told him he didn't deserve to move on," she said. "That some things shouldn't be forgiven."

"Did you ever act on that?"

"Are you asking me if I killed him?"

"Did you?"

"No." Flat. Immediate.

"Did Abram have any enemies?"

"He made them for a living," she said. "Kids. Parents. People who thought he went too far."

"Anyone in particular?"

Her gaze glanced briefly toward the photo of Liam. Then back. "No one who mattered more than he did," she said.

That was an answer. Just not a clean one. "Do you know anything he could've been blackmailed for?"

She seemed surprised at that question. "You mean did he do anything in his life that he would have paid to cover up?"

"Yeah."

"Not unless it was after we separated. Before that, he was a straight shooter. I may not have liked some of the things he did, but he was always honest and above board. I can't imagine anyone would have anything on him."

DuBois stood. He walked toward the door, then paused. "One more thing, did Abram seem afraid recently?"

"No," she said. "He seemed... focused."

"On what?"

She shook her head.

"I don't know," she said. "But whatever it was, he thought he could fix it."

Outside, the air felt cooler than it had when he arrived. DuBois walked back to his car, not rushing.

Evelyn Wilcox had motive. She had no alibi. No hesitation. No regret. But something didn't fit, or maybe he didn't want it to. But people who killed in anger didn't usually stage restraint. They didn't take wallets. They didn't leave clean scenes behind.

Still— He pulled out his phone and made the call. "Perkins," he said. "I want background on Evelyn Wilcox. Financials. Phone records. Anyone she's been in contact with the last month."

Chapter 32

Saturday evening

Sabre arrived at the group home in time to speak to Giovanni before DuBois got there. She was concerned that the detective wanted another interview so soon. She signed in at the front desk, stuck the visitor badge to her jacket, and waited while the house manager finished a phone call.

"Giovanni's in the common room," the woman finally said. "I'll walk you back."

They moved down the hall past closed bedroom doors and a television murmuring to itself. Giovanni sat on one end of a couch, shoulders hunched, eyes fixed on his hands. He looked thinner than she remembered, and he seemed tired.

"Giovanni," the manager said, "Please wait for Ms. Brown in the interview room."

After Giovanni left, the house manager said, "Can I talk to you a minute?"

"Of course." Sabre followed her a few steps back toward the hall.

"A probation officer was here last week," the manager said quietly. "Abram Wilcox."

"Wilcox was here?"

"Yes. He didn't have a scheduled visit. He just showed up."

"What did he want?" Sabre asked.

The woman frowned. "He asked questions about Giovanni. He asked how he was doing, and whether he was having trouble sleeping. And he asked if he ever talked about the accident."

Sabre felt a slow tightening in her chest. "Was he assigned to Giovanni?"

The manager shook her head. "That's why his visit stood out. It wasn't inappropriate exactly, but it wasn't routine either."

"Did Giovanni know he was here?" Sabre asked.

"Yes," the manager said. "He spoke to him briefly. After that, Giovanni was kind of *off* for a couple of days."

"Off how?"

"Quiet," the woman said. "More than usual."

Sabre thanked her, then asked, "Is Iverson here today?"

"No. But he'll be on duty tomorrow afternoon."

As she walked back down the hall, the house manager's words replayed in her mind.

He just showed up. He asked questions. It wasn't routine.

Wilcox had crossed a line, not a legal one, but a personal one. And Giovanni's silence hadn't helped him.

Sabre continued toward the interview room, her steps slower now.

Giovanni looked up when he saw her. "You're back."

"I wanted to check on you." Sabre took the chair across from him. "See how you're holding up."

He shrugged. "The same."

Sabre looked him in the eyes. "Did Probation come to see you last week?"

His shoulders stiffened.

"More specifically, did Wilcox come to see you?" she asked.

Giovanni's jaw tightened, and he stayed silent.

"Giovanni," Sabre said gently. "I already know he was here."

He stared at the floor. "He said he was here to see someone else, but he didn't talk to anyone else except Mrs. Stephenson. I didn't tell you because—" He stopped, swallowed. "I thought it made me look bad."

"How?" Sabre asked.

"Like I had something to hide," he said. "Like I did something."

Sabre leaned forward. "Did you?"

He shook his head quickly. "No. I swear. I didn't do anything."

"What did you talk about?"

"He just asked me things."

"Like what?" Sabre asked.

Giovanni hesitated, then spoke fast, like he needed to get it out. "If I remembered the night. If I thought about Liam a lot. If I ever got angry about what happened."

"And?" Sabre asked.

"I do think about it," Giovanni said. "Every day. But I didn't hurt Mr. Wilcox. I didn't go anywhere. I didn't—" He stopped himself. "I was scared it would sound wrong."

Sabre sat back, absorbing that. "You should've told me."

"I know," Giovanni said quietly. "I just didn't want you thinking I did something else too."

Sabre stood a moment later, feeling unsettled.

"Detective DuBois is coming here to question you again. He probably already knows about Wilcox's visit, so you need to be honest."

Sabre waited in the interview room with Giovanni, but a new thought had taken hold, unwelcome and persistent. *What if Giovanni had done something?* She didn't believe it yet. But she could no longer dismiss it either.

~~~

DuBois stepped into the interview room. It was small and over-lit, the table bolted down, the walls bare except for a laminated poster about anger management. Giovanni Taber sat on the far side of the table, shoulders tight, hands clasped like he was holding something in place.

Sabre sat beside him, legal pad open.
~~~

DuBois sat and got right into it. "The other day when we talked, you said the last time you saw Abram Wilcox was at a convenience store. A few weeks after the trial."

Taber nodded cautiously. "Yeah."

"Since then," DuBois continued, "I've learned Wilcox came to your group home last week and spoke to you directly."

The kid's eyes moved toward Sabre, then back.

"What you told me wasn't true," DuBois said. "Help me understand why."

Taber swallowed. "I didn't think that visit mattered."

DuBois waited.

"I mean, he wasn't supposed to be here. He just showed up, asked some questions, and left."

"You didn't think that was important?"

The kid lowered his head. "I didn't want it to look like I was connected to him."

"Connected how?" DuBois asked.

"Like I was involved in anything."

Sabre spoke softly. "You should've told us."

"I know," Taber said quickly. "It's just that every time his name comes up, things get worse for me."

DuBois studied him. The kid wasn't calculating. He was afraid.

"What did Wilcox want?" DuBois asked.

"He asked about the accident. He wanted to know if I remembered everything. Mostly, he wanted to know if I ever thought about Liam."

"And do you?" DuBois asked.

Giovanni's voice dropped. "Every day."

"Did Wilcox accuse you of anything?"

"No. But he looked at me like he was waiting for me to say something."

"What?" DuBois pressed.

"I don't know," Taber said. "Maybe an apology. But I've done that many times, and it just seems to make him angry."

"Did you tell anyone about the visit?"

"No." Taber shook his head.

DuBois shifted gears. "Let's talk about Tuesday night."

Taber stiffened.

"Where were you between five-thirty and nine?" DuBois asked.

"Here, like I told you last time," Taber said. "After dinner, I went to my room and watched TV."

"Was anyone with you in your room?" DuBois asked.

"No."

"Did you leave the property?" DuBois asked.

"No. I don't have a car, and you said yourself that Wilcox lived about three miles away." Taber's eyes widened. "I didn't go there."

"I'm still concerned that you didn't tell me Wilcox came here."

The kid looked down again. "I knew it would look bad."

"That's usually when it matters most." DuBois stood. "I'm not arresting you. But I'm not ignoring this either."

Out in the hall, Sabre closed the door behind them. "Do you think he's lying?"

"I think he's choosing his truths," DuBois replied. "He didn't remember that last time he said he was playing video games. This time he said he was watching TV."

"You caught that, did ya?"

"Choosing your truth always complicates things."

Chapter 33

Sunday afternoon

When JP went looking for the truth, he assumed that people would be protecting it. He wanted to double check Giovanni's alibi since the boy had lied about not seeing Wilcox recently. Perhaps there was more.

The group home seemed more settled than it had during the week. The lights were low, television noise drifted from the common room, and the rhythm felt like a place winding down. JP signed in and asked for Iverson.

They headed to a small room reserved for interviews.

JP got right to the point. "I need to know if Giovanni left the property Tuesday night."

"Like I told you last time, he didn't leave," Iverson said. "If he had, I'd know."

"I'm not saying you let him."

Iverson's eyes narrowed. "Then what are you saying?"

"I'm saying kids are good at finding cracks," JP replied. "And adults are good at not wanting to see them."

Iverson studied him for a moment, then sighed. "He had a window of opportunity after dinner. Not long though. If he slipped out, it would've been quick."

"Would you have approved it?" JP asked.

"No," Iverson said flatly.

"Then he wouldn't have asked, right?" JP said.

"Probably not."

"Can I speak to Jeremiah again?"

"I'll get him." Iverson stood. "You can stay here and talk to him. It's more private than anywhere else."

JP knew how kids that age worked. He was pretty certain if anyone knew anything, it would be Giovanni's roommate. He had decided to call his bluff.

The kid opened the door halfway, eyes cautious. "You again."

"Yep. I need to ask a few more questions about Giovanni."

"I don't know anything."

"I think you know more than you told me last time."

"Not really."

"Tell me this, if you were going to sneak out of here, could you do it without getting caught?"

"Probably."

"Would Giovanni cover for you?"

"I'm sure he would."

"And I'd bet you'd cover for him as well?"

Jeremiah hesitated. "I didn't cover for him if that's what you're getting at."

"I think you did."

The kid bristled. "I didn't lie."

"But you didn't tell everything," JP said calmly.

Silence stretched.

"I'm not here to get anyone in trouble," JP continued. "But right now, people think Giovanni might've hurt someone. And the only thing standing between him and that assumption is the truth."

The kid looked away.

"Iverson didn't know," JP said. "Which means if Giovanni stepped out, someone helped him keep it quiet."

"He didn't go far," Jeremiah said finally. "Just a couple of blocks."

"Why?" JP asked.

"He was meeting a girl."

"What's her name?"

"Kayleigh. She doesn't live that close by, and she works at the convenience store on Imperial near her house."

"How long was Giovanni gone?"

"Twenty minutes," the kid said. "Maybe thirty. He was back before Iverson made rounds."

"Did he have a ride?" JP asked.

"No. He walked." Jeremiah stood and started to pace. "I don't want to get him in trouble."

"You didn't," JP said. "You just waited a little too long, but this will help him, not hurt him."

Outside, JP stood on the sidewalk and looked in the direction Jeremiah had pointed.

Could Giovanni have had time to walk to meet the girl and either use her car or drive with her to Wilcox's house? Jeremiah said he was only gone twenty or thirty minutes, but he also said he'd cover for him.

JP drove east, parked across from the convenience store, and waited.

A young woman stepped out a few minutes later, sweater folded over one arm, phone in hand. She looked older than Giovanni, with reddish-blonde hair and tattoos on both forearms.

JP got out and approached slowly, hands visible. "Kayleigh?"

She froze. "Who are you?"

"My name's JP," he said. "I'm looking into something for Giovanni Taber. Did you see him Tuesday night?"

"If I say yes, will he get into trouble?"

"More likely the opposite. Don't worry. I'm not going to tell Iverson."

She hesitated, then nodded. "I saw him for a little while."

"Where?" JP asked.

"Here. He came to see me on my break. We talked. That's all."

"What time?" JP asked.

"Six-thirty."

"How long did he stay?"

"Till about seven."

"Did you go anywhere with him during that time?"

"No."

"What about afterward?"

"I went back to work, and he went home."

"Did you loan him your car?"

She frowned. "I don't have a car."

"Did he seem upset?" JP asked.

She answered quickly. "No. He seemed really happy. We don't get to see each other that much, so it was nice."

"Thank you. You've been very helpful."

"Is Giovanni in trouble?"

"Only if the truth doesn't show up," JP said.

When JP walked back to his truck, the pieces finally settled into place.

Giovanni had lied, but not to cover a crime. He'd lied the way teenagers did when they were afraid of getting caught doing something small that felt big in the moment. That meant the space between five-thirty and nine wasn't a blank anymore. At least part of it was accounted for. Unless, of course, Kayleigh was covering for him.

JP called Sabre to let her know what he'd learned.

"Do you think Kayleigh is telling the truth?"

"She could be talking with her tongue outside her shoe, but I don't think so."

Chapter 34

Sunday evening

Dinner unfolded the way it usually did when everyone was home. Gene told a story that started in the middle and wandered around before it found an ending. Conner argued about whether potatoes counted as vegetables. Morgan talked more than she listened. And Dené sat cross-legged on her chair, picking at her food.

It was ordinary, comfortingly so. Sabre let herself stay in it longer than she normally would. JP caught her eye from across the table, a look that said later. She nodded. Later was fine.

When the dishes were cleared and the kids drifted away, Sabre and JP lingered in the kitchen with mugs of coffee neither of them really needed.

"So, what did you learn about Giovanni?" Sabre asked.

JP leaned against the counter. "He stepped out Tuesday night, for about half an hour, to meet a girl at her workplace."

Sabre closed her eyes for a moment. "So, he lied about not leaving too."

"That kid's as full of wind as a corn-eatin' horse."

"At least it explains the gap. And if the timing's true, it might actually give him an alibi."

"DuBois probably won't clear him," JP said, "But he's also not building a case."

As they stood in the quiet kitchen, Dené wandered back in. "Can I ask something?"

Sabre turned. "Of course."

"It's about Mateo," Dené said. "Is he still in the hospital?"

"Yes"

Dené frowned. "He was acting weird at school that day."

Sabre's attention sharpened. "What do you mean by weird?"

"He kept saying how much it sucked when adults made decisions without telling him," Dené explained. "Like when they decided stuff, and he was transferred before he knew it."

"Did he say he was leaving?" Sabre asked.

"I don't think he knew until lunch time," Dené said. "Because earlier he was talking about the quiz we had coming up."

Sabre felt a shift, not alarm, but awareness.

After Dené went back to her room, Sabre leaned against the counter, staring at the darkened window.

"He didn't expect to be moved until the last minute," she said quietly. "Which isn't unusual, but I should've been given notice."

JP looked at her. "And it sounds rushed."

Sabre reached for her phone. "I want to take another look at the timing on the transfer. Who authorized it, and when."

"That's a different approach."

Sabre nodded. "We need to find out who knew about the transfer before Mateo did."

Chapter 35

Monday morning

Sabre finished her hearings at court and then drove to the Department of Social Services. She approached a clerk and introduced herself. "I'm updating my notes," she said. "I want to confirm the timing on Mateo Alvarez's transfer."

The clerk took a moment to check the computer files. "Placement approval came through early afternoon. It was a same-day move."

"How early?" Sabre asked.

"Around noon, maybe a little before."

"And transport?" Sabre asked.

"It was requested immediately."

Sabre thanked her and headed back to the lobby. There was nothing improper and nothing out of order. But speed was often sloppy.

She called Polinsky to get general information without naming Mateo.

"When a same-day placement opens," she said, "how much notice does the child usually get?"

"Not much," the supervisor said. "Sometimes none. We try, but once the bed's approved, we move."

"So, the child might not know until pickup," Sabre said.

"That's common," the woman replied. "Especially when the timing is tight."

Sabre pulled Mateo's file and focused on timestamps. *Placement approved: 11:22 a.m. Transport requested: 12:07 p.m. Pickup logged: 1:15 p.m.*

The process had been efficient and fast enough that no one had time to second-guess it.

She called Hannah, a caseworker she trusted, someone who'd been around long enough to see patterns form and break.

Sabre gave her the details, then asked, "Does that seem rushed?"

"Fast, yes. Wrong, no."

"But not typical," Sabre said.

"Only if someone was watching the board," Hannah said. "Waiting for a bed to open."

Sabre frowned. "Watching for a specific kid?"

"No. Watching for a window where a transport could be made."

Sabre walked back to her car with that phrase looping in her mind. A window.

Mateo hadn't known he was leaving because kids almost never knew ahead of time. But someone else had known the moment the system turned green, not because Mateo mattered, but because timing did.

She called JP. "I think the move happened fast because the system allows it to."

"And someone exploited that," JP said.

"Not the kid. The process. But I don't know who was watching," she added. "And I don't know why."

"But you know where the weakness is," JP said.

"I guess," she said.

"So, what now?"

Sabre's phone beeped with an incoming call. "Hold on a second." She took the other call.

"Hi Sabre, this is Paul Reyes. Can you come by my office? There's something I think you should know."

"Of course." Sabre clicked back to JP. "Officer Reyes, Wilcox's best friend, wants to see me. Can you come along?"

~~~

Sabre and JP found Probation Officer Reyes in a narrow office, door half-open, a stack of files balanced on the corner of his desk. He glanced up when she knocked, his expression unreadable. They stepped inside and closed the door. She introduced the two men.

"Nice to see you, Sabre, and to meet you, JP." He stood to greet them. "Thanks for coming in."

"Of course," Sabre said. "What's this all about?"

"Have a seat." They all sat down.

"You warned me about Wilcox before anyone else did. I assume you have more to report about him."

"Unfortunately." Reyes sighed. "Abram wasn't okay."

Sabre waited.

"He looked like he wasn't sleeping much, and he'd stopped eating lunch. He was staying late but not doing work. He'd just sit there, staring at a file he wasn't assigned to."

"Giovanni Taber's."

Reyes nodded. "Abram was fixated on it." The PO shifted in his chair. "He couldn't let go of the idea that Taber got away with something. Not legally, but morally. Abram was stuck there."

"Did he talk about taking action?"

"Not directly," Reyes said. "But he talked about fairness, about consequences, and how the system protected the wrong people."

Sabre thought of Giovanni, scared and already punished in ways no sentence could measure. "Did Wilcox have enemies?" she asked.

Reyes snorted. "We all do. We put conditions on people's lives, and they get mad. But upset enough to kill someone? Not usually. I can't think of anyone who would fit that mold."

"So, why are you telling me all this?" Sabre asked quietly.
~~~

Reyes met her eyes. "Because when I heard how Abram died, it didn't fit."

"Didn't fit what?" Sabre asked.

"Robbery," Reyes said flatly. "Abram wasn't careless. He didn't flash money and didn't bring trouble home."

Sabre absorbed that. "You think the murder was personal?"

"Yes," Reyes said. "And I think the motive, whatever it was, started long before that night."

Sabre decided to ask him right out. "Do you think Giovanni killed Wilcox?"

"I don't have any reason to think that."

"So, how does any of this make sense?"

"It doesn't," Reyes said, "but I think it's related somehow. Maybe because of the way he was acting, I'm reading too much into it."

"Have you told DuBois about Abram's behavior?"

"Not yet," Reyes said. "I wanted you to know first."

"Why?"

Reyes hesitated. "Because you represent the kid Abram was obsessed with. And I don't want to point a finger at Giovanni. And because Abram was my friend. I hate to make him look bad, but I'd like to know who really killed him."

JP spoke for the first time. "Is there anything else you can tell us about him? What was a normal day for him? Close friends? Family?""He had no other family in the area. And I was probably the only friend he had left after the accident. He drove everyone away. It was as if he wanted to be alone."

"But you didn't leave, right?" Sabre asked.

"He tried to get rid of me too, but I didn't let him. Although, he wouldn't really go anywhere with me anymore. He'd go to work and then go home. He didn't have much of a social life. He was working out at a gym just a few blocks from his house for a while, but then he quit that."

JP got the name of the gym from him. "Did he go anywhere else regularly?"

"He had a coffee house he'd stop at both going and coming from work."

"Do you know the name of the coffee shop?"

"I never went there, but I'd see the name on his cup every morning. It was called *Common Ground*."

"Clever," JP said.

~~~

Sabre left the office thinking about the victim. Wilcox hadn't just been grieving. He'd been unraveling. And his mental health issue had been building, obsessively, until it may have led to his death.

The murder hadn't been a crime of opportunity. It had been a crime of purpose. She just hoped Giovanni wasn't also a target.

Her phone buzzed. An alarm reminding her of their appointment with Mateo's doctors.
~~~

Chapter 36

Monday late morning

In the hospital conference room, JP stood near the window while Sabre sat at the small table, legal pad open. Across from them were two doctors, one trauma, one toxicology. Both were careful in the way people were when they knew their words might end up in court.

"I represent Mateo Alvarez," Sabre said. "I need to understand what you know."

The trauma physician nodded. "Of course."

JP watched the way the doctor folded his hands before he spoke. That was never a good sign.

"Mateo's injuries are serious," the doctor began. "But they're concentrated. We're not seeing multiple impact points across the body."

Sabre looked up. "What does that tell you?"

"It suggests the force was applied in a controlled setting," the doctor said. "Not chaotic. Not a lot of movement."

JP shifted beside her. "Meaning not in a moving van."

The doctor gave a slight nod. "It would be unusual to see this kind of contained pattern if he were being struck while the vehicle was in motion. You'd expect more variation. More scatter."

The toxicologist leaned forward, flipping a page in the chart.

"There's something else," she said. "The drug levels in his system."

Sabre's focus sharpened. "What about them?"

"He was sedated," she said. "Not heavily enough to knock him out completely, but enough to make him compliant. The levels indicate the drug had been in his system for a short time before the injuries occurred."

Sabre frowned. "You can tell that?"

"To a degree," the toxicologist said. "We're seeing distribution consistent with absorption already underway, not a fresh administration at the time of trauma."

"And there's no defensive injury pattern," the doctor added. "No forearm bruising, no signs he tried to shield himself."

Sabre's jaw tightened.

"So, he couldn't fight back."

"That would be our concern," the doctor said.

JP glanced at Sabre. "He was under someone's control first."

The toxicologist nodded. "That's what the evidence suggests."

Sabre didn't say anything for a moment.

"So, they weren't trying to hurt him at first," she said quietly. "They were trying to manage him. And if he wasn't beaten during transport..."

"Someone lost control," JP said quietly.

"That's one interpretation," Sabre said. "Another is that something went wrong." She closed her notebook. "Mateo was left alive," she said. "In a place where he could be found."

"Yes," JP said. "That's unusual if the intent was to permanently silence him."

"Thank you," Sabre said. "This helps."

After the doctors left the conference room, Sabre leaned back in her chair.

"Whatever this was about, it wasn't supposed to end with a kid in a drainage canal."

"No," JP said. "It was supposed to be clean."

Sabre turned to him. "Clean how?"

JP shook his head. "I mean, I don't think this was about hurting Mateo."

Sabre's voice dropped. "Me either. But it all fits if one of his parents tried to take him."

"That's true. If he decided not to go along, they might've sedated him."

"So, who would you bet on? Mom? Or Dad?"

"I don't know yet." JP picked up his hat. "Someone planned one thing and got something else. People who make that kind of mistake don't relax afterward."

"They panic."

"Exactly," JP said.

They walked out of the conference room together, the hum of machines and voices fading behind them.

Mateo Alvarez had been taken and then discarded. And whatever had gone wrong was still rippling outward, dangerously, through people who didn't want the truth catching up to them.

JP opened the truck door, already adjusting his thinking. The case hadn't revealed itself, but it had exposed a fracture. And fractures were where everything eventually broke.

"I got a call from Detective Miller, and I need to meet him at the station. Do you want to go along?"

"Sure, I've got time. But I'd like to check on Mateo first."

"I'll wait in the car," JP said. "I have a few calls to make."

~~~

Sabre checked in at the front desk and followed the directions to Mateo's room. The hallway was quieter than the ICU. Less urgent. More waiting. She paused just outside the door before stepping in.

Mateo lay in the bed hooked up to tubes and monitors. A steady rhythm of sound filled the room without drawing attention to itself. His eyes were closed.

A nurse glanced up as Sabre entered. "Are you family?"
~~~

"No," Sabre said. "I'm his attorney."

The nurse studied her for a second, then gave a small nod. "Keep it short," she said. "He tires easily."

Sabre nodded and stepped closer to the bed. For a moment, she just stood there. "Mateo," she said quietly.

His eyes flickered. Slow. Heavy. But they opened. He looked at her without recognition at first. Then something shifted. Awareness.

"You're okay," Sabre said, keeping her voice steady. "You're safe."

He blinked again. His lips moved slightly, but no sound came out.

"That's all right," she said. "You don't have to say anything." She watched him for another second. "You're at the hospital. People are taking care of you."

His gaze drifted, then came back to her. He looked confused.

Sabre didn't push. "We'll talk later, when you're ready."

He closed his eyes.

Chapter 37

Monday afternoon

JP and Sabre sat in a small interview room at the precinct.

Miller stood across from them, arms folded. "I have some new information on the Alvarez case," the detective said. "I thought you'd want to hear this."

"We appreciate that," JP said.

Miller slid a thin folder across the table. "Here's the updated medical notes from the hospital. I just got it, so, I haven't had a chance to go through it thoroughly."

"We just had a meeting with the doctors," Sabre said.

"Then you probably know more than I do about the injuries. Please update me."

JP took the lead. "They said the sedatives were in his system first, and the trauma came later."

"That doesn't sound like escalation," Miller said. "It sounds more like improvisation."

"That's what I thought," JP said. "If someone intended to hurt him, they wouldn't likely sedate him first."

"And Mateo was left alive and discoverable."

"That's not how it would have ended, if the violence was the point," JP said.

"And we found no evidence of a struggle in the van either," Miller added. "There was no blood or hair or skin that matched Mateo." JP's jaw tightened. "What is your working theory?"

"Someone met Mendoza at the stop. At some point, the kid got out of the van. It looks like the second set of footprints accompanied Mateo, and Mendoza got back in the van."

"How do you know which person went with Mateo?" Sabre asked.

"Because we were able to compare the shoe prints with the person who picked Mateo up at Polinsky."

"So, you're suggesting the second person was the one who beat up Mateo."

"It looks that way," Miller said. "If we could find Mendoza, we could get a lot more answers. So far, he's pretty elusive."

"I'm working on that," JP said. "I just may have a way to smoke him out."

They were halfway to the parking garage when Sabre slowed. "Do you think Mendoza panicked?"

"I think he might've been the last person in control before things went wrong," JP said.

Sabre nodded. "My theory is he took a job he didn't fully understand. Then he realized too late that he was in over his head."

"That jives with what his sister said." JP leaned against the concrete wall. "And when he realized it, he panicked and left or was told to leave."

"And if he panicked, he could've made decisions that weren't part of any plan."

"True," JP said. "But the sedation still bothers me."

Sabre frowned. "Why?"

"Because sedation takes forethought," JP said. "You don't improvise that. You bring the meds with you."

Sabre's eyes sharpened. "So, either Mendoza came prepared, or he wasn't the one to sedate him."

They stood in silence for a moment, the sounds of the precinct drifting out behind them.

Sabre broke it. "Do you think Mendoza is dangerous?"

JP considered that carefully. "I think he's scared. And scared people do dumb things."

"We have to figure out what's really going on, or Mateo may be in more danger." Sabre looked worried. "Then Mendoza isn't the end of this."

"No," JP said. "He's the hinge. And I have to find him to get that door opened. And I'm starting back at his sister's."

~~~

Rosalia Mendoza recognized JP the moment she opened the door. No chain this time. That, by itself, told him something had shifted.

"I told you before," she said. "I don't know where he is."

JP nodded. "I know."

Again, he didn't crowd the threshold. He stayed where he was, hands loose at his sides, the way he'd learned to stand when the point wasn't authority but patience. "I'm here because you know him, and at some point, he will get in touch with you."

Rosalia studied him for a long moment, then opened the door wider and stepped back. Not an invitation, yet.

"You said he was in trouble, but I don't know how I can help."

"He's in more trouble now," JP replied. "The police will be more inclined to think it was Luis who hurt Mateo if he doesn't give his side of the story."

Her eyes flashed. "Luis didn't hurt that boy."

"I don't think so either," JP said.

She crossed her arms. "Then why are you here again?"

"Because whatever Luis agreed to do," JP said carefully, "didn't include beating a kid and leaving him for dead. We know someone else was involved."

"He told me things went bad. He said he tried to stop it. That he should've stopped it."

JP let the silence stretch for a moment.
~~~

"Right now," JP said, "Luis looks like the last man in the chain. The one everyone points at because he's visible and scared."

Rosalia swallowed. "And the ones above him disappear."

"Exactly," JP said. "And the only way that changes is if Luis talks before someone else decides he's expendable. He can talk to me, or the cops, or a lawyer, but he has to come forward before whoever he's running from finds him."

Her eyes snapped to his. "Do you think someone would kill him?"

"I think that the person who panicked once is capable of panicking again. And this time, they won't leave a witness."

"He didn't mean for any of this to happen," she said. "He took a job because he needed money. He thought he was helping someone. And it was simple."

JP nodded. "Simple jobs don't involve sedatives."

She looked up sharply. "You know about that."

"Yes," JP said. "Which is why I'm telling you this now, before it's too late."

Rosalia stared at the floor for a long moment. "I can reach him," she said finally. "I don't know where he is, but I can get a message to him."

JP handed her a business card. "Tell him to call me. Or a lawyer. But tell him this too. If he didn't hurt that boy, his silence is doing the most damage."

"He is innocent."

JP didn't flinch. "Then the truth matters."

Rosalia pocketed the card.

"He's afraid," she said.

"I know," JP replied. "But fear isn't protection. It's a clock."

She nodded. "I'll tell him."

Chapter 38

Monday late afternoon

DuBois found Reyes in his office, nursing a Pepsi.

"You look like a man waiting for the other shoe to drop," DuBois said.

Reyes gave a dry laugh. "Feels like it's been hovering for weeks."

"Walk with me," DuBois said.

They stepped out, DuBois closed the door behind them, and he leaned back against it.

"I've been going through Wilcox's finances," DuBois said. "He was pulling cash regularly."

Reyes exhaled. "I was afraid you'd say that."

"Large withdrawals," DuBois continued. "Close together, and no pattern that makes sense for bills or emergencies."

Reyes nodded. "That lines up with the timing."

"Timing of what?"

"The shift." Reyes tapped his desk calendar. "The last week or so of his life, Abram was different. Before that, he was spiraling. He was fixated on something and very angry. He kept talking about fairness like it was something he was owed."

"Did he say what was bothering him?"

"When I would ask, he'd always come back to the death of his son, but I think that was his way of covering what was really going on. Don't get me wrong, that never left his mind, and I understand that. But sometimes, I think there was something else bothering him."

"But a week before his death?" DuBois prompted.

"He calmed down," Reyes said. "Not happy. Just relieved. Like something he'd been bracing for had finally passed."

Relief. DuBois let the word settle. "Do you think he was in therapy?"

"No. I asked him that straight out. He said he'd tried it a while back, but it didn't help. I left it alone because he was finally acting more like himself."

"Was he a religious man?"

"Not at all. He thought organized religion was a money-making gimmick. So, if you're asking if he found religion, that's a definite no."

"People don't get relief for free," DuBois said. "Not when they're that wound up."

"No," Reyes agreed. "Relief comes from a problem being handled."

"Or bought."

Reyes looked up sharply. "Do you think he was being blackmailed?"

"I think he believed he was solving something with money—whether he called it blackmail or not."

Reyes frowned. "Abram hated being cornered."

"Which makes him a perfect target," DuBois said. "Maybe someone came to him with leverage, and framed payment as a way out of whatever the issue was."

Reyes's voice dropped. "Pay and make it go away."

"Exactly," DuBois said. "And judging by Wilcox's recent mood, he thought it worked."

"Until it didn't," Reyes said.

DuBois nodded. "That's where it breaks."

Reyes leaned back in his chair. "So, what went wrong? He stopped paying? Or they wanted more?"

"It could have been either," DuBois said. "Or he realized too late that whatever he paid for didn't actually solve the problem."

Reyes' brow creased. "If it was blackmail, what was the leverage?"

"That's the part I don't have yet."

"Knowing Abram, it would have to be something pretty serious for him to buckle."

"You and Abram were close, right?"

"For years," Reyes said. "Back when he was married, we spent a lot of time together. Our wives were best friends."

"Were?"

"Abram and I stayed friends. The women didn't." He paused. "Evelyn took the divorce hard. She became bitter. My wife couldn't stand to be around it. And after their son died, it only got worse."

"I met her," DuBois said. "She came off cold. Detached. Do you think she's capable of killing Abram? Or blackmailing him?"

Reyes considered that. "She might know something deep in his past that we don't know." He took a breath. "I wouldn't cross her off your list just yet."

"If Wilcox was paying someone off, it could be anything, boundary issues, an obsession maybe, but something Wilcox didn't want to get out, professionally or personally."

Reyes went quiet for a moment. "Do you think he changed his mind? Decided he wasn't paying anymore?"

"Or decided the price wasn't worth it," DuBois said. "And the person on the other end didn't agree."

Reyes swallowed. "So, it escalated."

"Yes," DuBois said. "Because blackmail only works as long as both sides agree to the same rules."

"Abram thought he bought certainty."

"And certainty is dangerous," DuBois said. "Especially when the leverage doesn't disappear with the payment." DuBois stood and opened the door. "If this was blackmail," he said, "then Wilcox died because the deal fell apart."

DuBois stepped back into the hall, the noise of the building rushing in around him.

Blackmail wasn't just about money. It was about control. And whatever Abram Wilcox thought he'd paid to control had slipped out of his hands, hard enough to get him killed. But what was it?

Chapter 39

Monday late afternoon

DuBois stood behind the glass at a downtown bank branch, watching surveillance footage with a fraud investigator. The screen showed Abram Wilcox three weeks before his death, standing at the counter in a collared shirt, posture straight, hands folded neatly.

"Pause it there," DuBois said.

The image froze.

Wilcox didn't look nervous. He wasn't scanning the room and didn't seem impatient. He looked like a man finishing an errand.

"That withdrawal was five thousand in cash," the investigator said. "Anything over ten gets flagged."

"Did anyone talk to him?" DuBois asked.

"The teller would've asked standard questions about the purpose."

"Did Wilcox hesitate when asked?"

The investigator scrubbed back. Wilcox shook his head once at something the teller said. Then he smiled and signed the withdrawal slip.

"He didn't hesitate," the investigator said.

DuBois watched the next clip, which took place ten days later at a different branch. Wilcox seemed just as calm.

The third withdrawal, two days before Wilcox was killed, was when DuBois leaned in.

Wilcox bent slightly toward the teller and said something. The teller nodded and glanced toward the manager's office.

"Can you pull the audio?" DuBois asked.

"There is none."

"Any notes?"

The investigator pulled up the internal log.

The customer insisted on cash. He declined a cashier's check and then stated: 'This resolves it.'

DuBois stared at the words. Resolves what?

He left the bank and drove straight back to Probation Services.

Wilcox's supervisor, a man who'd been there long enough to wear burnout like a second suit, met him in a cramped office with a window that looked onto concrete.

"You're asking about Abram's last few weeks?" the supervisor said.

"Yes," DuBois replied. "What was his behavior like? Was he stressed? Was there anything out of the ordinary?"

The supervisor rubbed his jaw. "That's the thing. He was better."

"Better how?" DuBois asked, hoping to confirm what he'd heard from Reyes.

"Before that, he was wound tight," the man said. "Obsessed with the death of his son. And who could blame him? He was very angry. And then, suddenly, he wasn't."

"When?" DuBois asked.

"A week or two before he died."

That all lined up with what Reyes said. DuBois flipped a page in his notebook. "Did he say why?"

"No," the supervisor said. "Just that he'd 'handled something.' He talked about refocusing, and he asked about taking a couple days off."

"Did he ever say he felt threatened?" DuBois asked.

The supervisor shook his head immediately. "No. If Abram had been scared, I'd have known. He didn't hide that kind of thing."

DuBois asked to see Wilcox's delinquency caseload history again. The supervisor set him up at a computer.

He didn't discover anything too unusual, just the things that made life miserable for the clients, like probation violations, drug tests, curfew and missed school, as well as missed appointments. Anger lived here.

He flagged three recent cases and started making calls.

One parent answered, already furious. "He humiliated my son," the woman said. "He acted like he was God."

"Did you threaten him?" DuBois asked.

"No," she snapped. "I complained. That's not a crime."

Another call, this time a teenage boy on probation. "I hated that dude," the kid said. "He violated me for nothing."

"Did you confront him?" DuBois asked.

"No," the kid said. "I didn't want more time."

The pattern repeated. Plenty of resentment. Plenty of motive for anger. None of it escalated.

Before DuBois left the building, he asked around about the employees who knew Wilcox the best. By the end of the afternoon, DuBois sat across from a former coworker of Wilcox's, someone who'd shared breakroom conversations and court calendars with him for years.

"Did Wilcox talk about his son much?" DuBois asked.

The woman hesitated. "He talked about him all the time. At first, it was mostly in anger that he was gone. Then, toward the end, it was different."

"How?"

"More reflective, like he was finally at peace with it."

DuBois wrote it down.

Peace didn't come from nowhere, and it sounded a lot like *relief*.

He sat in his car in the probation department's parking lot afterward and jotted down notes: *Cash withdrawals. No fear. No threats reported. Angry parents. Angry teens. Nothing that explained murder.*

This hadn't been extortion in the classic sense. It seemed more like a man who believed he'd paid to make something stop.

Chapter 40

Monday late afternoon

JP parked a block away from Wilcox's house and walked the neighborhood, slow and ordinary, like he belonged there. He noticed the midday traffic, lawns with sprinklers on, and a dog barking from behind a fence. He wasn't sure what he was looking for, but he discovered nothing dramatic was going on. He guessed that told him something.

He drove to the gym and headed inside. The front desk kid barely looked up. "Membership question?"

"Something like that." JP flashed a friendly smile, along with his PI badge. "I need some information on a guy named Abram Wilcox. He used to work out here."

"That's the guy who got shot, right?"

"That's the guy."

The kid squinted at his computer screen. "Yeah. He froze his account."

"When?" JP asked.

"About three weeks ago." The young man typed something into the computer, then hit a few more buttons. "The reason listed for freezing the account was that he was *too busy and finally sleeping again.*"

"Does it say anything else?"

"Nope. That's it."

JP thanked him and drove to the coffee shop that Wilcox frequented.

The sign read Common Ground Café, the kind of place people drifted into without thinking and came back to without realizing why.

The inside felt lived in without being worn down. Warm light hung low over small wooden tables, each one just far enough apart to give the illusion of privacy. A soft hum of conversation blended with the steady hiss of the espresso machine behind the counter.

One wall was lined with mismatched chairs and a long counter facing the window, where people sat alone with their thoughts or their phones. Across from it, a corkboard crowded with business cards, notices about lost cats, guitar lessons, and other handwritten flyers gave the place a quiet sense of community.

It wasn't trendy. It wasn't polished. It was the kind of place no one paid attention to, and that's what made people come back.

JP ordered a coffee he didn't need and waited for the line to clear. Then he approached the clerk, showed Wilcox's photo, and asked if she had ever seen him.

The barista recognized the PO immediately. "Abram," she said. "Yeah. He came in almost every morning."

"Did you ever talk to him?"

"For months, he never said a word except to order. He wasn't unpleasant. He just seemed sad. Then a few weeks ago, he actually smiled."

"Was he ever with anyone?"

"He talked to a woman a few times."

That got JP's attention. "When was that?"

"I don't know. Maybe a month ago."

"Do you know who she was?"

The barista tilted her head. "She was one of a kind. She wore long scarves and big rings. She claimed to be a medium."

JP kept his face neutral. "As in..."

"... Talking to the dead," the barista said. "She told people she could help them find closure."

And take advantage of people's grief. JP unclenched his jaw to ask, "Do you know her?"

"Not personally, but she's a regular." The barista gestured toward the corkboard. "She posts her card up there."

JP walked over.

The card was simple, cream-colored with black ink. It read: *CLAIRE HAWTHORNE,*Spiritual Medium & Grief Counselor, Private Sessions Available. She listed a phone number and an address.

JP pulled down the card and went back to the barista.

"Do you know if they were meeting officially?" JP asked.

The barista shook her head. "I don't know. They talked a lot. He talked more to her than I ever heard him talk to anyone."

"Did you hear anything they said?"

"Once, I heard her say, 'peace came in different forms.'"

"When did they start talking? Was it before or after his behavior changed?"

"It was a few weeks before." She tilted her head. "I didn't think about that. Maybe she helped him somehow. Do you think?"

"Maybe she did." JP didn't believe the medium could communicate with his son, but maybe Wilcox had. At least, in his grieving state, he may have wanted to believe. And that may have been enough to relieve his pain. The sessions might also explain the bank withdrawals.

JP stepped outside with the card in his fingers. Next stop: Claire Hawthorne.

Chapter 41

Monday late afternoon

The address on the card led JP to a small office in a strip mall tucked between a nail salon and a travel agency that still had posters promising cheap flights that didn't exist anymore.

CLAIRE HAWTHORNE was stenciled on the glass in soft lettering. The building was the kind that tried to look more important than it was. Neutral paint. Narrow hallway. A directory near the entrance with small black lettering listing businesses no one really understood until they needed them.

JP found the suite number and stepped inside. There was a shared waiting area with three chairs along one wall and two more across from them. A small table sat in the middle, stacked with outdated magazines no one was reading. A water cooler stood in the corner with a paper cup dispenser that had been refilled unevenly.

Four doors branched off from the room, each with a nameplate. There was no receptionist, no one in charge, just people coming and going.

JP took a seat where he could see the hallway and most of the doors.

The place was quiet in that particular way office buildings were, where sound carried, but it didn't echo. Muffled voices behind closed doors. A chair shifting somewhere down the hall. Footsteps, then silence again.

And then a clicking sound. JP's eyes shifted slightly, but he didn't move his head. It came from somewhere beyond the door to his left, not loud but deliberate. JP leaned back in the chair, stretching one leg out just enough to look like he was settling in. The sound stopped.

A few seconds later, the door opened, and a man came out of the medium's office but didn't make eye contact. JP studied him, as always, when he was investigating. He never knew what things around him would mean later.

The man walked past without a word. The faint scent of something clean, almost clinical, followed him out.

JP went into Claire's office. It wasn't at all what JP expected. There were no neon signs, no crystal balls sitting in the open, and no theatrical nonsense designed to convince someone they'd stepped into another world.

Instead, it felt intentional. Quiet. Controlled.

The lighting was soft, but not dim, with lamps instead of overheads. Warm pools of light that left the corners just a shade darker than they should be. Not enough to notice at first. Just enough to feel.

A faint scent hung in the air, something like sandalwood, but cleaner. Subtle. Consistent. The kind of smell that stayed with you after you left.

A small round table sat in the center of the room. It wasn't dramatic or ceremonial. Just large enough that two people sitting across from each other would have to lean in slightly to speak.

Along one wall sat a narrow shelf that was carefully arranged, a few objects spaced with precision: a smooth stone, a single candle, a small, framed quote about "clarity" instead of destiny. No clutter. No distractions. Everything looked like it had been chosen, not collected.

There were no personal photos. No family. No history. Nothing that gave anything back.

Behind the table sat a simple desk. It was clean, almost sterile, with a notebook placed square to the edge and a pen resting exactly parallel to it. JP's eyes lingered on that longer than he meant to. Everything in the room had a place. And everything stayed in it.

The windows were covered, not blocked, just filtered. Natural light came through softened, diffused, as if the outside world had been gently pushed back. It wasn't mystical. That was the unsettling part.

But Claire Hawthorne looked exactly like someone who made a living being remembered. She wore the scarves, big earrings, and flowing skirts as the barista had described. She was in her mid-forties with sharp eyes and a calm posture. She rose when he entered, offering a polite, professional smile.

"May I help you?" she asked.

"My name's JP," he said. "I'm looking into the death of Abram Wilcox."

Her eyes registered recognition. "I wondered when someone might come."

She gestured to the chair across from her desk, and JP took a seat.

"Did you know him?" JP asked.

"I met him," she corrected. "Twice."

She was careful with her language, but people who lived in gray areas usually were. "At the coffee shop?"

"Yes. He was grieving, and it was obvious to me that I was sent to help."

"So, you approached him?"

"I did," she said. "I told him that he was carrying something unresolved. I could see it was the death of a teenage boy."

She had done her homework. "You told him that?"

"Yes. I could see the boy vividly."

"Did Wilcox confirm it?"

"He did, but he didn't need to. I already knew. So, I told him I could help if he wanted."

Of course you did. JP nodded. "Did he accept your help?"

"No," she said without hesitation. "He never came to see me. We spoke at the café. Briefly. He asked questions. Mostly philosophical ones."

"Like what?" JP asked.

She leaned back. "He asked if it was possible to make things right. If closure was something you could *create*."

JP kept his voice neutral. "What did you tell him?"

"That closure doesn't come from punishment. It comes from acceptance."

JP studied her. "Did you charge him for those conversations?"

"No," she said firmly. "I was merely comforting someone I saw in distress. There was no session, and he didn't pay me anything."

"No cash?"

"No," A trace of offense crept in. "I don't ambush people."

"Did Wilcox ever mention money?"

"No. He mentioned regret."

"Did he seem afraid?" JP asked.

Claire shook her head. "No. In fact, the second time I saw him, he seemed a little better."

"Like something had been resolved?"

"Like he thought it had."

That was the first honest thing she'd said that felt like it cost her nothing. JP stood, slipping the card back into his pocket even though he didn't need it anymore.

"Ms. Hawthorne," he said, "did you tell him to do anything?"

Her eyes held his. "Yes. I told him to forgive himself."

That was answer enough.

Outside, the afternoon sun felt sharper than it had a moment ago. The medium didn't act like a blackmailer or a conspirator. But she also didn't feel like someone who just "happened" into a grieving man at the right moment. JP wondered how many other sad people she had swindled.

Chapter 42

Tuesday morning

The panadería was the same as last time, windows fogged with heat, the smell of sugar and yeast drifting into the street. JP parked across the way where he could see the front counter and the bulletin board near the register without being obvious.

He waited and used his binoculars whenever someone went inside.

Morning customers came and went, a woman with a stroller, a construction crew grabbing pastries by the box, and a kid who handed the counter person a piece of paper. JP watched hands more than faces. He watched to see if anyone paused at the board or lingered longer than they needed to, but no one did.

An hour passed. Then another. If Mendoza had been using this place to pass messages, it wasn't happening this morning. Or not the way JP had imagined. He checked his watch, then pulled out his phone.

"Ron," he said when the call connected. "I need eyes on a bakery on Imperial. Watch the board by the register and anyone who posts or retrieves a note."

"How long?" Ron asked.

"The rest of the day," JP said. "Maybe tomorrow morning if nothing shakes loose. You'll need to call me if anyone posts, pulls, or stares."

"Got it," Ron said. "I'll blend."

When Ron arrived, JP explained what was going on. He also texted him the photo he had of Luis Mendoza, as well as one of his sister, Rosalia.

"I'll call if there's any news," Ron said.

JP started the truck and drove to Rosalia's house, knocked, and waited.

When she opened the door, she seemed disappointed. "You didn't find him."

"No," JP replied. "And that's why I'm here."

She stepped back and let him in. They stood in the small living room.

JP kept his voice low, "I need you to hear this clearly. The police don't think your brother beat that kid."

Rosalia's breath caught despite herself. "*They* don't, or *you* don't?"

"Neither of us," JP said. "The detective is certain there was a second man involved."

Her eyes searched his face. "You're sure?"

"As sure as anyone gets before the whole truth comes out," JP said. "But right now, Luis looks like the last man holding the bag."

Rosalia crossed her arms. "He's terrified."

"I know," JP said. "And I know why. But hiding isn't protecting him."

She shook her head. "If he comes forward—"

"If he doesn't," JP interrupted gently, "the story hardens. Evidence gets interpreted without him. And whoever did cross the line gets exactly what they want, another person to blame. Not only that, if they find your brother before we do, they'll probably kill him."

Rosalia looked away. "Do you think they'll do that?"

"Yes," JP said. "They drugged and beat up a teenage boy. Luis knows what they look like."

"You're sure the police know there was a second guy?" Rosalia asked.

"They do," JP confirmed. "They have footprints and tire tracks, even some medical evidence. They have enough to know Luis didn't act alone, but not enough to know why. Luis needs to talk before it gets worse."

Rosalia's voice dropped. "I'm not sure what to do."

"You need to reach him and let him decide. And the sooner the better."

She closed her eyes for a moment, then opened them again. "I don't know where he is, but I'll try to get a message to him."

JP nodded. "That's all I'm asking. And when you do, make sure he knows how fast the clock is running."

He moved toward the door, then paused. "Tell him this too. The kid's still alive. And the truth is coming whether he's part of it or not."

Outside, JP sat in his truck for a long moment before turning the key.

The panadería hadn't given him Mendoza, at least not yet, but Rosalia might.

Chapter 43

Tuesday morning

Sabre was halfway through her calendar and waiting for her next case when her phone vibrated. She listened, spoke a few words, then hung up and stood.

"What is it?" Bob asked from the bench beside her.

"Mateo is awake. Can you cover the rest of my cases?"

"Sure," Bob said. "What do you have?"

"Just reviews. You're on two of them, and my notes are on my pink slips in the files." She handed him four folders. "Are you sure you're okay with this? I hate to dump on you again."

"Get out of here. Your notes are so thorough a monkey could do them."

~~~

The drive felt longer than it should have. She kept hitting traffic lights and got behind a bus that wouldn't pull over. A traffic jam on the freeway slowed her down more.

When she stepped off the elevator on the hospital floor, Detective Miller was coming from the other direction.

"He's awake?" she asked.

"Far better than he's been," Miller said. "They called me ten minutes ago."

They walked down the hall together, shoes squeaking softly on smooth vinyl. "I'll be present when you question him," Sabre said.

Miller smiled. "I assumed you would."
~~~

The nurse met them outside Mateo's room and spoke quietly. "He's awake, but he's still groggy. Don't push him."

Mateo's room was dim, curtains pulled halfway. Machines hummed softly. The boy lay still beneath the blankets, his face pale, bruises faded to yellow and green along his jaw. Mateo's gaze drifted when they entered, unfocused at first, then sharpened.

"Hey, Mateo. I'm Sabre. Remember me?"

He nodded. Barely.

"This is Detective Miller," she said. "He's going to ask a few questions. If you get too tired, please let us know."

He focused on her slowly. "Am I... in trouble?"

"No," she said. "You're safe. I just want you to answer honestly, okay? Whatever you remember."

Miller stepped closer. "Mateo, I'm glad to see you awake. We've all been worried about you."

The boy tried to smile but didn't pull it off.

Miller kept his voice low. "Do you know where you are?"

"The hospital."

"Do you know why?" Miller asked.

Mateo frowned. "I got hurt."

Miller waited a beat. "Do you remember how?"

Mateo's brow creased, as if the effort caused discomfort. "Not really."

Sabre watched his hands clench and unclench beneath the blanket.

"Do you remember being in a vehicle?" Miller asked.

Mateo nodded. "A van."

"Do you remember anyone with you?" Miller asked.

"The driver."

"Male or female?"

"Male."

"Was the driver the only other person in the van?" Miller asked.

Mateo shrugged, then winced. "I think so."

Sabre's instinct was to intervene, to clarify, and protect, but she stayed silent. This was Miller's lane.

"Did anyone talk to you?" Miller asked.

"I was tired," Mateo said. "I think I fell asleep."

"Do you remember going anywhere else?" Miller asked.

Mateo was quiet for a long moment. "I don't know."

Miller asked where the van stopped, whether Mateo remembered getting out, and whether anyone else was there, but the answers blurred quickly into uncertainty and fatigue.

Mateo's eyelids drooped. "My head hurts."

Sabre rested her hand lightly on his shoulder. "That's all right. We can talk more later."

In the hall, the doctor met them, chart in hand.

"Will he remember more?" Sabre asked.

"Possibly," the doctor said. "Memory often returns in fragments. Smells. Sounds. Names. Sometimes days later."

"And sometimes not at all?" Sabre asked.

The doctor grimaced. "That's also possible."

"How soon will you know?" Sabre asked.

"When he starts sleeping normally," the doctor said. "When the swelling goes down. When the medication tapers. They're all factors, and even then, it may come back only in pieces."

Chapter 44

Tuesday afternoon

Ron had been parked across from the panadería long enough that the smell of bread felt permanent. He sat low in the seat, baseball cap pulled down, newspaper open but unread. After the morning rush, the place had hit a midday lull. He expected another after-work rush soon.

A woman crossed the street and slowed near the door. Ron straightened a little. She matched JP's description of Rosalia, with dark hair pulled back tightly. He checked the photo on his phone to confirm.

Ron waited.

She went straight to the bulletin board by the register and stood just long enough to look it over. She didn't appear to remove anything, but she might have posted something. Ron couldn't tell for sure. She ordered bread, paid, and left like it was an ordinary stop.

Ron counted to thirty, then went in. At first glance, the board looked just as JP had told him. Notices about lost dogs, rooms for rent, someone advertising housecleaning in block letters. Then he saw something in the bottom right corner, a small handwritten note that read: *mi hermano.*

Ron reached for it. The note was folded and tucked in just enough to be missed if you weren't looking for it. He opened it and read the message: *Por favor llámame.*

Call me. That was it. No number, no name. Ron put the note back exactly as he'd found it, then took a step back and memorized everything—the position, the tape, and the slight tear along the edge.

He went to the counter, bought a sweet roll, and stepped back outside. Then he pulled out his phone and called JP.

"I've got movement," Ron said.

"Talk to me."

"A woman matching Rosalia's description went inside," Ron said. "She checked the board, so I went in after."

"And?"

"There was a new note in the bottom right corner. It read *mi hermano*. Inside it just said, *Por favor llámame*."

"So, she asked her brother to call." JP paused for a moment. "Did you take it down?"

"Only to read it, then I put it back exactly where it was," Ron said.

"Good," JP said. "Stay on it. Don't spook anything."

Ron slipped the phone into his pocket and turned back to the bakery, eyes on the door, on the board, on anyone who paused longer than they should.

If Luis Mendoza came looking for his sister's message, Ron intended to see him first. He returned to his car and continued his surveillance. As the afternoon wore on, the clerk flipped the sign to *CASH ONLY* for a while, then back again. Someone wiped down the counter. Someone else restocked the pastry case.

The bulletin board stayed untouched.

Ron shifted his position twice, careful not to draw attention. He watched every customer who slowed near the register. No one reached for the board.

At closing time, the clerk pulled the last tray of bread and locked the door from the inside. The lights went dark a few minutes later.

Ron waited another ten minutes anyway but saw nothing. He called JP.

"No sign of him," Ron said. "She came. He didn't."

JP didn't sound surprised. "He won't move when it's busy."

"You want me to stay?" Ron asked.

"No," JP said. "Go home. Be back just before they open."

"First customers, first look."

"Exactly," JP said. "That's when he'll check, when there are no witnesses."

Ron started the car and pulled away, already planning where he'd park at dawn. The note was still there, and hopefully, someone was going to read it.

~~~

Wednesday morning

Ron was parked and settled by 6:15 a.m. The sky was just starting to lighten, that gray-blue hour before the weather decided what kind of day it would be. The lights inside the panadería flicked on one by one, and at six-thirty sharp, the metal grate rattled up.

The first customers appeared to be regulars. A man in paint-splattered jeans, followed by a woman with a reusable bag and a quick order. A young Latino boy, about ten years old, entered, picked up several loaves of bread, then disappeared briefly behind another customer before leaving.

Ron watched everyone, but no one matched Rosalia's or Luis' description. No one lingered at the counter. No one looked twice at the bulletin board.

Around 7:00 a.m., there was a brief lull. Ron crossed the street, pushed through the door, and let the warmth and smell of fresh bread wash over him. He ordered a coffee and a pastry, waited while the clerk worked the register, then drifted toward the board like he was killing time.

The bottom right corner was empty. No handwritten note, no folded paper, and no tape.
~~~

Ron felt the shift, not panic, but confirmation. Someone had taken the message.

He stepped back outside. The morning had fully arrived now. Traffic was picking up with people heading to work, and the city was erasing the quiet.

He waited until he was back in his car before calling JP. "It's gone."

"How?" JP asked.

"I don't know," Ron said. "I didn't see anyone who fit the description for Mendoza or Rosalia."

There was a pause. "Someone took it," JP said slowly. "Just not who we expected."

"Exactly," Ron said. "Which leaves us with a few options."

"Let's figure this out. How long was it after opening?"

"Within the first half-hour," Ron replied. "I watched everyone go in, but I didn't see Mendoza."

"One of those customers could've picked it up for him. Perhaps it was a courier, a friend, or a relative. Did you see anyone go to the board?"

"No. Except I couldn't be certain about the kid because part of the time he was blocked by another customer."

"That could be our courier," JP said.

"There's another possibility," Ron said. "Maybe Luis knows the owners and/or an employee. He could've come in before opening or after closing yesterday."

JP was quiet for longer this time. "That one bothers me," JP said. "So, the question now is: Will he show up again?"

"You want me to stay?"

"Yes. Here's why. If Mendoza's cautious, he'll wait. He'll watch the place the way we are. He'll want to know who's watching whom."

"I become the scenery," Ron said.

"Exactly," JP said. "Don't do anything different. You can get coffee or another pastry. But be forgettable."

Ron glanced at the bag on the seat beside him. "I'm already diabetic bait, and I'm over caffeinated."

JP chuckled, then sobered. "If he comes back, he'll be leaving a note because he's afraid to *call* Rosalia."

"All right," Ron said. "I'll sit."

"Call me if anything feels even a little off," JP said.

Chapter 45

Wednesday morning

JP was in his truck when the phone rang. Rosalia Mendoza's name lit the screen, and he answered immediately. "Rosalia."

"I need to see you," she said.

JP backed out, already shifting gears in his head. "Where are you?"

She gave him an address near the bay, busy enough not to feel like a trap, quiet enough for a private conversation.

"I'll be there in fifteen," JP said.

~~~

When JP arrived, he spotted Luis Mendoza near the far edge of the parking lot. He looked scruffier than he did in the photo JP had in his phone, older too. His shoulders were drawn in, hands jammed deep into the pockets of a hooded sweatshirt, like he was trying to hold himself together.

Rosalia stood a few feet away, arms crossed, watching the road.

JP parked, stepped out, and waited.

Luis spoke first. "I didn't hurt the kid." No greeting, just the words tumbling out like he'd been holding them in too long. "I swear to you."

JP moved toward him. "Then tell me what happened."

Luis swallowed. "I was told to pick up a boy. Just take him and drop him somewhere else. The guy said he was trying to save his son from a druggie mom."
~~~

"How did you get pulled into this in the first place?"

Luis glanced at Rosa, then back at JP. "A man approached me. About a month ago."

"Where?" JP asked.

"Outside a job site," Luis said. "He knew my name and who I worked for. He said his son was in real trouble, that they wanted to place him with his mother who was still using drugs, and he wanted the boy to come home to him."

"Why you?" JP asked.

"I was already inside the county transport system," Luis said.

"How much did he offer you?" JP asked.

"Three thousand."

JP didn't react. "What exactly were you instructed to do?"

"Pick up the kid and transport him to a spot just off the freeway and drop him," Luis explained. "He said all the arrangements would be made and the kid would just get in the van."

"So, when did you realize something was wrong?"

"I told the kid that his dad was fixing a mistake, and that he was going to live with his father."

JP waited.

"The kid looked at me like he was trying to understand something that didn't make sense." Luis shuddered. "Then he said, 'My dad's dead.'"

JP felt the click in his own head, the moment when a story collapses under its own weight.

"How did you respond?" JP asked.

"I didn't," Luis said. "Not right away. I thought maybe he meant… I don't know, estranged, you know *dead to him*."

"But?"

"But he didn't say it like that," Luis said. "He wasn't upset. He was just correcting me. Like I'd gotten a fact wrong."

"So, what did you do?"

"I asked him how long," Luis said. "He said his dad died years ago, and that there wasn't anyone who could just come get him."

JP waited.

Luis shook his head. "That's when I knew this wasn't a family fixing a mistake," Luis said.

"So, you called it in," JP said.

"Right away. I told the guy I thought we had the wrong kid."

"And he didn't tell you to abort?"

"No," Luis said quietly.

"Who did you call?" JP asked.

Luis shook his head. "I don't know his name. I never had it, just the number."

Luis went on. "He told me help was coming. That he would take care of it."

JP felt the slow burn of that settle in. "Who came?"

"A different man, not the one who hired me."

"Describe him," JP said.

"He was older, calm, and very sure of himself," Luis said. "About sixty, white, medium height, slightly overweight. Clean shaven and partially gray haired."

"What then?" JP asked.

"I told him the kid's father was dead. That this wasn't right."

"And what did he say?"

"That's the thing. He took one look at the boy and said, 'That's not the one.'"

"So, I asked him what we should do now that we had the wrong kid. And he said, it didn't matter."

Something inside JP hardened. "What did he mean by that?"

"I don't know. He just said they couldn't let the kid go. That it was already in motion."

Rosalia wiped at her eyes angrily. "You should've come to me."

"He told me he knew where you lived." Luis didn't look at her. "That if I interfered or went to the police, my family would pay for it. I was trying to protect you."

JP held up a hand, steadying the moment. "And then?"

"He asked if the transfer had been logged yet. I didn't even know what that meant," Luis added quickly. "I told him I just drove the van."

"And?"

"He said, 'Then we're early.'"

JP folded his arms. "Did he explain what that meant?"

Luis shook his head. "He just took out a syringe and said it would calm the kid down. But the kid wasn't fighting him or anything. At least, not yet. I tried to stop the guy, but he just walked up to the kid and jabbed him with the needle. The boy got sleepy fast."

"Was he completely passed out?"

"Not then, but he was fading. The guy turned to me and told me to disappear, or it wouldn't end well for Rosa. So, I did."

Silence stretched between them.

"Did you ever hear the name of the kid you were supposed to pick up?" JP asked. "Or anyone else's?"

Luis frowned, searching his memory. "No names, but the kidnapper made a call, and when he got off the phone, he said, 'She'll handle it.'"

She? That was interesting.

"Did you ask him about the *she* reference?"

"No. I was afraid to ask anything at that point." Luis looked up at him, desperate. "Am I going to prison?"

JP knew it was a possibility, but maybe not if he cooperated. "You're going to need a lawyer," JP said. "And you need to tell all this to the police."

Luis' shoulders slumped. "He said they'd kill us."

JP met his eyes. "They might eventually kill you and your sister anyway, just to silence you." JP handed him Jerry Leahy's card. "This attorney is good. You can trust him."

Rosalia gripped her brother's arm. "We'll do it. Together."

JP nodded. "Good. Because the truth don't chase a man. It just waits till he runs outta road."

Chapter 46

Wednesday late morning

Miller's interview room was small and clean and deliberately unwelcoming. JP had always appreciated that about police stations. They weren't designed for comfort. They were designed to get to the truth. JP and Miller chatted while they waited.

Jerry Leahy arrived first, suit jacket off and sleeves rolled. Mendoza walked in behind him, shoulders hunched, eyes scanning like the room might bite.

JP introduced everyone.

Miller waited until everyone sat. "Mr. Mendoza. Do you understand you're here voluntarily?"

"Yes."

"And you have legal representation?" Miller glanced at Jerry.

"And my client intends to cooperate," Leahy said.

Miller nodded. "All right. Start at the beginning."

Mendoza did.

JP stayed quiet while the story unfolded—the approach, the job site, the assurance that it was a family matter. The story he'd repeated without understanding it. Then the moment that changed everything.

"When the kid said his dad was dead, that's when I knew I had the wrong one. So, I called the number I'd been given. I never knew the man's name."

"I'll need that number, although it's probably no longer good."

Mendoza gave it to him.

"What happened when you called?" Miller asked.

"He said help was coming," Mendoza said. "And a few minutes later, someone else showed up." Mendoza described the man the same way he had for JP.

"What happened next?" Miller asked.

"I suggested I take the kid to where he was supposed to be, or drop him off somewhere, but the guy said it didn't matter that it was the wrong kid. They couldn't let him go. Then he threatened me and my family if I didn't cooperate."

"Mateo was drugged. Who did that?" Miller asked.

"That was the man who showed up," Mendoza said quickly. "I tried to stop it, but it happened too fast."

"And then?"

"He told me to leave," Mendoza said. "So, I did. I ditched the van and went into hiding."

"Have you had any more contact with anyone regarding this matter?"

"No. But word on the street is someone besides the police is looking for me."

"I'll need to know where you're getting that information." Miller closed his notebook.

"I don't have any specifics. People just talk. I've been warned that someone is asking around about me."

"Do you think the older man who showed up was the one calling the shots?"

Mendoza shook his head. "No. He had to call someone else to get the *go-ahead*. And I think it was a woman because he said, 'She'll take care of it.'"

Jerry leaned forward. "My client is willing to provide call records, locations, anything you need. But he needs assurances."

"Like what?"

"His family needs protection. I want limited immunity for my client, subject to verification."

Miller looked at Mendoza. "I'm going to treat you as a witness and a person of interest for now. You need to provide more details and work with a sketch artist. Maybe we can find the man you're talking about."

"What about my client's family?" Leahy asked.

"The best I can do, at this point, is send police cars to his sister's neighborhood. Hopefully, their presence will be enough to deter." Miller looked directly at Mendoza. "You might want to suggest she stay somewhere else for a while."

"Thank you." Mendoza turned to JP. "I didn't mean for any of this to happen."

JP nodded. "A man can leave a mistake behind, but the conscience don't forget the road home."

Miller stood. "Wait here while I set up the sketch artist. Can you describe the first man too?"

"Not well. He wore a hat, sunglasses, and kept his head down. He also came to me late in the day, and it was not good lighting. But I'll do what I can."

Miller turned to JP. "Let's talk for a second."

JP walked out of the office with Miller, who said, "Who does the abductor sound like to you?"

JP shrugged. "The physical description doesn't fit the father, but everything else does. The kid thinks he's dead, but we don't know that. Unless you've learned otherwise."

"Detective Perkins couldn't find a death record."

"Nothing?" JP asked.

"No death certificate, no coroner's report, nothing tied to his name, his date of birth, or any known identifiers. If he's dead, it's not on paper."

"I'm guessing you've checked the prisons as well?"

"I had Perkins run Alvarez through everything," Miller said.

"And?"

Miller leaned back slightly. "He's not in federal custody. Nothing in the system with the Bureau of Prisons."

JP gave a small nod. "All right."

"Not in California State prison either. We checked Corrections and got no hits, not under his name, not under any obvious variations. Don't get me wrong. He has been there, just not in the last five years."

JP's grip tightened a fraction on the brim of his hat. "So, he's not locked up anywhere official."

"Not anywhere easy," Miller said.

JP let out a slow breath through his nose. "People don't just vanish clean."

"Not unless someone helps them."

JP turned that over for a second. "What about county?"

Miller shook his head. "Too many holes. We can start chasing jails, but if he's sitting in one under an alias or a typo, we could burn days and still miss him. You're welcome to tackle it if you've got time."

JP gave a faint, humorless smile. "Or he's not in a cell at all. There's a good chance he's either dead or in Mexico."

"Exactly. But if he is alive, and he wants to keep Mateo from going back to his 'druggie' mother, hiring someone wouldn't be a stretch."

"We already know Rafael's got connections," Miller said. "He could've hired someone to do the dirty work."

"True," JP said. "But Mendoza swears a woman was calling the shots. So, maybe Brandy and Rafael are working together. The story fits Rafael. The gender fits Brandy."

"Yeah. Time to take another hard look at both of Mateo's parents. I'll see what else I can dig up on the streets about Rafael."

"You do that. I'm going to see if I can shake Franny Kirk loose."

Chapter 47

Wednesday afternoon

The room was quiet in the way hospitals tried to make things feel safe, muted beeps, soft footsteps, light filtered through half-closed blinds.

Mateo was awake when Sabre sat down. His swelling was down enough that his face looked more like the boy she remembered from her earlier encounters. He was awake now and not drifting.

"You look better," she said. "How are you feeling?"

"Like I ran into a wall." His voice was hoarse. "Twice."

She smiled. "That sounds about right."

"My head doesn't spin as much," he said. "At least not as fast."

"That's okay. Slow is good."

Mateo frowned, like something had bumped loose. He studied her for a moment. "You were my lawyer."

"And I'm still your lawyer."

He nodded, accepting that the way kids did when something stayed true long enough to be reliable.

They sat quietly for a bit. Sabre took her time. Memory didn't respond to pressure; it surfaced when it felt safe.

"Mateo," she said gently, "do you remember anything new?"

His eyes slid toward the window. "I keep thinking I do. Then it goes away."

"That's normal," she said. "Just tell me what sticks."

"There was a van," he said. "And a man. The driver and another voice. Not loud. Like... not talking to me."

"Talking to who then?" Sabre asked.

Mateo shrugged. "Someone on the phone, I think. Or maybe the driver. I don't know."

"What do you remember about the conversation?"

"It was calm. He wasn't yelling or anything."

"Did you hear any words?"

He squinted, frustrated. "I don't remember."

"Anything else?"

Mateo shook his head. "I can't see him in my mind. I can't see anyone. But I heard a voice, and then a pause. Then the voice again, but no one talked back." Mateo stared at the ceiling. "I keep hearing it when I'm half asleep."

"That's fine. We're not in a hurry. Let's try to figure out where you heard it, okay?" She paused. "Could it have been at Polinsky before you left?"

Mateo shook his head.

"Are you sure?" she asked.

"Yes," he said. "Polinsky's loud. It wasn't loud."

"Do you remember being alone with the driver?" she asked.

Mateo thought for a moment. "Yeah. We talked a little."

"Could the voice have been his?"

"No. It was definitely a different voice." Mateo reached for his water. "Luis speaks with a Mexican accent. The voice on the phone didn't. And I don't think it was in the van."

"Where then?" Sabre asked.

Mateo hesitated. "Outside."

"The voice was outside the van?" she asked. "While you were in the van?"

"I think so."

"Do you remember when or where?" she asked.

Mateo pressed his lips together, thinking hard. "We were stopped. I remember that."

"Did you see anything?" Sabre asked.

"No," Mateo said. "It's all pretty blurry."

"Could you tell how many people were outside? How many voices you heard?"

"Just one voice."

Sabre kept her tone calm. "Do you remember any words at all?"

Mateo squeezed his eyes shut, then opened them again. "No. Just the sound. Like they were talking about something, but not to me."

"Was the voice angry?" she asked.

"No. That's what's weird. It was calm."

"And after that?"

Mateo shrugged weakly. "I got really sleepy."

"That makes sense."

Mateo looked at her. "Did I do something wrong?"

"No. Of course not."

He seemed relieved by that.

The nurse appeared at the door, giving Sabre a gentle look. Time.

Sabre stood. "That was really helpful," she said. "You did great."

Mateo looked uncertain. "It doesn't feel like much."

"You don't have to make sense of it yet. I'm sure more will come back to you. Just rest your brain. Let it heal."

As she stepped into the hall, Sabre paused, heart beating a little faster.

A stop. A second person outside the van. A calm voice. It all matched with Mendoza's version.

Chapter 48

Wednesday afternoon

Mendoza sat stiffly in the chair, hands clasped, eyes fixed on a spot just past the sketch artist's shoulder. They started with the second man.

"Take your time," the artist said. "We'll build him piece by piece."

Miller stayed near the wall, notebook closed. He would soon have images to work with.

"He was older than me," Mendoza said. "In his early sixties, maybe."

"How tall?" the artist asked.

"About five-ten."

"Can you guess his weight?"

"I'm not good at that, but he was a little heavier than he should be. Not a lot, maybe twenty or thirty pounds over, most of it around his belly."

"Did he have facial hair?"

"No. And he had thick hair, but it was starting to gray."

"Anything else? A scar? Tattoo?"

"No. Nothing really stood out about him. Everything was just average, except he looked like a scrapper."

The artist nodded and kept working.

Miller watched the face take shape slowly.

"That's him," Mendoza said finally. "That's close anyway."

They moved on to the man who recruited him. "What do you remember?"

"Not much. I didn't see him that well. But I remember thinking he took care of himself."

"How?" the artist asked.

"He had good posture," Mendoza said. "And his shoes were good quality. He stood like he was used to people listening."

"How tall?"

"I'd say six foot."

"Weight?"

"He was lean, not skinny, but not muscular either."

"Anything else you can remember about him?"

"He wasn't dramatic or threatening, the kind you'd forget five minutes after passing him on the street." He paused for a second. "He seemed to have a limp. It wasn't very bad. I barely noticed it."

After the same kind of questioning, they had a simple sketch of the recruiter.

"I just can't be sure," Mendoza said. "I couldn't see his eyes because he wore sunglasses."

"I think this is the best we're going to do," the artist said.

"Are you sure you never saw him before?" Miller asked Mendoza.

"No," Mendoza said. "But he didn't act like someone new to this."

"How so?"

"He didn't ask questions," Mendoza said. "He didn't need directions, and he didn't hesitate."

Someone like that didn't drift into a situation by accident, Miller thought.

After the civilians left, Miller ran the sketches through every system they had, which included prior arrests, parole records, even DMV photos. Facial recognition flagged half a dozen possible matches for the older man, then discarded them just as quickly. But no hits on the recruiter.

Miller tried again from a different angle. Contractor lists, state employees, and prior law enforcement contacts, but still nothing.

That didn't mean he was clean. It just meant his image wasn't documented anywhere.

Later, Miller stood in his office, the sketch propped on his desk. No record meant no paper trail. The men's insulation meant planning. The older guy wasn't a thug hired off the street. He was someone who knew how to stay invisible.

Miller picked up his phone and made a note to widen the search, not for the men's faces, but for their behavior. Who had access? Who knew transport schedules? Who could step in when a job went wrong without leaving fingerprints behind?

Chapter 49

Thursday, early morning

JP got into his truck and headed out. He wanted to watch places where kids were visible, like Polinsky Receiving Home, group homes, probation waiting areas, and school pull-outs. In such places, a kid could be seen, remembered, and recognized, without a log entry.

He drove to Polinsky first and sat in the lobby, just to watch.

Staff moved in predictable patterns. Security at the doors. Intake clerks behind glass. Volunteers coming and going with badges that said *visitor*. People who didn't trigger alarms. But no one stood out as suspicious.

He left and drove to a county building that handled juvenile transfers. A place nobody thought about unless something went wrong.

After some small talk, he asked casually, "How long does it usually take for a transfer to show as complete?"

"It depends," the clerk said. "It could be minutes, could be an hour, sometimes longer if it's at the end of the day."

"And before it's logged?" JP asked. "What does it look like?"

The clerk shrugged. "Like the kid's in limbo. Picked up but not placed."

JP nodded, like that info was just trivia. But it was a window. And someone had known exactly when it opened.

JP walked out with a narrowed list forming in his head. He didn't have names yet, but he had categories. People who could see Mateo in the system *before* he got into the van. People who knew when the paperwork lagged. People who didn't need to be present to act.

JP got back into his truck. Maybe this wasn't about who grabbed the kid. Maybe it was about who knew *when* a kid could vanish without anyone noticing right away.

Back in his office, he analyzed what he had discovered, looking for overlap. That was often the trick, finding the thin strip where two different kinds of access crossed.

He started with three columns on a legal pad. *Who can see kids before transport. Who understands transfer timing. Who can act without being logged.*

Then he started crossing out categories of people. Transport drivers were easy. They were too visible, too traceable. Which explained why Mendoza was brought in. County clerks were next. They had too many eyes on them and too many checks.

Some roles stayed on the page longer, people who weren't assigned to the transport, but moved easily through juvenile spaces. Not all, just the ones who worked close enough to juvenile halls to be present, but not so close they had to sign for anything. People who moved through secure spaces because no one questioned why they were there.

JP circled *adjacent authority.*

He called a former county supervisor, someone who'd worked intake years ago. Someone who'd once explained how things really worked when the manuals stopped helping.

"Who hangs around Polinsky without being assigned?" JP asked.

The answer came quicker than he expected.

"People with reasons," the ex-supervisor said. "And people with grief."

Abram Wilcox came to mind.

"If you lose a kid in the system," the man continued, "you don't just stop showing up. You hover. You look. You watch."

JP thanked him and hung up.

He stared at the legal pad on his desk, then added a fourth column across the top: *Who would be watching.*

The first three were already there: transport staff, group home staff, and probation/caseworkers.

Now he started filling the fourth; parents, former parents, and people who'd lost custody but never really left. People who knew where to stand without being noticed.

He tapped the pen once, thinking. The man on the phone had been a former group home supervisor, someone who'd spent years around intake and transfers. Not policy. Just practice.

JP wrote another line beneath the columns: *Who understands the delay.* He circled it. Not everyone knew this part. When a kid left Polinsky, the system didn't update instantly. Intake logs, transport logs, placement confirmations, they didn't sync in real time. There was always a gap. Sometimes ten minutes. Sometimes longer. That was the window.

JP pulled up the county access portal on his laptop, the one Sabre had legitimate access to, which he used when she was sitting across from him. He wasn't looking for names yet. He was looking for *patterns.*

He filtered recent transport days. Then cross-checked: delayed arrivals, late confirmations, and re-logged entries. It wasn't clean data. But it didn't need to be.

He made another list on the pad:

People present during transfer windows:

- parents signing paperwork
- relatives denied visitation
- probation walk-ins

- contractors and drivers

Then he narrowed it again. Who shows up repeatedly? Who lingers? Who watches? The list got shorter. Not clean enough to act on, but tighter.

JP leaned back in his chair. This wasn't someone grabbing a random kid.

This was someone who understood:

- when a child was in motion
- when no one was fully accountable yet
- when a delay wouldn't trigger an immediate alarm

Someone who knew how long they had.

JP folded the paper and slid it into his pocket. He wasn't ready to bring this to Miller. Not yet. Because two questions still sat there, clearer now than before. *Why that day? Why that kid?*

But if he could finally catch Franny Kirk, he would have something to share with Miller. He got in his truck and drove to her apartment complex.

He found Franny leaning against the railing outside her apartment, cigarette in hand, eyes tracking everything in the lot below. She didn't look surprised to see him, just annoyed.

"Are you Franny?" JP asked.

"Depends who's asking."

"JP Torn." He gave her a slight nod. "Mind if I talk to you a minute?"

She took a drag, exhaled slowly. "You a cop?"

"Private investigator."

"Same difference." She flicked ash over the rail. "Make it quick."

JP leaned beside her, casual. "Are you and Brandy Alvarez close?"

Franny shrugged. "We get by."

"She says she was with you the afternoon her son went missing."

Franny didn't even look at him. "Yeah. That's right."

JP nodded like he expected that. "It gets rough with cops asking questions, people talking. Sometimes it's hard to keep stories straight when things get loud."

"My story's straight."

"I'm sure it is." He paused. "The problem is the rest of the pieces don't line up."

That got her attention. Just a riffle of the eyes.

JP kept it easy. "Look, I'm not here to jam you up. But if Brandy's alibi doesn't hold, people start digging. And when they dig, they don't always stop in the right place."

Franny took another drag, slower this time. "Sounds like a *you* problem."

"Could be," JP said. "Could also become a *you* problem real quick."

Silence stretched. The cigarette burned down between her fingers.

"A kid was seriously hurt," JP added, quieter now. "This isn't some probation check-in. This matters."

Franny's jaw worked. "I didn't touch that kid."

"I didn't say you did." JP met her eyes. "But you are covering for someone who might know more than she's saying."

She looked away, down at the lot again. A car door slammed somewhere below.

"She wasn't with me," Franny muttered.

JP didn't move. "Okay."

"She came by the next day and asked me to say she was. Said she had to go make money." Franny snorted. "Didn't want it getting around she was back out working."

"Working the streets," JP said.

"Yeah." Franny crushed the cigarette out on the railing. "I didn't ask questions."

"But you knew she wasn't here."

"I knew she wasn't here," she said, sharper now. "That's it."

JP nodded once. "That's enough."

Franny finally looked at him. "I'm not taking a hit for this."

"Then don't," JP said. "If anyone asks, you tell it straight."

She held his gaze a second longer, then gave a tight nod. "Yeah. I will."

JP pushed off the railing. "Good."

He started down the walkway, mind already working it through. *Brandy's alibi was gone. Maybe she was working the streets, or maybe she was abducting her son.*

JP paused halfway down the walkway, then turned back. "One more thing."

Franny was already reaching for another cigarette. "Figures."

"Rafael Alvarez," JP said. "Have you seen him around?"

She shook her head immediately. "Nope."

"Not lately?"

"Not ever, really." She lit up, took a quick drag. "I don't know him like that."

JP studied her. "But you've seen people coming and going."

Franny gave a short laugh. "This place? There's always people coming and going."

"Anyone stick out?"

She shrugged. "Couple guys. Different cars. In and out. Could be him, could be anybody. I don't keep a guest list."

JP tilted his head. "Did Brandy mention him being back?"

Franny's eyes flicked to his, then away. "No."

"It didn't come up at all?"

"She doesn't tell me everything," Franny said, a little sharper. "And I don't ask."

"Fair enough."

He turned and headed off again.

Chapter 50

Thursday mid-morning

Sabre and Detective Miller walked into the hospital room. Miller kept the sketch of the older man face down.

Mateo lay propped up against the pillows, color still uneven in his face. He looked better than he had the last time, but *better* was a relative term. The boy watched them approach, like he was still deciding whether the world was safe.

"Hey," Sabre said gently. "How are you feeling today?"

"Okay." Then, after a second, "Tired."

"That makes sense," she said. "You've been through a lot."

Sabre pulled a chair closer but didn't sit right away. "There's something we want to show you. You don't have to say anything if you don't want to, and you can stop anytime."

Mateo nodded, agreeing without committing.

Miller, who stood a few feet back, handed her the sketch. Sabre turned it over so Mateo could see it.

The boy flinched with a sharp intake of breath, his shoulders tensing.

Sabre waited.

Mateo stared at the sketch; eyes fixed on it in a way that suggested recognition without context.

"He's mean," Mateo said quietly.

Miller stepped forward. "Do you recognize him?"

Mateo's eyes didn't leave the page. "Yeah."

"From where?"

He studied the drawing. "I don't know."

"Do you remember anything about him?"

Mateo swallowed. "No. I don't remember what he did. Or what he said. Or where I know him from."

"That's okay," Sabre said. "It'll come back to you."

"But I know I know him," Mateo said, more insistently now. "Because... it feels bad."

Miller stepped forward. "What feels bad?"

Mateo's fingers tightened on the blanket. "It makes my stomach hurt," he said finally. "Like when you know something's wrong, but you don't know why."

Sabre felt a chill between her shoulder blades.

"Did he hurt you?" Miller asked gently.

Mateo shook his head. "I don't remember."

"Is there any memory of him talking to you?" Sabre asked.

Mateo frowned again. "I don't think so. Or maybe he did. I don't know." He looked frustrated now, embarrassed by the gaps. "It's like my brain won't go there."

"That's normal," Sabre said quickly. "Your body remembers things your mind isn't ready for yet."

Mateo glanced at the sketch again, then looked away. "I don't like him," he said. "I don't want to look at him."

"That's fine." Sabre turned the sketch face down and handed it back to the detective.

"You did really well," Miller said. "That helps more than you know."

Mateo had already retreated inward, eyes on the window, jaw set like he was holding something in.

Chapter 51

Thursday mid-morning

Law enforcement didn't trust coincidences. So, when the tech opened the screen with the location report, DuBois' first instinct was irritation.

Giovanni Taber's phone had pinged off a tower less than three blocks from Abram Wilcox's house on the night Wilcox was killed. Not right on top of it, but close enough to make a straight-faced denial uncomfortable.

DuBois leaned back in his chair and stared at the screen. The timestamp fell inside the broader window, early evening, before patrol canvassing, before neighbors started calling things in. Before the scene went loud.

"What is the accuracy radius?" he asked.

"About a hundred meters," the analyst said. "With urban density, it could be off some, one way or the other."

"So, not across town," DuBois said.

"No."

Taber had told him, firmly, that he hadn't been near Wilcox since the trial. Then he'd fessed up when they found out Wilcox had gone to see him at the group home.

Kids lied. That wasn't new. But DuBois hadn't pegged Taber as careless.

He pulled Taber's first interview and listened again, then the second one, headphones on, office door closed. The kid sounded scared, but consistent. Defensive, but not evasive.

DuBois took the headphones off. He hated this part. He checked the basics next, the group home logs, sign-out sheets, and staff notes that he and Perkins had obtained. It showed a gap that night, a shift change, a staffer stretched thin.

If Taber had been near Wilcox's house, there could be an explanation, innocent, dumb, or just teenage nonsense. But there was also motive, and proximity, and now, data evidence.

DuBois opened a new working note in the file.

Re-evaluate Taber as potential suspect. Do not confront without counsel. Corroborate before escalation.

A moment later, he added one more line. *Evidence is circumstantial but non-trivial.*

DuBois closed the file. He wasn't ready to say Taber killed Wilcox. But he was done pretending the kid wasn't standing closer to the fire than anyone wanted to admit.

DuBois picked up his phone and called Sabre.

She answered on the second ring. "What's going on?"

"I need to give you a heads-up," DuBois said. "We pulled phone location data tied to the Wilcox homicide," he continued. "Taber's phone shows a ping in Wilcox's neighborhood the night he was killed."

There was a pause on the line. "How close?"

"Within a few blocks," DuBois said. "It wasn't inside the house, so it's not definitive, but it was close enough that I can't ignore it."

Sabre exhaled slowly. "Giovanni told us he hadn't been there."

"I know," DuBois said. "I'm not calling this probable cause. And I'm not charging him with anything."

"But you want to talk to him again?"

"Yes," DuBois said.

"I'll need to be present."

"Understood."

She was quiet for longer this time. When she spoke, her voice had sharpened. "You understand that this puts him in a very vulnerable position."

"That's why I'm calling you."

"And you also understand that kids lie sometimes because they're scared, not because they're guilty."

"I understand that too," DuBois replied. "But right now, I have a fact I can't reconcile with his statement. He needs to explain it."

"When?"

"This afternoon, around three," DuBois said. "If that works for you."

"See you then."

He ended the call and stood a moment longer, phone still in his hand.

He didn't know yet whether Taber was guilty.

But he knew this much: Once a fact entered a case, it didn't leave just because it was inconvenient. And Giovanni Taber had just become very inconvenient.

Chapter 52

Thursday afternoon

Sabre arrived at the group home early, during the lull that came between school hours and dinner, when staff rotated and kids drifted. She signed in, chatted with the house manager, and was shown to the small interview room.

Giovanni stood when she walked in, then hesitated, unsure whether he was supposed to. She gestured for him to sit, then took the chair across from him. "I need to talk to you before Detective DuBois gets here."

His shoulders tensed. "Am I in trouble?"

"Not right now," Sabre said. "But you need to be careful."

That got his attention.

"DuBois has more questions about Abram Wilcox," she continued. "Specifically, about where you were the night he was killed."

Giovanni swallowed. "I already told him."

"He has new information that doesn't line up with what you said."

Giovanni looked down. He didn't argue. That worried her more than denial would have.

"I'm going to ask you again," Sabre said quietly. "And I need the truth. Did you have anything to do with Wilcox's death?"

"No," Giovanni said vehemently. "I swear. I didn't go to his house. I didn't want him dead."

"Did you see him that night?"

"I did not."

Sabre leaned back. "If you were somewhere you weren't supposed to be, that's one thing. If you lied about it, that's something we can manage. But if you were involved in his death, even indirectly, that's different. You need to understand that."

He nodded quickly. "I understand, and I didn't do it."

"Then when the detective asks you questions," Sabre said, "you answer honestly. Don't try to outsmart him. Don't fill gaps. Just say what happened."

Giovanni took a breath, steadying himself. "Okay."

There was a knock at the door, and DuBois stepped in.

"Hey, kid," he said. "Sabre."

She stood. "Vinny."

DuBois took the seat Sabre vacated, angling his chair just slightly toward Taber.

"I'm going to ask you some questions," DuBois said. "And I need the truth this time. Lying to me is making you look bad."

Taber's eyes flashed with worry.

"Let's start simple," DuBois said. "Were you anywhere near Abram Wilcox's neighborhood the night he was killed?"

Taber hesitated for a half second, then said, "Yes."

Sabre felt it in her chest but didn't react.

"Why?"

"I snuck out," Taber said. "I wasn't supposed to, and I knew I'd get in trouble if anyone found out."

"Where did you go?" DuBois asked.

"To see someone," Taber said. "A girl who lives and works a few blocks from there."

DuBois made a note. "Why didn't you mention that before?"

Taber's hands clenched together in his lap. "Because I wasn't supposed to be out. And when I heard Wilcox was dead, I panicked."

"Why would that make you panic?"

Taber looked at Sabre, then back at the detective. "Because everyone already thought I was the reason his son died. I figured they'd think I killed him too."

DuBois studied him for a long moment. "Let's back up. What's the girl's name?"

"Kayleigh Lopez. She goes to my school."

"Where does she live?" DuBois asked.

"On Cedar, near Wilcox's street. It's just a few blocks over."

"How close did you get to his house?" DuBois asked.

"Not that close." Taber shook his head. "We stayed near the corner store."

"Why that area?" DuBois asked.

Taber looked even more uncomfortable. "Because we all used to hang out there."

"All?" DuBois said.

"Me, Liam, and Kayleigh." Taber's voice dropped. "Before the accident."

The room went quiet.

"You're saying you were in Wilcox's neighborhood because it was familiar," DuBois clarified.

"Yes. And it was close to Kayleigh's house. It wasn't about his dad. It was about Liam."

DuBois made another note. "You told me the last time you saw Wilcox was at a store after the trial. Was it the same store?"

"Yes."

"Why didn't you mention the store was connected to his son?"

"I didn't think it mattered. I was there with Kayleigh that time too."

Sabre leaned forward. "Did you see Mr. Wilcox the night he died? Anywhere, even at a distance, or just in passing?"

"No," Taber said quickly. "I didn't see him. If I had, I would've left."

"Why?" DuBois asked.

"Because he scared me," Taber said. "Just the way he looked at me sometimes. Like he was always measuring something."

DuBois closed his notebook. "We'll have to verify what you told us. Names. Times. Locations. You have to understand, it's hard for me to believe anything you say because you've lied to me several times now. Is there anything else you might want to add?"

Taber shook his head.

DuBois stood. "If you do remember anything else, tell Sabre immediately. Not later."

"I will."

After DuBois stepped out of the room, Sabre stayed a moment longer, watching Giovanni try to steady his breathing.

He rubbed his hands together, staring at the table. "I didn't do this."

"I know," Sabre said gently. "But it's good that you're finally telling the truth."

"I'm still scared."

"Don't worry. He'll find the real killer." She hoped that was true.

But Giovanni had placed himself near Wilcox's world again. And that was exactly the kind of coincidence that made innocent people look guilty. And she couldn't shake the feeling that, although Giovanni's explanation could be true, it might not be enough.

Chapter 53

Thursday evening

JP noticed the truck on the third turn. The first time could've been a coincidence. Maybe even the second. By the third turn, two blocks apart, the same dull-gray Dodge Ram eased through the light just after him, and coincidence ran out of credit.

JP kept his speed steady, one hand light on the wheel, eyes moving the way they did when his instincts kicked in before his brain caught up. The Dodge stayed two cars back, keeping a professional distance.

JP took a random right turn, and the truck followed. He took another turn, into a residential area this time, with no reason for through traffic. The vehicle was still behind him.

"Okay," JP muttered. "Let's dance."

He slowed a touch, letting the truck close the gap. In the side mirror, he caught a glimpse of the driver—male, baseball cap pulled low, face turned just enough to avoid being seen.

JP turned onto a frontage road that ran parallel to the freeway. It was long and straight, with nowhere to duck out easily. If the driver was going to make a move, this was where it would happen.

Another mile, then JP did something small but unmistakable. He checked his mirror and made eye contact, just for a second.

The truck surged forward.

No more pretending. The Dodge closed in fast, crowding his rear bumper, then swung to the left like it was going to pass.

"Don't," JP said aloud.

The truck pulled alongside him, close enough that JP could see the driver's profile, then see the passenger lean over and say something he couldn't hear.

Then the truck drifted. A controlled bump, and the metal kissed his truck with a grinding thud.

JP gripped the wheel, tires screaming as his truck fishtailed toward the shoulder. Gravel exploded beneath him. He fought the slide, heart hammering, but his hands were steady, years of reflex taking over.

The Dodge accelerated past him. JP's truck slammed sideways into the dirt embankment. He rode it out, foot off the gas, steering into the skid until the truck finally shuddered to a stop in a cloud of dust.

JP sat there for a moment, breathing hard, and listening to the ticking engine. Instinctively, he pulled his gun from his belt and scanned the area. He saw no one.

He checked himself, hands shaking but working, ribs sore but intact. He shoved the door open and staggered out, still looking around him.

The Dodge was gone. Whoever it was hadn't wanted him hurt. They'd wanted him warned.

JP leaned against the truck and laughed, short and sharp. "Message received," he said.

He pulled out his phone with fingers that still trembled and called Sabre.

She answered immediately. "JP?"

"Yeah," he said. "I'm okay."

"What happened?"

He summarized the encounter, then said, "They think I know something." He glanced down the empty road, the dust still settling around him. "And they don't scare easy."

"Who?"

"I can't ID them, but I'm sure they're connected to Mateo. I must've hit a nerve somewhere."

"Unless it's something from your past?"

"That's always possible, but I'm moving forward with this one, and I'll see where I might've struck a nerve."

"Is your truck drivable?"

"Let me see." JP looked around for gas or oil leaks. Everything seemed intact, except for the scrape of paint along the side. He got back in the driver's seat and moved forward. "I'm good. I'll see you soon."

He called Detective Miller and reported the incident. JP gave him the facts only—gray Dodge Ram, newer model, no plates visible, and a driver skilled enough to control speed and angle during a deliberate sideswipe.

"I'll put out a BOLO."

"And could you please check on Mendoza. If they're warning me, they may want to silence him."

"I'll do that first and get back to you."

JP drove toward home, watching carefully for a tail, but saw none. He straightened, pain blooming along his ribs, and smiled grimly. "Message received," he said to the empty stretch of asphalt.

Just before he pulled into his driveway, his phone rang. It was Miller.

"Mendoza is fine."

"They wanted me scared," JP said. "Not dead. And I think I know why."

Miller waited.

"They think I can flush out Mendoza."

There was a brief silence. "That's a theory," Miller said.

"It fits," JP said. "They'll come after anyone who gets close to the guy they're afraid of."

Chapter 54

Thursday night

At his home, JP sat in the driveway and assessed his injuries. His side throbbed where the seat belt had snapped him back, but nothing felt broken. He picked up his cell again. He had one more call to make before he went inside.

DuBois answered with his usual calm.

JP cut to the chase. "Someone ran me off the road."

"Start at the beginning," DuBois commanded.

JP recounted the incident.

"And you think this is about what?" DuBois prompted.

"My gut says Mateo. But I could be missing something, so I can't ignore Wilcox. Either way, it's someone who wants me to stop asking questions."

"Why would anyone come after you on the Wilcox case? You're not really involved in it."

"Unless I uncovered something I didn't realize. But I can't think what that might be. That's why I'm certain it's Mateo's abductors. But I wanted to let you know just in case."

"I appreciate that. Stay reachable," DuBois said. "And don't go lone wolf on me."

JP almost smiled. "I'll try."

As he walked into his house, his phone rang again.

This time it was Rosalia, her voice stretched tight with panic. "JP," she said. "Someone's been in my house."

He was already turning around when Sabre approached.

"What happened?" JP asked into the phone.

"I came home, and the door was open," Rosalia said. "Everything's a mess. Drawers dumped. Cushions cut. I don't know what they may have taken."

JP stiffened. "Get out of the house. Now. Go to your neighbor's. Don't touch anything."

"Do you think they were looking for Luis?" she asked. "Or something he has?"

"Rosalia," JP snapped. "You're not safe there. Leave now."

"I already did," she said. "I'm across the street."

"Good. Stay put. I'm calling this in."

He ended the call and looked up at Sabre.

"What happened?" she asked.

He told her what Rosalia had said. "I need to go to her."

"Are you sure you're okay?"

"I'm fine."

Gene walked out, boots on, jacket pulled tight. "I'm going with you."

"You're still recovering from your accident. I can do this."

"I'm in better shape than you right now," Gene said. "Let's go. You can tell me all about it on the way."

JP gave Sabre a quick kiss, then walked to his truck with Gene next to him.

"Are you driving or me?" Gene asked.

JP tossed him the keys, then called Miller as they pulled onto the street.

"Rosalia Mendoza's place was ransacked," JP said. "I'm heading there now."

"I'll meet you there."

~~~

Rosalia's house looked normal from the outside. The porch light was on, the curtains were still, and nothing was broken or kicked in.

Inside told a different story. Drawers were pulled out and dumped. Couch cushions were slashed just enough to search,
~~~

not enough to destroy. The bedroom closet was open, hangers pushed aside. The desk in the corner sat half open, papers scattered like someone had rifled through them impatiently.

Miller walked the room slowly, hands behind his back, eyes sharp. "I wonder what they were looking for."

Rosalia stood near the kitchen doorway, arms folded tight across her chest. She looked shaken but holding steady, the way people did when fear hadn't fully hit them.

"I can't see that they took much," she said. "At least... nothing important."

Miller turned. "Walk me through what is missing."

Rosalia thought for a moment. "I had twenty dollars in my desk drawer. It's gone."

Gene raised an eyebrow. "Just that?"

Rosalia nodded. "Everything else is here. My jewelry, which isn't worth much. We have a few electronics, a laptop, a TV, an iPod. They're all here."

Miller glanced at JP. "That's confirmation."

"Of what?" Rosalia asked.

"That they were looking for a person or information, not valuables to sell."

"This is probably about Luis," JP said. "Same timing as what happened to me."

"What did they do?" Rosalia asked.

JP gave a quick explanation.

Miller stepped aside and spoke quietly into his radio, then turned back. "Crime scene techs will do a light sweep for prints."

Rosalia swallowed. "Am I safe here?"

JP didn't lie. "Not for now."

She sighed, like she'd already known the answer. "I can stay with some friends. They live across town."

Miller looked at JP.

"We'll follow you," JP said. "To make sure you get there without problems."

Miller handed her a card. "Call me if anything feels off. Even if you think it's nothing."

Rosalia took it with both hands. "Thank you."

~~~

They drove in a loose formation, Rosalia in front, Gene behind her, with JP watching the mirrors. No one followed.

Rosalia's friend, Stella, lived in a small duplex with a narrow driveway and motion lights that snapped on the moment they pulled in. Rosalia got out, relief flickering across her face.

"I'll be okay here," she said.

JP waited until she was inside and the door locked before he turned away.

Gene didn't start the truck right away. "Do you think the ransacking was a warning?" Gene asked.

JP met his eyes. "It was a search. And they didn't find what they wanted."

"Which means they'll keep looking."

JP nodded. "Yeah. And now they know where pressure works."

"It can't be a coincidence that you and Rosalia were targeted at the same time."

"Someone is making a point, and they want us to know what it's about."

JP and Gene drove home in silence. The house lights were on when they pulled in, safe and familiar for now. JP reached for the door handle, then turned to Gene. "Thanks, bro."
~~~

Chapter 55

Friday morning

Detective Miller stood near the door, arms crossed, watching Mendoza with the kind of patience that came from knowing silence usually did most of the work. In the interview room, Mendoza waited patiently. His shoulders were hunched, hands folded on the table like he was trying to take up less space.

"Your sister's house was ransacked last night."

Mendoza's head snapped up. "What?"

"Drawers were dumped, furniture was cut open, but no apparent forced entry," Miller said. "They took twenty dollars and nothing else as far as we can tell."

Mendoza stared at him, his breath shallow. "And Rosa?"

"She's safe," Miller said. "But the perps were likely looking for you."

"I didn't tell anyone where she lives."

"You didn't have to," Miller said. "Someone already knew."

Mendoza dropped his gaze to the table. His fingers curled, then flattened again.

"This is why we offered protective custody," Miller said. "It's still on the table."

Mendoza looked up sharply. "No. If I go into custody, they'll watch Rosalia harder. They'll think she knows something. She doesn't. I won't do that to her."

"You're already doing it by staying quiet."

"I told you everything I remember."

"Everything you *noticed*," Miller corrected. "Not the same thing."

Mendoza didn't answer.

Miller exhaled and stepped back. "I can't force you into protection," he said. "Not without charges. But I need you to understand something."

Mendoza looked up again.

"Whoever scared you into silence is still moving," Miller said. "They're escalating. And right now, you're not just a witness, you're leverage."

"Then let me go."

Miller hesitated, then nodded. "We'll be watching."

He opened the door. "Someone's here to take you home."

JP was waiting in the hallway when Mendoza stepped out.

They didn't speak until they were in JP's truck, doors shut, engine running. The cab felt too small, the silence heavier than before.

"They hit Rosalia's house," Mendoza said quietly.

"I know. I'm the one she called."

Mendoza stared straight ahead. "I didn't mean for any of this to happen."

JP didn't soften his voice. "Intent doesn't stop consequences."

Mendoza flinched. "I know."

JP waited until the tension settled just enough.

"Luis," he said. "The person you think is after you, I think that's the same guy who ran me off the road last night."

Mendoza turned, eyes widening. "They did what?"

"Exactly what they wanted," JP said. "They let me live."

Mendoza swallowed. "I don't know names."

"I'm asking for *details*," JP said. "Anything that felt off. Anything you dismissed because it didn't seem important at the time."

Mendoza closed his eyes, forcing himself to think. "The older guy asked questions about things that didn't make sense."

"Like what?"

"Like whether the transport had been logged yet," Mendoza said. "Whether anyone would notice if we went off route. He already knew the answers; he just wanted to hear me say them."

JP felt the familiar tightening in his chest. "Anything else?"

"He kept checking his phone. Like he was waiting for instructions."

"From who?" JP asked.

Mendoza shook his head. "I don't know. Like I told you before, it was a woman."

JP kept his face neutral, but his mind was already moving.

Mendoza turned toward him. "Am I dead?"

JP met his eyes. "Not if we're smarter than they are."

Fear and relief collided in Mendoza's expression.

JP put the truck in gear and drove off.

"The person you're afraid of," JP said. "The one who showed up after you called for help. He wasn't improvising."

Mendoza's hands tightened in his lap. "He asked precise questions."

"About what?" JP asked.

"The paperwork," Mendoza said. "Whether the transfer had been logged yet. Whether the foster home had already been notified."

JP glanced at him. "He knew how the system worked?"

"Yes," Mendoza said. "That's what scared me."

"What else?"

Mendoza gave it some thought. "He corrected me."

"On what?"

"On the route," Mendoza said. "I thought the fastest way was the freeway. He said there was a frontage road that kept the van out of the system longer."

"You sure?" JP asked.

"Yes. He acted like he'd done it before. Like he knew where the highway cameras were."

After a moment, Mendoza added, "And one more thing. When I told him I thought I had the wrong kid, he didn't ask who the kid *was*. He asked who the kid *was supposed to be released to*."

"The thing is, Mateo probably wasn't the wrong kid. He thought his father was dead."

"So, the guy that hired me might've been telling the truth?"

"Maybe some of the truth, but regardless, there's far more to this than we know."

JP thought about what Mendoza had said about what the enforcer had asked. *That was a whole new angle.* "He asked about the receiving end?"

"Yes," Mendoza said. "Like that's where the problem was."

JP pulled the truck into a side street to mull it over. Who would benefit from knowing the release side of the system better than the transport side? That was a different kind of suspect.

Chapter 56

Friday late morning

The call came while Sabre was at her office desk. She had finished early in court that morning.

"Ms. Brown," the voice said. "Juvenile Hall intake. Giovanni Taber was brought in about thirty minutes ago. He requested you."

Sabre sighed. "What's he booked on?"

"Probation violation."

"I'm on my way." She hung up and called JP.

"I'll meet you there. I'm close by."

Sabre walked the two blocks to juvenile hall. JP pulled up right after she arrived.

"DuBois called me," JP said as he got out of his truck. "He didn't give details. Just said there was probable cause."

~~~

Giovanni sat alone in the interview room; hands clasped so tightly his knuckles were pale. He looked up, relief and fear colliding on his face. "This isn't just about violating my probation, is it?"

"That's what they're charging you with." Sabre took a seat. "But you're right. They think you have something to do with Mr. Wilcox's murder."

"I didn't do it."

"I know," Sabre said. "But you need to answer *our* questions carefully and honestly."
~~~

A fast nod. "Okay."

"Start from the beginning," she said. "What exactly did you do the night Mr. Wilcox was killed? Don't lie to me again. I want the whole truth."

Giovanni looked ashamed. "I snuck out to see Kayleigh. She was working late at the market."

"What time did you get there?"

"Around 6:30," he said. "Maybe a little after."

"And then?" Sabre pressed.

"We talked," he said. "Then I waited outside until her shift ended."

"Did you go inside the store?" Sabre asked.

"No," he said quickly. "I waited outside."

Sabre noted that.

"When her shift ended," Sabre said, "what did you do?"

"We walked toward her place."

"Toward? Not to?"

Giovanni hesitated. "We didn't go inside."

"Did you walk her home?" Sabre asked.

"Yes," he said. "I mean, part of the way."

Sabre leaned forward, anger evident in her voice. "Giovanni. Be precise. Your story keeps changing, and so does Kayleigh's. I need to know the truth."

He exhaled. "I walked her almost all the way. Then I left."

"What time?" Sabre asked.

"I don't know," he said. "It was getting dark."

"Wait a minute," JP cut in. "It was getting dark, and you left her out there by herself?"

"Not really."

"So, what did you really do?" Sabre asked.

"I got her real close where I could still see her."

"Your story isn't adding up."

He shrugged. "That's what happened."

"Did you drop her off before seven?" she asked.

"Yeah," he said. "Probably."

JP shook his head. "Kayleigh says she went back to work, and you left."

Giovanni's eyes widened. "She said that?"

"Now, you're saying you walked her almost all the way home. Did you walk her home or back to work?"

He rubbed his face with both hands. "I didn't want it to look bad."

"Bad how?" Sabre asked.

"Like I was out too long," he said. "Like I wasn't where I was supposed to be."

"So, you stretched the timeline," Sabre said quietly.

"Yes," he said. "But I didn't go anywhere else. I went straight back."

"Did you pass Mr. Wilcox's street?" Sabre asked.

He froze. "No," he said. "I didn't go near his house."

"There was someone there wearing a hoodie. Was that you?"

"No."

Sabre held his gaze. "Did you hear anything? See anything unusual?"

"No," he said. "Nothing."

She studied him for another moment. "Was Kayleigh helping you?"

"With what?"

"To get Wilcox to stop bothering you."

"No. She wasn't involved in anything. I wasn't either. I just tried to stay away from him."

"Yet, you went to his house that night," JP said.

"I didn't go *to* his house. I was in the neighborhood, that's all."

Sabre didn't raise her voice, but she could see Giovanni's shoulders were tense.

"Originally, you said you left her a couple blocks from her house," Sabre said. "But the way you describe it now, you were closer."

He stared at the table. "We walked around the block."

"Which block?" Sabre asked.

His jaw tightened. "I don't know."

"Yes, you do," she said calmly. "Because if you didn't, you wouldn't be dancing around it."

The teenager swallowed hard.

"Detective DuBois already has evidence that you were on or near Wilcox's street," Sabre said. "What are you hiding?"

"I'm not hiding anything about Wilcox," Giovanni said. "I swear."

"Then what *are* you hiding?" she asked.

Silence.

Sabre softened her tone. "Giovanni, you're not in trouble for being a teenager. You *are* in trouble for lying."

He dragged a hand over his face. "I didn't want it to sound like we were doing something we weren't supposed to."

"So, you walked longer than you planned," she said. "You doubled back. You ended up closer to Wilcox's house than you want to admit."

He nodded, barely.

"And when I asked you before," she said, "you lied again."

"Yes," he said quietly.

Sabre leaned back. "Here's the problem," she said. "Every time you lie to protect yourself from embarrassment or whatever it is you're hiding, you make it look like you're trying to protect yourself from a murder charge."

He looked up, eyes wet. "I didn't hurt him."

"I believe that," she said. "But right now, my belief isn't enough." Sabre stood. "And if Kayleigh knows the whole truth, it will all come out whether you want it to or not. You need to stop making it worse."

Giovanni nodded, ashamed, scared, and still very much a teenager.

Chapter 57

Friday afternoon

When Sabre entered the hospital room, Mateo was sitting up and looking more alert than last time. She pulled a chair close and sat where he could see her without turning his head. "Hey," she said gently. "I'm Sabre. Remember me?"

"Of course. You're my lawyer, and you visited me the other day."

"The doctors say you're remembering more. But you don't have to tell me anything that makes you uncomfortable," she said. "I just want you to tell me what comes to you. Even if it doesn't make sense."

He swallowed. "It's still kinda fuzzy."

"That's okay."

He stared at the ceiling for a moment. "I remember the van stopping," he said. "The driver got out."

"Do you know why?"

Mateo shook his head. "No. But I remember we had pulled off the main road, and it was kind of isolated."

Sabre let the silence sit. She'd learned that if she rushed, kids shut down. If she waited, they filled the space themselves.

"There was the other man," Mateo said. "The one you had the drawing of."

"Did you remember something else about him?"

"I remember him leaning through the door of the van."

"What else do you remember about him?"

Mateo's brow creased. "He had a pen. It was bright and shiny, and he clicked it." Mateo mimicked the sound under his breath. Click. Click.

"He was holding something else," Mateo said after a moment. "I didn't know what it was at first."

"Can you describe it?"

"It was clear," he said. "Small. Like from the nurse's office."

"A syringe?"

Mateo nodded. "Yeah."

"Did he say anything?" Sabre asked.

Mateo frowned. "He said something to the driver, but I don't know what it was. Then he jabbed me with the syringe."

"Did it hurt?" Sabre asked.

"No," Mateo said. "That's the weird part. It didn't knock me out or anything. I was still awake, but everything went foggy. Like when you wake up too fast."

"That's all I remember," he said. "After that, it's just blank, so maybe I did pass out."

"That's more than enough," she said. "You did great."

Mateo looked relieved, like he'd been afraid of disappointing her.

The doctor came in a few minutes later to check Mateo's vitals.

Sabre said quietly, "He's getting some of his memory back."

"It's a little better every day," the doctor said. "That's the way it works sometimes. First, some fragments, smells, sounds, objects. Things that don't seem important."

Sabre glanced back at Mateo. A pen. A click. A syringe. That was a lot.

She thanked the doctor and stood to leave. As she reached the door, Mateo spoke again.

"Remembering those things made me uncomfortable," he said. "I don't know why."

"That's okay," Sabre said. "Sometimes your body remembers before your brain does. Together we'll figure it out."

~~~

Sabre drove to see Detective DuBois, checked in, and waited for DuBois to call her into his office. She had to talk to him about Giovanni.

"You arrested my client on a suspicion," Sabre set her briefcase down, but remained standing. "Not evidence."

DuBois leaned back in his chair, expression unreadable. "First of all, I didn't arrest him. His probation officer violated him, because Taber lied about his movements the night Wilcox was killed."

"He lied about sneaking out," Sabre said. "That's not homicide."

"But it is a probation violation, and the truth puts him within walking distance of the victim's house," DuBois countered. "What did you expect?"

Sabre *had* expected that. "Did any witnesses actually see him approach the house?"

DuBois didn't respond.

"You don't have one," Sabre said. "Do you have anything that places him at the scene?"

DuBois' eyes narrowed. "What I have is a young man with motive, proximity, and a demonstrated willingness to lie."

"What motive?" Sabre said. "Giovanni lost his friend. And has no reason to hate the friend's father."

DuBois studied her. "People snap."

"Not like this," Sabre said. "Not without leaving evidence at the crime scene. And the effort to make the murder look like a robbery? My teenage client is not that sophisticated." She took a step closer to the desk. "Giovanni didn't have access to a weapon. He didn't have transportation. And he didn't have time to do anything beyond getting back to his group home before curfew."

DuBois exhaled through his nose. "You're very sure of him."
~~~

"I'm sure of the math," Sabre said. "Lies don't equal murder. Fear doesn't equal intent. And proximity doesn't equal guilt."

A beat passed.

"I'm not saying you're wrong to question him," Sabre continued, softer now. "But you're trying to make him fit a crime that doesn't behave like he does."

DuBois stood, signaling the conversation was over for now. "The evidence will decide that."

Sabre met his eyes. "Then let it."

~~~

JP was waiting in the living room when Sabre returned home. He didn't ask how it went. He could read it in her face.

"They're holding him?" JP asked.

"On a probation violation." She made air quotes.

JP was quiet for a moment. "So, they like him for the homicide, but they don't have enough to charge him, so they locked him up for a probation violation?"

"Exactly. And they're building a narrative out of discomfort."

"What doesn't fit?"

"Everything that requires forethought." She ticked them off on her fingers. "Giovanni doesn't plan. He reacts. He panics. He covers stupid things because he's afraid of getting into trouble, not because he's hiding something bigger. That's not enough. Besides, he had no access to a weapon," Sabre continued. "No vehicle. No way to control the scene. And no reason to believe killing Wilcox would make his life better."

"It would make it worse."

"Agreed," Sabre said. "This crime required someone who believed the outcome would fix something."

Sabre started to pace. "We need to find what DuBois is missing."

"Already working on it."
~~~

Chapter 58

Saturday morning

JP sat across from Mendoza at the small table in Jerry Leahy's office. Leahy had called the meeting, and now he sat at the head of the table, jacket off, sleeves rolled, watching everything and managing the questioning.

Mendoza's shoulders were tight, and his eyes were fixed on the wood grain like it might give him instructions.

Leahy leaned slightly toward him before JP spoke. "Luis," he said, "you answer what you're comfortable answering. If you don't understand a question, you say so. If you need to stop, we stop."

Mendoza nodded.

JP waited until Leahy leaned back again, and then said, "You've told us a lot about the man who intercepted Mateo. I want to hear about the man who hired you."

Mendoza frowned. "I had never met the man before."

"But he found you," JP said. "Where were you when the recruiter approached you?"

Mendoza glanced at Leahy, who nodded. "I was at the yard. The subcontractor lot, where we check in for assignments. He was standing near the gate, like he'd been there before."

"And he knew what your job was?"

"Yeah," Mendoza said. "He didn't come at me like a criminal. He came at me like a father."

"What do you mean?"

"He said there'd been a mistake," Mendoza continued. "That the system was about to ruin a kid's life, and nobody would listen. He said he'd tried everything the right way."

"What did he say about the kid?" JP asked.

Mendoza swallowed. "That he was his son. He said the boy was about to be given to his drug-addicted mother. That he wasn't safe there."

JP leaned forward just slightly. "Did he say anything else?"

"He said the kid was afraid to go home with her. That she had a boyfriend who beat him and his mother. He was very convincing."

JP stayed quiet.

"He told me the boy would be alone in the van," Mendoza said. "That nobody would check right away. He said all I had to do was drive him to an interception spot. He said, 'This will look like a delay.'"

"Did he say where to stop?" JP asked.

"No," Mendoza said quickly. "He said someone else would let me know. They would call after we left Polinsky."

"Did they?"

"No, because I pulled over and called before they did. That's when I thought I had the wrong kid."

"What did the first man look like?" JP asked.

"In his late forties or early fifties, maybe. He was clean and wore nice shoes. He wasn't flashy, but not cheap either. Oh, and he had a limp. Just a little one, like an old injury."

JP nodded. "Anything else?"

"He wore a watch," Mendoza said. "Plain metal band. He kept touching it when he talked."

"And the payment?" JP asked.

Mendoza reached into his jacket and pulled out an envelope, worn at the edges. "He gave me this. Right there in the yard. He said it was good faith, and the rest would come after."

JP didn't touch it. "How much?"

"A thousand." He let out a bitter laugh. "That's how I knew he was serious. He wasn't bargaining. He was trusting me."

"I'm afraid we have to turn that over to the detective," Leahy said.

"I know. I couldn't spend it anyway once I realized what was going on."

Leahy got a small plastic bag and had Mendoza drop it in. "They'll check for prints, but it's probably too late for that anyway."

JP nodded. "Is there anything else?"

"He kept saying, 'I'm not asking you to hurt anyone. I'm asking you to help me fix a mistake.'" Mendoza looked up, eyes raw. "I believed him."

"And the man who showed up later?" JP asked.

"That one scared me," Mendoza said.

"Why?"

"Because he didn't talk about family. He talked about endings."

JP leaned back. "So, the first man sold you a story, and the second man enforced it."

Mendoza's eyes were wide now. "I didn't know that's what it was."

"You didn't need to." JP stood. "You just needed to do your part."

Mendoza swallowed. "What does that mean?"

"It means the person you should be afraid of is the woman pulling the strings."

Chapter 59

Saturday late morning

The hospital room felt strangely temporary now.

Sabre stood near the window while the nurse finished removing the last monitor from Mateo's chest. He sat upright on the bed. His shoulders were squared in a way that told her he was bracing himself. Fifteen years old and already practiced at waiting for the other shoe to drop.

"You're clear," the nurse said kindly. "No more wires. You get to leave today."

Mateo didn't smile.

Sabre had seen that look before. Relief held back by caution. Kids who'd learned that good news didn't always stay good.

The social worker, Filippa, waited just outside the room with a small duffel and Mateo's paperwork. She caught Sabre's eye and gave a thumbs-up. Everything was ready.

Mateo slid off the bed and stood.

"You remember the Venables?" Sabre asked as they walked down the hall. "You had a visit to their home a few weeks ago when we were considering your placement."

He nodded. "They had the dog."

"Still do," Sabre said. "And the lemon tree out back."

His shoulders loosened a little. "I liked them a lot."

Outside the hospital entrance, Filippa opened the back door of the county sedan. Mateo hesitated, then climbed in, pulling the duffel onto his lap.

Sabre leaned down so she was level with him. "I'll see you there," she said. "I promise."

Mateo searched her face. "You'll really be there?"

"Yes. I know the way."

That earned her the faintest smile.

She watched the sedan pull away, then turned toward her own car. She'd been to the Venables' house more times than she could count. She had appeared at birthdays, emergencies, regular visits to other foster children, and the quiet check-ins that never made it into reports.

By the time she arrived, the social worker's car was already parked out front.

Mr. Venable stood on the porch, hands tucked into the pockets of his jeans, posture relaxed but attentive. Mrs. Venable hovered just inside the doorway, giving space but ready to step in.

Mateo climbed out of the sedan and looked around. "This is it."

Mrs. Venable stepped forward. "Welcome, Mateo."

They went inside together. The house smelled like coffee and something baking, *banana bread*, Sabre thought.

Mateo stopped in the doorway of the bedroom, taking it in. The desk lamp was on. The bed made with a Star Wars bedspread. A corkboard on the wall with nothing pinned to it yet.

"My stuff can go here?" he asked.

"Of course," Mrs. Venable said. "And you can move things around if you want. This is your room."

Mateo stepped into the room and set down his duffel.

Sabre leaned against the doorframe, feeling better about Mateo by the minute.

She turned to the boy. "I'll check in soon. And if you need me before that—"

"I know," he said. "I can call."

"Yes," Sabre said. "Anytime."

Outside, Filippa finished her notes and handed Sabre a copy. "Everything's official," she said. "I'll follow up next week."

Sabre thanked her and watched her drive off.

For a moment, it was just Sabre and the Venables on the porch.

"He's quieter than the last time we saw him," Mr. Venable said.

"He's been through an ordeal," Sabre replied. "But this is a good place for him."

Mrs. Venable nodded. "We'll take it one day at a time."

Sabre believed them. She always had.

As she walked back to her car, she let herself feel the relief she'd been holding back since the hospital. Mateo was where he was supposed to be. He was safe, seen, and not alone. The Venables were her favorite foster parents.

Sabre pulled out her phone and called JP. "He's home. The Venables have him."

Chapter 60

Saturday late afternoon

JP didn't tell Sabre where he was going. Not because he wanted to keep secrets from her, but because he wasn't certain himself.

He drove with the radio off, windows up, eyes working the mirrors the way they always did when his gut wouldn't settle. The city was already hot, the air shimmering off the asphalt, but the inside of the truck felt colder than it should. He told himself it was nothing.

He cut through a neighborhood he didn't need to be in, looped around a block twice, and watched the same blue sedan show up in his rearview on the second pass. Not close or aggressive. Just... present. *Not again.*

JP kept his speed steady. He didn't brake-check or turn his head. He drove like a man with nowhere urgent to be.

At the next light, he turned right. The sedan also turned right.

He kept going another three blocks and took a left into a small shopping strip, with a nail salon, pawn shop, and liquor store with metal bars on the windows. He pulled into a space near the far end where he could see the lot and the street. He got out like he was stretching his legs.

The blue sedan rolled by without stopping. JP watched it disappear.

He climbed back into his truck and waited. Five minutes. Ten.

A woman walked out of the nail salon, phone to her ear, arguing with someone in Spanish. A teenager leaned against the pawn shop wall pretending he wasn't waiting for anything.

JP watched the street. Nothing.

Then his phone buzzed with an unknown number. He let the call go to voicemail.

JP stared at the screen until the backlight dimmed. Then he hit play, put it to his ear, and listened.

At first, it was just dead air. Then a sound rose underneath it. A faint rhythmic clicking. He couldn't quite make out what it was.

JP sat up straighter. The clicking stopped, and a man's voice came on, calm and close to the phone. The tone of someone leaving a reminder, not a threat.

"You're working too hard," the voice said.

JP held his breath.

The voice continued, almost conversational. "People get hurt when you pull the wrong thread."

After a final click, the line went quiet again.

JP lowered the phone, his fingers tight around it.

He wasn't certain which case the message was about. But he knew one thing with clarity: Someone was watching him now, and they were close enough to call and leave something that felt personal.

JP stared at the street, letting his eyes take in everything he'd ignored the first time, the parked cars, the tinted windows, the angles.

Then he called Sabre.

She answered on the first ring. "JP?"

"I'm fine," he said before she could ask. "But I need you to hear me."

Her voice sharpened. "What happened?"

"I just got a voicemail," JP said. "From a blocked number. A man who sounded calm."

"What did he say?"

JP repeated it word for word.

"What do you want me to do?" Sabre asked.

JP watched a white delivery van roll through the intersection, slow enough that he could see the driver's sunglasses, fast enough that he couldn't see his face.

"Lock the house down tonight," JP said. "Gene too. I don't care if it makes everybody mad. I want the kids where we can see them."

Sabre exhaled. "Okay."

"And call Ron," JP added. "Tell him I might need him on short notice. Not surveillance yet. Just ready."

"JP—" Sabre started.

"I know. I don't like this either."

He hung up before she could argue, because if he let her talk, it would pull him back into normal. And normal was gone.

JP started the truck and pulled out of the parking lot, taking the long way back, making turns that wouldn't make sense to anyone watching.

He wasn't headed home yet. Not until he was sure he wasn't bringing company with him. The voicemail man wasn't just trying to scare him. He was trying to steer him.

And JP Torn didn't like being steered.

He made one more turn, then another, and watched his mirrors until the city blurred into patterns. If they wanted him predictable, they picked the wrong man. And if they wanted him afraid—JP's hands tightened on the wheel—they were about to learn something else. They weren't the only ones who knew how to hunt.

He kept going until the neighborhoods thinned and the roads widened. He drove the speed limit and didn't do anything dramatic. He just didn't give anyone a destination that led anywhere personal.

By the time he pulled into a grocery store parking lot on the far edge of town, the tension in his shoulders had settled into something colder and more useful. Fear was loud. Control was quiet.

He parked near a cart return, cut the engine, and sat long enough to be sure no one had followed him in. A man loading groceries glanced his way, then went back to wrestling a case of bottled water into his trunk. Everything seemed normal and boring.

JP got out and walked inside. He bought a few random things a person could always use—coffee filters, duct tape, a loaf of bread—and paid cash.

Outside, he tore the receipt in half and dropped it into two different trash cans on opposite ends of the lot.

Then he called Ron. "You busy?"

"No. Sabre called, so I cleared my afternoon."

"Good. I need you to do something for me."

"Whatever you need."

JP gave him the address for the Venable foster home. "I need you there tonight to watch who comes and goes. Don't follow anyone. Just tell me if someone shows up who doesn't belong."

"When do you want me there?"

"Now," JP replied. "Mateo went there today. I'm afraid he may not be safe."

JP hung up and made the call he'd been avoiding.

Sabre answered immediately.

"I'm not coming straight home," JP said.

"I figured."

"I changed my routine," JP continued. "I used different roads. I made different stops. If anyone's watching, they won't get a clean line on me."

"Do you think this is about Mateo's case?"

He leaned against the truck, eyes on the street. "Yeah."

"Is Mateo safe?"

"I think so, but I just sent Ron over for surveillance."

"Should I tell the Venables?"

"I suppose that would be prudent."

"Be careful," Sabre said.

JP smiled faintly. "I always am. Just not in the ways people expect."

He ended the call and climbed back into the truck.

JP started the engine and pulled out of the lot, turning in the opposite direction from home. If they were still watching him, that meant they were nervous. And nervous people made mistakes. JP intended to be there when they did.

Chapter 61

Saturday evening

Ron parked two houses down from the Venables' home, far enough away to not be spotted, close enough to see who belonged and who didn't.

It was early evening, that in-between hour when the neighborhood settled into itself, garage doors rising and falling, sprinklers ticking on, a kid pedaling a bike in slow, lazy circles. The Venables' place looked like it should: porch light off, curtains open, a dog's tail occasionally flashing past the front window.

In these situations, Ron liked boring. He set his phone on the dash, screen dark, and watched.

Twenty minutes passed. Then thirty. A silver SUV rolled through, slowed, then kept going. A jogger cut across the corner and disappeared. Everything seemed normal.

At forty-five minutes, a dark Honda sedan came down the street not looking normal at all. It slowed just enough to read the house numbers, then rolled past the Venables' driveway, continued to the end of the block, and pulled over beneath a jacaranda tree where the branches drooped low enough to hide the windshield.

Ron waited.

Two minutes later, the Honda rolled back up the street. Same pace. Same pause at the Venables' house. Not a stop, just long enough to notice the open curtains, the light on in the back room. Then it kept going.

Ron felt a familiar prickle at the base of his neck. He reached for his phone, then decided to wait.

Ten minutes later, the sedan came back. Same path. Same pause. This time, the driver cracked the window and lifted a phone, angling it toward the house. The movement was small and easy to miss if you weren't looking for it. Ron was looking.

Ron snapped a quick photo of the back end as the car passed, capturing a partial plate and a dent above the left taillight. Then he made the call.

"I've got a vehicle doing slow passes."

"How many?" JP asked.

"Three," Ron replied. "They appeared to be checking for something or someone."

"What's the description?"

"An older dark Honda sedan. I couldn't fully read the plates, but I've got part of it. The driver took a photo of the house."

"Anyone approach?" JP asked.

"No," Ron said. "They were just watching, like they're confirming something."

JP exhaled. "Stay put. I'm on my way."

"And if it comes back again?"

"Don't engage."

Ron slid the phone back into the cup holder and kept his eyes on the street.

Five minutes passed. Then the Honda came back. This time, it turned into the Venables' driveway.

Ron's heart kicked hard.

The car stopped at the base instead of pulling all the way in, engine running. The driver just sat there, window down, arm resting casually like he was waiting for someone.

The dog barked inside the house. A porch light flicked on. The sedan backed out and pulled away.

Ron let out a breath he hadn't realized he was holding and immediately called JP.

"It pulled into the driveway this time, not all the way though. The guy sat there for a minute, then left. My guess is he wanted them to know he was here."

"That's another message," JP said.

Ron shifted in his seat, suddenly aware of how exposed the street felt.

Someone wanted the Venables, and the kid inside, to feel vulnerable.

And Ron knew how that ended if nobody pushed back.

JP arrived five minutes later. They waited together for about an hour, but no one returned. Ron left to get some sleep, and JP stayed the remainder of the uneventful night.

Chapter 62

Sunday afternoon

Ron had done enough surveillance to know most days were boredom wrapped in caffeine. Today was no exception. He'd been parked half a block from the Venables' house since that morning when he relieved JP so he could get some rest. Same routine. Newspaper on the passenger seat. Phone charging. Windows cracked.

The home looked exactly how it should: neat lawn, trimmed hedges, quiet street. Mateo had not come outside once, so Ron assumed he was still in there.

At 3:12 p.m., the dark Honda sedan approached. It didn't circle or idle. Instead, the driver parked directly across from the Venables' and shut off the engine.

Ron adjusted his rearview mirror until he could see a male, mid-forties, wearing a baseball cap. The man was watching the front door.

Ron sent JP a text.

--Honda sedan. Parked. Watching.

JP responded almost immediately.

--Don't spook him. Stay soft.

The man sat there for twelve minutes. Long enough to be deliberate.

At 3:26 p.m., a delivery truck came down the street. The sedan driver leaned forward. When the delivery truck passed the Venables' driveway, the man relaxed.

Ron's pulse ticked up. *The guy was waiting for movement.*

At 3:31 p.m., the front door opened, and Mrs. Venable stepped outside. The man in the sedan stiffened and focused. She walked to the mailbox alone. The man's shoulders eased.

At 3:34 p.m., the sedan started a slow roll and glided down the block.

Ron counted to ten, then started his engine. He didn't follow aggressively. He let distance build. Two blocks. Three.

The sedan turned right without signaling. Ron followed. The sedan accelerated. They hit a busier street, and the traffic swallowed them.

Ron stayed three cars back. The sedan suddenly braked hard. Ron braked too, but the car behind him didn't. Horns started honking at the near collision.

The Honda darted into a left turn lane and cut across traffic. Ron couldn't follow safely. He watched the sedan disappear through a yellow light and exhaled slowly. The man had known he was being followed.

Ron checked his mirror and didn't see a tail or second vehicle, just regular traffic.

He pulled into a gas station and called JP. "He clocked me," Ron said.

"Are you sure?"

"He braked me into traffic and bailed."

"Did you get the license?"

"Three letters. H-K-something, then 276. It was a mid-size white sedan. He wasn't looking for the Venables," Ron added. "He was looking for Mateo."

"I think you're right. I'll call Miller."

~~~

Sabre and Detective Miller stood in the Venables' living room while Mateo packed upstairs.

"We've had credible surveillance activity outside your home," Miller said. "A vehicle parked and observed your home for a while."
~~~

Mr. Venable tensed. "Because of Mateo's abduction?"

"Most likely," Sabre said.

Mrs. Venable sat forward. "Do you think someone is trying again?"

"We don't know," Miller answered. "But we're not going to wait to find out."

The room fell quiet.

Mateo's backpack zipper rasped faintly upstairs.

"What do you recommend?" Mr. Venable asked.

"We move Mateo tonight," Miller said. "To a temporary relocation with a controlled environment."

"And us?" Mrs. Venable asked.

"I recommend you stay somewhere else for a few days," Miller replied. "We'll do a sweep here and increase patrol, but you shouldn't assume this house is invincible."

"We'll stay with our daughter," Mrs. Venable said. "She's a Riverside PD officer."

Sabre stepped closer to her. "I'm sorry this is happening."

Mateo came down the stairs, backpack slung over one shoulder. He stopped when he saw everyone gathered. "What's going on? Why do I have to leave?" he asked.

"We're moving you somewhere more secure for a while," Sabre said. "Just until we're sure things are quiet."

He looked toward Miller. "Because someone was watching us?"

"Yes. Did you see someone?"

"I saw a car pull into the driveway last night. I just thought it was someone turning around."

"Have you seen that car before?"

"I don't think so." Mateo turned to Sabre. "Will I get to come back here?"

"Absolutely."

"Okay then."

~~~
~~~

Three hours later, Miller walked the perimeter again before Mateo stepped outside.

Mrs. Venable hugged him tightly. "You'll come back," she said.

"I know," he replied.

The boy got into an unmarked police SUV with two plainclothes officers who looked like they could've been his parents.

Sabre watched the vehicle pull away. The house seemed normal again within seconds.

Miller stood beside her. "They'll check," he said quietly.

"I know."

Sabre stayed until the Venables locked up and drove off. When she finally got into her own car, her phone buzzed. It was JP.

"He's in Polinsky in a special area," JP said. "Under a different name."

"Good."

"Do you think the perps noticed?"

"Yes," she said.

"Then it's about to move," JP replied.

Sabre looked back once at the now-dark house. It already felt like a target.

Ron arrived just as she was about to leave but parked nearby and didn't approach.

Sabre sent him a text: *Be careful, Bro.*

Chapter 63

Sunday evening

Ron sat two houses down in his dark SUV, engine off, scanner low. He had a clear line of sight to the Venables' driveway and front porch. The lights were out, and their car was gone. A patrol unit rolled past twice in the first hour, then the checks tapered off, a routine presence and predictable.

At 11:47 p.m., the street went still. No more traffic, no late walkers, and no dogs barking.

At 12:02 a.m., headlights appeared at the end of the block. The vehicle rolled slowly past the Venables and kept going.

Ron didn't move.

Three minutes later, the same vehicle came back at the same slow crawl. This time, the headlights went off before it reached the house. Ron had his camera ready. The car coasted the last twenty feet, stopped, and turned off its engine. For half a second, the rear plate lit up like a photograph waiting to happen.

Ron pressed the shutter. Rapid burst.

He texted JP: *Dark Honda sedan is back. Lights off. Stopped near house.*

A door opened and the passenger stepped out wearing a dark hoodie over a cap pulled low and gloves. Ron aimed his camera—set on low-light and high ISO—at the intruder. Another fast burst of images.

The man moved along the shadow line of the sidewalk, past the driveway, and cut through the side yard.

Ron stayed still except to click his camera.

The person reached the side window, and Ron heard a muted pop, tempered glass broken cleanly.

The intruder slipped inside.

Ron called Miller. "House breach," he whispered. "One inside."

"Units are already in the area, and they'll be there shortly," Miller replied. "Do not engage."

Ron had no desire to be a hero, especially for an empty house. Instead, he eased his vehicle forward just enough to see the front door without pulling into the driveway. He kept his camera at the ready.

An upstairs light flicked on briefly. Then it went off. A minute later, he saw movement downstairs. Something heavy dropped.

Thirty seconds passed, then footsteps. The back door slammed open. Ron caught a glimpse of the intruder sprinting across the yard toward the fence. Ron stayed put.

The fence rattled. A thud on the other side. An engine roared to life, and the vehicle took off without headlights.

A patrol unit turned onto the street just as the vehicle accelerated away.

Another patrol unit approached from the opposite direction and stopped in front of the Venables' house. Ron got out and walked toward him, hands visible.

"I'm the reporting party." Ron quickly explained why he was there and mentioned that Detective Miller was on his way.

"We can both talk to him when he gets here," the officer said, a little skeptical. "Did you see the suspect?"

"Yes. I saw one male wearing a dark hoodie. He entered through a side window and fled out the back."

"Did you see the vehicle?"

"It was a dark Honda sedan, the same one I saw last night." Ron gave him the license plate number. "Detective Miller checked it out. It was stolen."

"Of course."

"The lights were off when he parked down the street."

Another unit soon arrived, and the officers went into the house, instructing Ron to stay in his vehicle.

After the scene was secure, Miller arrived, spoke to the officers, and cleared Ron. Then Miller walked through the side yard, studied the broken glass, and went inside.

When he returned, he said, "Most of the disturbance took place in Mateo's room. The closet was emptied and drawers overturned. The rest of the house was barely disturbed."

"Just as we expected," Ron said. "They needed to know if Mateo was still here."

Miller glanced toward the broken window.

"And now they know he isn't. But this just rose to attempted witness tampering."

Chapter 64

Monday morning

Sabre stood at the counsel table in the courtroom with Giovanni beside her, his hands folded, eyes forward. He wore a button-down shirt that San Diego Juvenile Hall kept for court appearances, sleeves too long and a collar pressed flat as if that could keep him out of trouble.

Across the aisle, an Assistant District Attorney flipped through a file just for show.

The clerk called the case. Antonio Hernandez, a judge Sabre had been in front of for years, looked down at the calendar and then at Giovanni.

"Probation violation," he said. "Sneaking out. Lying about whereabouts."

"Yes, Your Honor," the ADA said. "And the circumstances surrounding the violation raise serious concerns."

Sabre waited. Let him say it.

"The minor placed himself within proximity of a homicide scene," the ADA continued. "He initially lied to law enforcement. We believe detention is appropriate, pending further investigation."

The judge's gaze shifted to Sabre. "Counsel?"

Sabre stood. "Your Honor, this is not a detention case. Giovanni Taber is a scared teenager who made a bad personal decision, compounded it with a lie, and is now being squeezed because the police are unhappy that they haven't solved the case yet."

The judge's eyebrow twitched.

"Giovanni has no history of violence," Sabre went on. "No access to a vehicle. No access to a weapon. He returned to his group home voluntarily and complied once confronted." She paused, then added, "Detention should not be used as a holding cell for unresolved investigations."

The ADA interjected. "With respect, Counsel is minimizing the seriousness—"

"I'm contextualizing it," Sabre countered. "Sneaking out to see a girl is not evidence of homicidal intent. Lying out of fear is not proof of escalation."

She pivoted, just enough to include Giovanni without spotlighting him.

"His friend lost his life," Sabre said. "Giovanni lives with that every day. And right now, this court is being asked to punish him, not for what he did, but for what someone hopes he did so they can wrap up a case they can't solve."

The room went quiet.

Judge Hernandez leaned back, eyes moving between the two attorneys.

"I don't like what I'm seeing here," he said finally.

The ADA stiffened.

"This court does not detain minors because it's convenient," the judge continued. "And it does not allow the probation system to be used as leverage while law enforcement figures out its theory."

He looked directly at Giovanni.

"That said." The judge's tone sharpened. "Sneaking out was a violation. Lying was a mistake. And both of those choices have consequences."

Giovanni nodded. "Yes, sir."

"I'm releasing you back to the group home for now," the judge said. "Effective immediately."

Sabre exhaled.

"But hear me clearly," the judge went on. "You are on thin ice. You will comply with every condition. You will tell the truth, even when it's uncomfortable. And if I see you back here on another violation, I will not be nearly this patient."

"Yes, sir."

The judge turned back to the calendar. "I'm continuing this hearing for thirty days. I expect progress by then, from everyone."

The gavel came down.

As they stepped into the hallway, Giovanni let out a big sigh. "I'm sorry," he said quietly. "For lying."

Sabre stopped and looked at him. "Thanks for saying that."

As she watched the group home manager take him down the hall, Sabre felt the familiar mix of relief and unease.

Giovanni was free. But the pressure hadn't lifted. The police still didn't have another viable suspect. She and JP needed to find the truth to make it all end.

Chapter 65

Monday late morning

The last-minute schedule changes before Mateo had been picked up still bothered JP. Consequently, he found himself back at the transport company. This time, the office manager gave him the name of the original driver assigned to Mateo's transfer without much resistance. "Ken Gibson," she said. "He called in sick that morning."

"Before or after the shift started?" JP asked.

"About forty minutes before pickup."

"Convenient," JP muttered.

She bristled. "We can't control who gets the flu."

JP was already headed out. Now that he had the name, finding the address in a database would be easy.

~~~

Ken Gibson lived in a faded apartment in National City. The kind of place where the lawn tried but never quite succeeded. JP knocked, and the door soon opened halfway.

The man was in his thirties, with tired eyes and grease under his fingernails.

"Are you Ken Gibson?"

"Yeah."

"My name's JP Torn. I'm looking into the transport job you missed last week."

Ken's posture became guarded. "I was sick."
~~~

"So, the paperwork says." JP held his gaze a second longer than comfortable. "Your illness just seems too convenient."

"For what?"

"For that particular day and time."

"Are you from HR or something? Because I really need this job."

"I'm a private investigator who's trying to find out what happened to a teenage boy on his way to a foster home."

Ken exhaled. "I wasn't sick, not that it should matter to you. I had an accident on the way in."

"What kind of accident?"

Ken stepped outside, closing the door behind him.

"Someone ran a red light, clipped my rear quarter, and spun me into a pole."

"Was there a police report?"

Ken shook his head. "The guy took off. I didn't get plates."

"Was your car totaled?"

"Almost."

JP studied him. "But you told your boss you were sick."

Ken rubbed the back of his neck. "I've been late a lot because my car's been giving me problems. If I'd said accident, they would've wanted reports, insurance, photos. As a driver, I didn't want that on my record."

JP thought about his own recent incident with another vehicle. "Who knew where to find you on that road?"

"No one besides my friends and family. Why?"

"Because you were supposed to be driving the transport van that abducted a kid."

Ken looked at the sidewalk instead of JP. "A couple weeks ago, a guy approached me."

"Where?"

"Outside the yard at the end of shift."

"What'd he want?"

"He asked if I liked my job." Ken gave a dry laugh. "He said he had something easier. A quick pick-up that paid well."

"How much did he offer?"

"Three grand."

The recruiter again. "What were the details?"

"He didn't offer many. He just said it was a kid. Something about a family situation that the system messed up."

"Did he mention a name?"

"No."

"Did he mention a date?"

"No."

"What did you say?"

"Not much, but then I said no right off." Ken looked up finally. "I don't kidnap kids."

JP watched him carefully. "Describe the man for me."

Ken swallowed. "He was in his late-forties, maybe early fifties. Clean cut, a normal looking guy with a slight limp."

"How tall?"

"Six-foot, maybe. About like me."

"Did he have an accent?"

"No."

"Did you get a good look at him?"

"Not really. It was kind of dark, and he was wearing sunglasses and a cap pulled low. He kept his head down most of the time."

"Did anything stand out?"

Ken frowned. "He kept saying, 'It'll be logged. It'll look routine.' Like that was supposed to make it better."

It'll be logged. That's exactly what Mendoza had said.

"Did you ever see him again?" JP asked.

Ken shook his head. "I can't be sure, but there was a car behind me the morning of the accident."

JP didn't blink. "What kind?"

"It was a dark SUV. I couldn't tell the make. I remember thinking it was riding me too close."

"And then?"

"And then a silver sedan ran a red light and hit me."

JP didn't speak for several seconds. "Do you think that was random?" JP finally asked.

Ken's jaw tightened. "I did until you started asking questions. Now, I'm not so sure."

"So, someone approached you to commit a crime. You said no. Then just before that crime was committed, when you were scheduled for a transport, you're in a hit-and-run."

Ken sighed. "Seems like I was targeted."

JP stepped back. "Did you ever tell anyone about this?"

Ken shook his head. "Is the kid okay?"

JP met his eyes. "He was hurt pretty badly, but he's going to be fine."

Ken leaned back against the door, looking sick. "I guess I should've reported the accident to someone when it happened."

JP walked toward his truck. One thing was clear now: The recruiter hadn't just tried once. And when the first driver refused, he removed him from the schedule.

Chapter 66

Monday afternoon

JP sat in Miller's office and laid out his visit to the waylaid transport driver. "Ken Gibson was scheduled for the route," JP said. "He gets offered money to take a kid. He says no. The morning of the transfer, he's in a hit-and-run."

"You're saying someone removed him," Miller said.

"I'm saying it wasn't a coincidence."

Miller didn't respond. He just stood up and grabbed his keys.

"Let's go look."

~~~

Later, JP sat with Miller in the Traffic Division. The intersection camera had caught more than Ken remembered.

They watched it three times. The silver sedan was already at the red light when Ken's car approached. Waiting.

Miller paused the frame. The car crept forward for half a second before the light turned green. Then it accelerated hard.

The impact sent Ken's vehicle spinning exactly as he'd described.

The sedan corrected its own skid and drove off.

Miller rewound. "Zoom the plate," he told the tech.

The image sharpened, pixelated, sharpened again. Partial at first. Then enough to read it.

Miller exhaled slowly. "That's not bad for city cameras."
~~~

He ran the plate, and three minutes later he said, "The vehicle was reported stolen two days before the accident."

"Who's the owner?"

Miller turned the screen so JP could see.

Aubrey Harrington, age 82, Mission Hills

JP stared at the address.

"That doesn't fit," Miller said.

"No," JP agreed.

~~~

By afternoon, Miller had already sent an officer to speak with Aubrey Harrington. Her sedan had been taken from the church parking lot on a Tuesday morning, her volunteer day. She'd parked in the east lot like she always did, and when she came out two hours later, it was gone. She had filed a report, insurance had processed it, and the vehicle had never turned up.

She had no criminal history, no known associations, and no financial irregularities. She was just an elderly widow who baked cookies for her church.

Miller relayed all of that to JP in the parking lot outside the precinct.

"Still want to talk to her?" Miller asked.

JP nodded. "Sometimes people don't know what they know."

~~~

Aubrey answered the door herself when JP went to visit her. She was a small woman with sharp eyes and an even sharper mind.

"You're here about my car," she said before JP could speak.

"Yes, ma'am."

"The police officer who was here earlier said it was used in something terrible."

"Did anyone approach you before it was stolen?" he asked gently. "Anyone asking about it? Offering to buy it, maybe?"

She shook her head. "No."

"Did you notice anyone watching you at the grocery store or church or anywhere?"

"No."

She invited him in, and JP stepped inside.

The house told the same story her records did. Lots of framed family photos, a cross-stitched scripture, and an old piano.

"Do you think someone targeted me?" she asked.

"No," JP said honestly. "I think someone just needed a car."

JP thanked her for her time, encouraged her to be careful, and walked to his truck. He sat there for a long moment before starting the engine.

The stolen car told him something important. The abductors had planned everything well in advance but were also willing to improvise.

Someone had:

- Approached a driver weeks in advance.
- Tried to bribe him.
- Removed him when he refused.
- Used a stolen vehicle.
- Abducted and beaten a foster child.
- Threatened Mendoza's family
- Ran JP off the road, and ransacked Rosalia's home
- And was circling around Mateo.

"Who are you?" he muttered, as he drove to the church where the car had been stolen.

He stood at the edge of the lot, scanning the layout. It wasn't a bad place to take a car. It was open and predictable with plenty of foot traffic and no dedicated security guard. If someone needed something low-profile, this would do.

The parish secretary let him review archived footage from the week of the theft, even though the police had already done so. The system didn't hold much because it looped every thirty days, but someone had saved a segment when the police report was filed.

JP sat at the office's small desk and watched the screen. He was looking for loitering. The camera covered the middle section of the lot. Aubrey's silver sedan was parked three rows in, and the camera only caught the back end.

Cars came and went, along with minivans, pickup trucks, and one delivery van.

About twenty minutes into the footage, a group of teens in orange vests crossed through the frame. They carried trash grabbers and black bags, doing court-ordered service. They had their backs to the camera so JP couldn't see their faces.

They split up. Two of the boys slowed near Aubrey's car, then continued on their way, heads down, walking the perimeter. They finished their assigned strip and disappeared off camera.

JP let the footage continue.

Ten minutes later, a man in a baseball cap walked through the same row of cars. But he was too far from the camera to get a clear look at his face. He paused near Aubrey's sedan. The man bent, as if tying a shoe. Then he stood and moved on. Five minutes later, the vehicle backed out of the space and drove off.

JP rewound and watched it again. He sat back, knowing the police had searched for the man in the cap, but to no avail. There wasn't enough resolution to identify him.

JP thanked the secretary and stepped back outside into the late afternoon light. He stood where the sedan had been parked. If someone was scouting for a low-profile vehicle, this was the kind of place you'd find one.

This wasn't a breakthrough. It was a data point. And for now, that was all it was.

Chapter 67

Monday evening

Luis Mendoza hated sleeping in someone else's house. Rosalia's friend, Stella, had given them refuge. Rosalia was in the back bedroom, and Luis took the couch in the living room. He appreciated the kindness, but he was having trouble sleeping. Every sound felt like a footstep. Every closing car door made his pulse spike. He kept replaying the scene in the drainage canal—the second man stepping out of the shadows, the syringe, the way the man sounded both calm and annoyed when he said, "You picked up the wrong one." Like it was Luis' fault.

Luis had thought this would fade. But it wasn't fading. It was tightening. By the third night, he couldn't take the walls anymore.

"I'm going for a walk," he told Rosalia quietly.

She sat up immediately. "Luis—"

"I won't go far."

"You said that last time."

"I won't," he said again.

He needed air, so he headed out and walked a few blocks. A corner market was still open. Fluorescent light spilled out onto the sidewalk. He stood outside pretending to check his phone. That's when he saw the black Ford parked half a block down with the engine running.

He knew that vehicle. The passenger door opened, and a man stepped out. The enforcer. Even though his spine cringed, Luis turned and calmly walked in the opposite direction. He didn't run even when he sensed the Ford moving slowly behind him, matching his pace.

He cut into an alley, and then he ran. But he heard footsteps behind him closing in fast.

Luis burst out of the other end of the alley and saw Rosalia's friend's street ahead. The car was already turning onto it. They were triangulating and knew where he was staying.

Luis sprinted. He reached the house just as the sedan stopped. He slammed the front door behind him.

"Stella!" Luis yelled.

"She's gone," Rosalia shouted from the hallway.

"Back door!" Luis yelled.

The front handle rattled hard.

Rosalia grabbed the kids. Luis shoved open the kitchen window. It was small, but wide enough. He pushed the older child through. Then the younger. Then Rosalia.

The front door splintered.

Luis didn't look back. He squeezed through the window, dropped hard into the side yard, and ran. He caught up with Rosalia and grabbed the oldest. Rosalia was running with the little girl in her arms.

The car's engine revved. Someone shouted angrily from inside the house.

Luis grabbed Rosalia's hand and cut through the neighbor's yard, over a low fence, and through another alley. They didn't stop until they reached the main road. Then they ducked behind some bushes.

Sirens sounded in the distance.

"Do you think someone called it in?" Rosalia asked.

Luis bent over, hands on knees, lungs burning. "Maybe. There was a lot of noise."

"Was that him?"

Luis nodded. "Yes."

"Are you sure you told the police everything?"

He straightened. "Apparently, I didn't tell them enough."

Rosalia pulled out her phone and called Stella to warn her not to go home.

Luis dialed JP. "They found me," he said. "It's the same guy. The one that hurt Mateo."

"I'll be right there," JP said.

~~~

JP picked up the Mendoza family and delivered them to a safehouse Miller had directed him to. The exchange took less than five minutes. Two patrol units boxed the lot. An unmarked SUV idled at the curb. Rosalia clutched her kids so tightly the younger one started to protest.

"It's temporary," Miller told her. "You'll soon be back in your own place."

Luis agreed to stay put.

JP watched the SUV pull away.

"They're getting bolder," Miller said quietly.

"They're cleaning up," JP answered. "Anyone who knows anything about their crime. They came after me, Mateo, and now Mendoza. The only one left is ..."

Miller looked at him. "Gibson."

JP was already moving. "We need to check on him."

~~~

Gibson lived in a small duplex off Highland Avenue with a one-car driveway. The porch light was off, and that worried JP.

He knocked. No answer. He knocked harder and called out, "Gibson!" Still nothing.

Miller stepped past him and tried the handle. It was unlocked.

The detective looked at JP. "Are you armed?"

"Always."

"Good. Stay behind me."

JP drew his weapon, low and close to his body.

Miller drew his weapon fully and entered first.

"San Diego Police!" Miller called out as he crossed the threshold.

JP followed, staying offset behind Miller's shoulder. No independent clearing. He moved when Miller moved.

The living room was neat, with no sign of a struggle. The hall light was on. Miller advanced first. JP covered rear angles and door frames.

A bedroom door stood open. The bed was half-made, and one pillow was on the floor. The nightstand drawer was pulled out just enough to show it had been opened. Gibson's phone sat on the dresser, his keys next to it.

JP felt something cold settle in his chest.

"He didn't leave on his own," Miller said.

"No," JP replied. "He was interrupted."

They moved toward the kitchen. The back door was slightly ajar. The screen was bent, but not kicked in. Miller opened it carefully. Outside, the yard showed faint drag marks in the dirt and boot impressions near the fence.

"They took him," Miller said.

JP crouched, studying the ground. "There are two sets of prints, one larger and heavier. The recruiter and the enforcer maybe?"

Miller looked at him. "Why the hell would they take Gibson?"

"They don't know what he told us or what he might tell us."

Miller made a call, requesting a full response, crime scene team, and BOLO.

JP headed out front and scanned the street. It was dark, quiet, and normal. Miller came out and stood beside him.

"They're done warning us," JP said.

Chapter 68

Tuesday early morning

The call came in at 5:42 a.m. A garbage truck driver had found a male body in an alley behind a small commercial strip near University Avenue. DuBois was halfway into his jacket before dispatch finished reporting the location.

The early morning air was still cool when he arrived. Patrol had the alley taped off, and two officers stood near the dumpsters. The body lay on his back beside a delivery van.

DuBois crouched and examined the single gunshot wound to the chest. It looked like he's been shot at close range. No obvious signs of a struggle and no scatter of shell casings nearby.

"ID?" DuBois asked.

"His wallet's here," one of the officers said. "The name's Ken Gibson. The photo on the license matches."

DuBois took the license. *Gibson.* The name hit. He'd heard it last night. A BOLO had been issued when a witness in a child abduction case had gone missing.

DuBois stood and called Detective Miller.

"I've got a body," DuBois said. "I think it's your missing witness. At least his license reads Ken Gibson."

"Where?" Miller asked.

DuBois gave him the cross streets.

"Time of death?" Miller asked.

"Prelim says between ten and midnight."

~~~

Miller exhaled. "I'm on my way."

By the time Miller arrived, the ME had begun initial documentation.

DuBois walked Miller through the facts without commentary. "No robbery staging," DuBois said. "His wallet's intact. Cash still inside."

Miller looked down at Gibson's chest wound.

"You had a BOLO out," DuBois said. "Was he a witness in the Mateo Alvarez abduction?"

"Gibson was initially approached to be the driver, but he turned it down. Then he was in a hit-and-run accident and couldn't make it to work. They replaced him with Luis Mendoza."

"Have the perps targeted anyone else?"

"Mendoza's sister's house was ransacked. JP was run off the road. And someone broke into the victim's foster home."

DuBois processed the new information. "This was maintenance."

Miller looked at him. "Yes. Someone is eliminating the risks."

"All right," DuBois said. "Let's see if we can figure out who thought Gibson was a problem."
~~~

Chapter 69

Tuesday late afternoon

The house was suddenly quiet. Gene had taken Conner and Morgan to soccer practice, and Dené was in her room, the music low.

Sabre stood at the kitchen counter, hands wrapped around a mug of tea. JP was across from her, elbows on the wood, phone facedown between them.

"Gibson's dead," she said again, as if repetition might make it smaller.

JP looked as distressed as she felt. "He was trying to do the right thing, and it cost him his life."

Sabre had seen bodies before, clients who didn't make it, parents who didn't survive their own chaos. She'd stood in courtrooms where outcomes felt like slow executions. But this wasn't system failure. This was someone deciding who lived. And JP had been run off the road two days ago.

"It could've been you," she said.

"It wasn't."

"That's not the point."

Sabre moved to the window. The backyard was still, the late afternoon light falling across the grass. It all seemed so ordinary, even indifferent.

"I keep thinking about Mateo," she said. "He was supposed to go to a foster home. That was it, a placement, a routine transfer."

Silence settled between them.

"Maybe this is where I step back," she said finally.

"You've said that before."

"Not like this." She turned toward him. "They ransacked Rosalia's house. They tried to get Luis. They killed Gibson. And they ran you off the road." She swallowed. "At some point, this stops being about justice and starts being about ego."

JP shook his head. "You didn't create this."

"No," she said. "But I'm standing in the middle of it."

He studied her. "Are you saying you want to quit?"

She let out a breath that almost became a laugh. "I don't know what that would even look like."

"You'd still take cases," he said. "And you still wouldn't stop when things got dangerous."

Sabre met his eyes. "And that's the part I don't know how to do."

In the hallway, a door closed, life continued.

JP reached for her hand. "You think walking away would make them stop?" he asked.

"No."

"You think whoever's behind this is going to say, 'Sabre's tired, let's pack it in?'"

She managed a small smile. "That's not funny."

"I'm not trying to be." He squeezed her hand. "This isn't about your career. It's about someone who thinks they can keep themselves out of trouble by removing people."

"And what if they don't stop?" she asked.

"Then we finish it."

That sounded so simple, but terrifying. She rested her forehead against his shoulder. "I don't want the kids paying for this."

"They won't," JP said.

"How do you know?"

"I don't," he admitted. "But the only thing worse than standing in the middle of this chaos is stepping out and pretending it's someone else's job."

Sabre closed her eyes. Suddenly, her cases started to flash before her, babies in hospitals, Giovanni in detention, Mateo flinching at a sketch, Rosalia's kids climbing through a kitchen window, Gibson in an alley, and JP being chased. "I don't know how much more I can take," she said.

JP wrapped his arms around her. "Sweetheart, we've been through much worse. Why is this triggering so much?"

"I don't know, but it's hitting me hard," she said. "And we don't seem to be any closer to figuring it out."

JP picked up his phone. "I'll check in with Miller."

Sabre squeezed his hand. "Be careful. I can't lose you."

He gave her the look he always did when she said that. "I always am."

Chapter 70

Tuesday evening

After dinner, Gene took the kids for ice cream. JP sat at the kitchen table, files spread in front of him.

Sabre sat down with him and said, "Go through it again."

He looked up. "What part?"

"All of it."

He gave her a half-smile. "You don't do anything halfway."

"No," she said. "I don't."

He exhaled, then began.

"Two men are approached to transport a kid to someplace other than his foster destination. Gibson refuses to take the job. Mendoza agrees to it. There's a glitch in the system, and Mateo ends up in the transfer, maybe he was the target, maybe not. He leaves Polinsky at 1:15 p.m. Unit 417 logs out. GPS drops near the frontage road. Mendoza pulls off because he realizes something's wrong."

Sabre nodded.

"The enforcer shows up. Tells him it's the wrong kid, which Mendoza had already thought was the case, but now we don't know for certain."

Sabre's fingers tightened around her mug.

"The guy threatens Mendoza and his family if he doesn't cooperate." JP's voice stayed level. "The enforcer gives Mateo something in a syringe to make him sleepy. For some reason, Mateo gets beaten up. We're not sure why. Maybe he fought back. Maybe he saw something he shouldn't have. Or maybe the enforcer just took his anger out on him. Mateo is hospitalized and can't remember except bits and pieces."

"Then what?" she asked.

JP rubbed his hand over his jaw. "They dump Mateo. Mendoza takes off and ditches the van. Later, Rosalia's house gets vandalized. Gibson gets taken and killed."

He stopped.

Sabre sighed. "You missed the part where you get run off the road and then the threatening phone call you received."

JP blinked. "Right. Someone followed me and sideswiped me. I'm sure it was a warning."

"And one you should probably heed."

"Sure, honey."

"So, it wasn't anything serious?" she scowled.

"Oh, no. That driver was as serious as the business end of a .45. But I ain't gonna run like a scalded dog."

"Of course, you're not." Sabre sighed. "And the call you got?"

JP replayed it in his mind. "A male voice, not angry, just matter of fact. He told me I was working too hard. And that 'people get hurt when you pull the wrong thread.'"

JP frowned. "There was a sound in the background."

"Like what?"

He tilted his head, trying to retrieve it. "A clicking sound, like a pen, but he made a double click with it. Click, click, pause, then click, click."

Sabre's eyes widened. "Mateo said the man who came to the parked van kept clicking a pen."

JP went still. "I heard that same rhythm somewhere else," he said.

"Where?"

He stood and paced. "I don't know." JP suddenly stopped. "Wait. It was when I went to see the medium."

Sabre blinked. "What?"

"I was in the waiting room. Someone in the hall kept clicking a pen. Over and over. A double click, just like during the phone call."

"Did you see who it was?"

He shook his head. "Not really. I was reading a brochure."

They looked at each other. Neither of them spoke for several seconds.

"The medium had been talking to Wilcox," JP said.

"It doesn't mean the cases are connected," Sabre said.

"But it means something. It can't be a coincidence."

She walked to the window and stared out at the dark yard. "The medium worked with grieving parents. That's why she approached Wilcox in the coffee shop."

JP moved over to her.

"I don't know what to think," he said. "But I know that clicking pen was the same rhythmic pattern."

"Okay," Sabre said quietly. "Let's assume the sound isn't a coincidence."

JP nodded.

"That means someone who was near the medium made that call to you."

"Which would mean the call was about the Wilcox case," JP said. "Unless the sound Mateo heard was the same pattern, and that would mean ..."

Sabre finished his sentence. "That the enforcer in Mateo's case is somehow connected to Wilcox."

JP swallowed. "But how?"

Sabre looked at the clock. "It's too late to contact Mateo now. I'll do it first thing in the morning."

Chapter 71

Wednesday morning

Sabre and JP went to see Mateo in protective custody. "I need you to focus for a minute," she said gently. "On the sound of the clicking pen you heard from the man outside the van."

The boy shifted, uncertain. "Okay."

"Can you demonstrate what it sounded like?" She handed him a pen.

Mateo lifted his hand and mimicked it. *Click. Click.* Pause. *Click. Click.*

"Was it nervous?" Sabre asked. "Fast?"

"No," Mateo said. "Slow. Like he didn't care." He did it again. *Click. Click.* Pause.

JP tapped his finger against the counter. *Click. Click.* Pause. "That's the same cadence."

~~~

Sabre, JP, and Miller met with DuBois in his office.

Sabre laid it out. The clicking rhythm Mateo described. Then JP heard the same cadence outside the medium's office.

DuBois scowled. "You think the same person is in both lanes?"

"We think the sound is in both lanes," Sabre corrected. "But most likely made by the same person."

DuBois didn't look convinced. "I don't see how a clicking pen merges an abduction with a homicide."
~~~

"It might not," Sabre replied. "But it's not the only thing. Whoever abducted Mateo had insight into how the transfers work. Wilcox has dealt with many of them and could easily have had access to someone who could help him."

"Help him abduct Mateo?" DuBois looked even more skeptical.

"Not necessarily him. We think Mateo was the wrong kid."

JP cut in. "So, if you have anything else on Wilcox, we'd like to see it."

DuBois gave him a look. "Anything else how?"

"His movement, his routine, places he went that didn't make sense."

DuBois hesitated, then reached for a separate folder. "I pulled vehicle data. His SUV had a passive tracking system. But there was nothing special. He went to the grocery store, to work, to the bank."

He slid a printed sheet across the desk.

JP pulled the paper closer. Latitude and longitude meant nothing at a glance. But addresses did. He scanned, seeing a bank, his home, the probation office, a lot of what looked like home visits to the minors Wilcox supervised. Then JP spotted something and went still.

"What?" DuBois asked.

JP cross-checked the dates. There were five visits. Three were within an hour of a large cash withdrawal. The other two were the day after withdrawals.

"Can you pull the address for this coordinate?" JP asked.

DuBois tapped at his keyboard and the map loaded. "It's the Commercial Center off College Avenue. Does that mean something to you?"

JP didn't take his eyes off the screen. "That's where the medium's office is. She consulted with Wilcox after his son died."

DuBois frowned. "That never came up."

"It wouldn't," Sabre replied. "It's not illegal."

DuBois looked back at the map. "You're telling me Wilcox was visiting a psychic after pulling cash?"

"I'm telling you he was at that strip mall repeatedly," JP said. "Three times were within an hour of a withdrawal. The others were the next day."

DuBois stared at the screen a moment longer, then turned to Miller. "You're awfully quiet. What do you think of all this?"

"It's too big a coincidence for me to dismiss." Miller turned to JP. "You said you went to see the medium?"

"Yes."

"When?"

"Last week."

"Why?"

"I was tracking Wilcox's steps to help clear Giovanni."

DuBois let out a long breath. "I didn't connect that mall because I didn't know about the medium."

"And she may not matter," Sabre said. "But the sound does."

"So, you're convinced that Wilcox *wasn't* being blackmailed."

"I think he was probably paying for services," JP said.

Miller shook his head. "For what?"

No one answered. But the sound sat between them. *Click. Click.* Pause.

DuBois closed the folder. "We'll pull surveillance from that complex. Every camera. Every entrance. We'll find out exactly what Wilcox was doing there."

The cases still weren't officially connected. But they were no longer strangers.

Chapter 72

Wednesday afternoon

At the mall security office, DuBois stood behind the technician's chair while the footage buffered across three monitors. Miller leaned against the back wall. JP stood slightly apart, arms folded, saying nothing.

"Start with the first date," DuBois said.

The technician tapped the keyboard. He brought up camera 14, exterior entrance, south lot. Wilcox's SUV rolled into the frame. "That timestamp is less than an hour after the first large cash withdrawal," DuBois said.

On the screen, Wilcox parked, sat for a moment, then stepped out. He walked straight toward the side entrance that led to the second-floor offices.

"Follow him," DuBois said.

The technician switched the view to a different camera and displayed the interior hall footage. It was grainy, but they could see enough. Wilcox walked past the nail salon, past a dental office, and stopped outside the frosted-glass door of the medium's office.

He went inside, stayed for about twenty minutes, then walked out alone to his car and left.

"Next date," DuBois said.

The second visit followed the same pattern. Wilcox went in the same entrance, the same office, in and out alone. Nothing unusual.

"Third one," DuBois said.

The technician fast-forwarded. Wilcox's SUV entered the lot again. This time it was in the early evening. Wilcox parked and went inside. The hallway camera picked him up. The frosted door opened, and he entered.

"Roll it forward," DuBois said.

The technician jumped forward five minutes, seven, ten. Then the office door opened. Wilcox stepped out, and someone followed him. The clean-cut man was in his mid-forties with a slight limp. They walked side-by-side down the hall.

The two men exited together into the parking lot. The exterior camera picked them up and caught them standing beside Wilcox's SUV, talking for about four minutes.

Then Wilcox got into his SUV, the man stepped back, and Wilcox drove off.

The man turned and walked away, crossing the lot toward the east exit.

"Get me every angle on that guy," DuBois said.

The technician pulled additional camera footage, including the front entrance, the side lot, and the parking aisle. From those, he stitched together a partial face image. It was clear enough to see features, but not clear enough for certainty.

DuBois ran it through several databases with facial recognition. The system spun but got nothing.

"No match," the technician said.

DuBois nodded. "Print some stills."

~~~

An hour later, Mendoza sat in the interview room with his attorney, Jerry Leahy. Mendoza's eyes were tired, but alert.

DuBois slid the still frame across the table. The man in the image stood beside Wilcox's SUV, head angled slightly down, pen in hand.

"Do you recognize him?" DuBois asked.
~~~

Mendoza tensed. "That's the guy who approached me and paid the money."

"The one who told you it was a family matter?" Miller clarified.

Mendoza nodded. "That's him."

Miller and DuBois exchanged a look. JP felt vindicated.

After Leahy and Mendoza left, DuBois said, "So, we have Wilcox meeting with the man who recruited Mendoza."

JP spoke. "We know the recruiter, aka the pen-clicker, is connected to both Mateo's abduction and the medium Wilcox met with. That means the two cases are definitely connected. It's likely that whoever killed Wilcox probably killed Gibson too. And both men, the recruiter and the enforcer, were likely involved."

"But we don't know either of their names or their history," Miller added. "And we don't know why they abducted Mateo."

DuBois gathered the photos. "All right," he said quietly. "Now we find out who they are."

Chapter 73

Wednesday afternoon

Sabre was finishing a calendar call when her phone vibrated. It was from Polinsky.

"Ms. Brown?" the staff member said. "Mateo asked if he could speak with you. He said it's important."

Her stomach tightened. "Did he say what about?"

"Just that he remembered something."

Ten minutes later, she was in her car.

Mateo was waiting in one of the small interview rooms. He looked pale, but steadier than he had the week before.

"Are you doing okay in here?" she asked gently.

He nodded. "They're good to me, but it's not like being at the Venables."

"I know. They're anxious to get you back as well."

"Really?"

"Yeah, really. You don't need to worry about that."

Mateo sat up a little straighter.

"You said you remembered something."

"A lot of things have been coming back to me all of a sudden."

Sabre sat down across from him. "Start wherever you want."

Mateo swallowed. "It was when the van stopped. The driver got out. I couldn't see him, but I could hear them."

"Who?"

"The man I told you about. I didn't see him yet, but I heard him. He was outside the van near the front."

Sabre leaned forward. "What did he sound like?"

"Kind of mad."

"At the driver?"

Mateo nodded. "He said he messed up."

"Did he say anything else?"

Mateo frowned, concentrating. "He said, 'You were supposed to check.'"

Sabre felt her pulse pick up. "Check what?"

"I don't know."

"And then?"

Mateo's eyes flicked to the table. "He told the driver to get back in the van, then he made a call."

Sabre's voice softened. "Could you hear what he was saying?"

"Some of it." Mateo closed his eyes. "He said, 'It's the wrong one.'"

"And then?"

"He said, 'I know.'"

"Do you know who he was talking to?"

Mateo opened his eyes. "I think it was a woman because when he talked to the driver, he said, 'She'll take care of it.' Or something like that."

Sabre waited.

"When he was talking on the phone, he said her name."

"What name?"

"Slater."

"Did he say Mr. Slater?"

"No. Just Slater."

"Are you sure?"

Mateo nodded. "He said, 'Slater, it's the wrong one.'"

"Did the driver hear that?" Sabre asked.

"I don't think so. He was already back in the van on the other side."

"And then what happened?"

Mateo's voice got quiet. "The other guy, not the driver, got in the van, and that's when he jabbed me with the syringe."

~~~

Less than an hour later, Sabre walked into DuBois' office and closed the door behind her. "I saw Mateo. And he remembered something the enforcer said on a phone call. He said, 'Slater, it's the wrong one.'"

"You're certain Mateo said Slater?" DuBois asked.

"Yes."

"And he was talking to a woman?"

"That's what Mateo believes because he heard the word *she*."

DuBois didn't look surprised. Instead, he reached into a file folder sitting open on his desk. "When JP led us to the medium, Claire Hawthorne, I did a full background on her, including financials, associates, and her personal information."

DuBois slid a photograph across the desk. "This is Daniel Slater."

Sabre studied the image. He was in his mid-forties, clean-cut, with a controlled expression. The kind of man who didn't sweat in photographs.

"Who is he?" she asked.

"The medium's husband."

DuBois pulled another image from a folder. It was a picture of Wilcox exiting the medium's office. The man walking beside him was a match to Slater's DMV photo. "It's not a clean shot," DuBois said. "But close enough. This man walked Wilcox to the parking lot on his third visit to see the medium."

"And Mendoza identified him as the recruiter," Sabre said.

"That's correct. I ran Slater as well. He has no criminal convictions, but he has several civil disputes. He had a debt restructuring five years ago with a quiet foreclosure that disappeared before it went public."
~~~

"And?" she asked.

"And since Slater is married to the medium," DuBois continued, "that means Wilcox wasn't just seeing a grief counselor."

"He was seeing a couple," Sabre said.

"And that couple met with him multiple times after large cash withdrawals," DuBois added.

Sabre felt the final piece fall into place. "Did you run Slater's phone?"

"Working on warrants now."

"Financials?"

"Already subpoenaed."

"Any known associates?"

DuBois flipped another page. "One name keeps coming up, a contractor who's done security work for them. Off-the-books stuff."

"So, what are we looking at?" Sabre asked.

DuBois' voice was calm. "A grieving probation officer. Large cash withdrawals. Visits to a medium and her husband." He paused. "Then Wilcox is dead."

"After the husband abducts Mateo," Sabre added.

"For the first time," DuBois said, "those lines intersect."

Chapter 74

Wednesday night

Sabre sat at the kitchen table with a legal pad. She hadn't written a word. The kids had retreated to their rooms, so the house was quiet except for the hum of the dishwasher.

JP stood at the counter, arms crossed, staring at nothing in particular.

"Say it again," she said.

He didn't have to ask what she meant. "Wilcox was paying the medium. Not for grief counseling, but for a job."

Sabre finally made a note.

"The medium passes the gig to her husband," JP continued. "Slater recruits the enforcer. He recruits Mendoza to handle transport. He creates layers and distance between himself and the crime."

"And Giovanni," Sabre said quietly. "Was the target."

She reached into her briefcase, then slid a folder across the table toward JP. "I checked something earlier."

JP came around and sat across from her.

She opened the file. "I have the group home movement logs. They're internal, nothing official. But about a week before Mateo was transferred, Giovanni had a pending placement review."

JP's eyes sharpened. "Transfer?"

"Possibly," she said. "It was being discussed. Not approved yet. But the paperwork had been initiated."

"And?"

"It was delayed due to an administrative issue. A missing signature stalled it." She sipped her tea. "Two days later, Mateo's transfer was scheduled."

JP stared at the paper. "The transfer was run through the same company and was the same type of movement."

"Yes."

JP let out a breath. "So, Slater was waiting for the transfer for Giovanni, but when the van was switched to another transfer, they didn't realize it was for a different kid."

"Exactly. And no one was ever after Mateo, certainly not his parents."

JP rubbed his hand over his jaw. "Wilcox paid the medium to make Giovanni disappear. Slater set it up. The enforcer handled the hard part, and Mendoza gets pulled in as the middleman."

"And when the wrong kid gets in the van," Sabre said, "everything fractures."

JP looked up at her. "But why does Wilcox end up dead?"

"I'm not sure why that happened. Maybe they fought over money. Maybe Slater wanted to get paid even though he didn't get Giovanni. Maybe Wilcox changed his mind after the screw-up. We may never know."

JP's phone rang, and he picked up the call. "Yeah." He listened. "Understood," JP said. "When?" A pause. "We'll be ready." He hung up.

"DuBois?" Sabre asked.

JP nodded. "Warrants are being drafted for Hawthorne and Slater. After DuBois questions them, they'll round up the enforcer."

"They're moving," she said.

A small voice came from the doorway. "Who's moving?"

Sabre turned to see Dené looking worried. She probably hadn't heard everything, but she'd heard enough.

"Mateo?" Dené asked softly. "I heard his name. Is he okay?"

Sabre smiled. "He's fine, and he's safe."

"How do you know?"

"Because I saw him earlier today."

"But that was earlier," Dené argued. "How can you be sure?"

"Because Polinsky has great security."

"Why would someone take him?" Dené asked.

JP answered. "Sometimes people think hurting someone will fix something."

Dené frowned. "That's just dumb."

"Dumb as a bag of doorknobs."

Dené chuckled, then looked serious. "I just hope he's okay. I miss seeing him at school. Promise me he's safe?"

"I promise. Now, go to bed, honey," Sabre said softly.

Dené nodded and went back down the hall.

JP looked at Sabre. "They're cornered," he said.

"That's what worries me," Sabre said. "Cornered people do desperate things."

Chapter 75

Wednesday night

Sabre knew something was wrong. It wasn't the silence. Their house had old hardwood floors, and sounds carried easily. She could usually hear Morgan humming or the television from the living room. It was just a gut feeling.

She hurried down the hall into the girls' bedroom. Morgan was alone on the bed, scrolling on her phone. She looked up, and guilt flashed on her face.

"Where's Dené?" Sabre asked.

Morgan looked distressed. "She went to see Mateo."

Sabre's heart missed a beat. "How does she know where he is?"

"You told her he was at Polinsky. She thought she could ride her bike there and back before anyone noticed."

Sabre realized what she had said earlier. It stuck in her throat. "I guess I did."

Morgan nodded. "She said she had time."

"How long ago did she leave?" Sabre demanded, moving ahead of her fear.

"Like... twenty minutes." Morgan swallowed. "She made me promise not to squeal. But I told her I would tell if you asked."

"You should've told me before she left!"

JP stepped into the doorway. "Polinsky?"

Gene was right behind him. "What's going on?"

"Dené rode her bike to Polinsky to see Mateo," Sabre said flatly.

Gene cursed under his breath. "At this time of night?"

Conner stepped out of the hallway, already alert. "What happened?"

"Nothing yet," JP said. "And we're keeping it that way."

Sabre turned to Conner. "Stay here with Morgan and let us know immediately if Dené returns. Keep the doors locked. Don't open them for anyone."

~~~

They took three vehicles, each taking a different route.

Sabre's hands shook as she drove, but her mind was sharp. Dené was impulsive, but loyal to a fault. If she thought she could help Mateo, she would.

When Sabre turned into the Polinsky lot, she saw the bike immediately, its blue frame leaning crookedly against the outer fence. Sabre breathed a small sigh of relief. Dené had made it here.

JP's truck pulled in from another entrance almost at the same time.

Sabre ran up to the door. It was locked. She knocked frantically. The front desk staff looked up, and in seconds, a security guard answered the door. He recognized Sabre and greeted her.

"My cousin," Sabre said, breath tight. "She's thirteen and would've come in on a bike within the last half hour."

Security looked at the young woman behind the desk. She shook her head. "No visitors are signed in. It's past visiting hours."

Panic gripped Sabre. "But have you seen her?"

The young staff member shook her head. "Sorry, but no."

"Her bike is here. Please check the cameras!"

"Okay," the security guard said.

Sabre turned and went back outside.
~~~

JP was crouched by the bike. "She made it here," he said quietly. "The kickstand's not down, like she just jumped off quickly."

"She didn't go inside," Sabre said.

As JP stood, his phone rang, and he answered. "Yeah."

He didn't speak for several seconds, and his face hardened. "You've got my attention," JP said. "Where is she?"

A pause. Sabre could hear only faint static.

"No," JP said, voice flat. "That's not how this works."

Another pause. Sabre felt her pulse in her ears.

"What do you want?" JP asked.

A longer silence. JP's eyes shifted to Sabre. "He wants you to take Mateo out."

Sabre's stomach turned. "Then what?" she whispered.

JP's expression darkened further. "And he wants to know where Mendoza is."

The line went dead.

Sabre's breath came shallow. "Did he say anything else?"

"They were watching us," JP said. "They hoped they would get *you*."

Gene's car pulled in next to them. He jumped out. "What happened?"

JP looked at him. "They have Dené."

Gene swore like the ex-con that he was.

"They want Mateo, and they want Mendoza's location," JP said.

"But we're not giving them up," Sabre said coldly.

JP's eyes hardened. "I'm calling DuBois," he said.

Sabre looked at the empty stretch of lot beyond the fence. "I'll call Miller."

Chapter 76

Wednesday night

The call woke DuBois from a light sleep in his recliner, and he knew it wouldn't be good.

JP didn't waste words. "They took Dené."

DuBois bolted out of his chair. "Location?"

"Her bike was left outside Polinsky, but she never made it inside. She was trying to see Mateo."

"Why?"

"Because they're friends, and she felt bad for him. I received a call from the kidnapper. They want Mendoza's location, and they want Sabre to get Mateo out for them."

DuBois strapped on his weapon. "I'm on my way."

~~~

Twenty minutes later, he pulled into the Polinsky parking lot. Miller was already there, phone in one hand, notepad in the other.

"Did you do a call trace?" DuBois asked.

"It's a burner," Miller said. "Short duration. The cell tower ping puts it within a mile radius of here."

DuBois scanned the surrounding streets. "They must've been watching."

"Yeah," Miller replied. "They were probably looking for Sabre."

JP stood near the bike, still as stone.

DuBois stepped up to him. "What's the timeline?"
~~~

"She left the house twenty minutes before we realized she was gone," JP said. "The bike ride from our place is fifteen, maybe twenty. Maybe forty-five minutes total."

"So, they grabbed her from the lot before she made it inside. Which means, they've had her about half that time." DuBois turned to the Polinsky security supervisor. "What do you have for camera coverage?"

"Front lot, main entrance, side gate. We're already pulling it up. Let's go in and see what we've got."

Inside the security office, the footage rolled. DuBois, Miller, JP, and Sabre watched Dené ride into the lot, lean her bike against the fence, and look toward the entrance. After a pause, a dark SUV rolled past the outer curb.

Dené glanced at it, as if someone had said something to her. Then she looked back at the entrance.

The SUV continued past the camera's edge. Two seconds later, a hand reached into the frame, the footage jolted, and Dené disappeared from view.

The SUV reappeared in the far camera exiting the lot. No struggle visible.

"See the partial number on the plate?" Miller said. "It's the same first three as a stolen vehicle from last night."

"They're panicking." DuBois turned to JP. "You understand what this means."

"They can't get to Mateo or Mendoza," JP said. "So, they grabbed leverage."

"Which means she's alive."

JP's jaw tightened. "For now."

~~~

Back outside, DuBois made the calls that set the machinery in motion. He issued a BOLO and a grid search within a three-mile radius. He requested unmarked units to canvass intersections and flag traffic cameras.
~~~

Miller had already asked for a cell tower dump. He made another call. When he hung up, he said, "Protective custody on Mendoza is secure."

Sabre stood a few feet away, arms folded tightly across her chest. Her silence worried DuBois.

"Hopefully, they won't hurt the girl," he said.

Sabre looked at him. "They already have."

He couldn't argue with that.

Miller approached. "We've got traffic cam footage two blocks west," he said. "SUV matches the partial plate. It's headed toward the industrial corridor."

DuBois nodded. "Send units, but no lights or sirens."

Sabre looked confused.

"We don't want to alert them," DuBois' expression didn't change. "But they don't get to dictate police procedure. Once they don't need her anymore, they'll have to dispose of her."

"We're also not waiting."

The detective looked at JP. "You need to stay behind."

JP's gaze hardened. "No."

DuBois stepped toward him and whispered, "If you charge off half-cocked, you could get her killed."

The words hung between them.

JP didn't flinch. "I won't."

DuBois studied him for a long second. "Then we do this by the book."

Chapter 77

Wednesday night

The warehouse looked abandoned. Miller had parked and killed the engine two buildings down. DuBois' unmarked sedan slid in behind them. Two patrol units ghosted wider to seal the back.

JP stood just outside the vehicle, phone still in his hand.

"JP kept him talking long enough," Miller said, glancing at him. "We got a partial ping off the call."

"Not exact," DuBois added, stepping out. "But tight enough to work with."

JP nodded once. He'd heard enough of those conversations to know what that meant. They were close, but not certain.

Miller pointed down the block. "A traffic cam picked up a vehicle matching the plate Ron had obtained. It hit coming into this corridor ten minutes before the call," he said. "And it didn't come back out."

"That narrows it," DuBois said.

"Then we ran the ping against the grid," Miller continued. "This building lit up."

JP looked at the structure. Boarded windows, rusted roll-up door, and no signage. It was quiet in the wrong way.

"Thermals?" DuBois asked.

Miller checked the tablet. "Heat inside," he said. "Rear quadrant. Two for sure. Maybe three."

JP and Miller both exited their vehicles and stared at the structure. "She's in there."

"Yeah," Miller said. "But we're not rushing it."

JP's pulse didn't slow. They moved quietly on foot until they reached the nearest side. A door was partially open, and no guards were visible. Miller took point. DuBois covered the rear angle.

JP stayed near the door, as instructed—until he heard a sharp metallic scrape, followed by a muffled thud from deeper inside.

Miller's hand went up in hold gesture.

Now JP heard a man's voice. Low and irritated.

"Move her," the guy said.

JP didn't think. He just bolted.

"JP!" Miller hissed.

But it was too late. JP cut left instead of following the main corridor, slipping through a gap in stacked pallets that smelled like oil and dust. He kept low, moving quietly, years of training kicking in.

He reached a secondary door that overlooked the back room. Through the cracked frame, he saw Dené on the floor, zip-tied. A man with a gun tucked into his waistband hauled her upright by the arm.

The enforcer was repositioning her toward a rear exit, where he likely had a vehicle. That meant a vanishing point.

JP didn't have time to call for backup. If that door opened, they'd lose her. He stepped into the room.

The enforcer turned, but he was too slow. JP rammed him hard, driving his shoulder into the man's ribs before he could bring up his weapon.

They crashed into shelving. Metal exploded sideways. The gun skidded across the concrete. The enforcer swung wild.

JP took the hit and answered with one of his own.

The man pulled a knife seemingly from nowhere. JP saw the flash. He twisted, and pain ripped through his forearm, but he didn't let go. He drove the man into the wall and pinned him.

Footsteps thundered. Miller burst through the main doorway and shouted,

"Drop it!"

The enforcer snarled and tried to break free. JP shifted his weight and slammed him down hard. Miller's boot slammed down on the man's wrist. The knife clattered away.

DuBois was on the thug a second later. "Hands!" DuBois barked. The enforcer resisted. DuBois drove a knee into his back. Click. Cuffs. And the struggle was over.

JP's breath slowed, and he turned to Dené on the floor. She was wide-eyed, but relieved. He crossed to her and cut her ties.

"You okay?" he asked.

She nodded, tears forming.

He helped her up. "You're grounded, you know."

She gave a laugh that became a cry.

Miller stepped toward JP. "What the hell was that?"

JP didn't answer.

DuBois walked over. "Protocol," he said coldly. "We had perimeter. We had containment."

"He was moving her," JP countered.

"You don't know that."

"I heard him say it, and I saw him moving toward an escape."

"You don't freelance in a hostage situation," DuBois snapped.

JP held his gaze. "She was about to go out that door."

DuBois looked toward the rear exit. It was cracked open. A set of fresh tire marks cut through the dust. Slater was gone.

The room went still.

DuBois looked back at JP. "You got lucky."

"No," JP said, looking at Dené. "She did."

Outside, sirens finally pierced the air as marked units closed in. A few minutes later, paramedics checked Dené. No injuries beyond bruised wrists.

Sabre's car screeched into the lot. She jumped out and didn't stop running until she had Dené in her arms.

JP flexed his forearm and winced.

DuBois stepped beside him. "You ever go all cowboy on me again, McCloud," DuBois whispered, threatening, "I'll charge you myself."

"Fair." JP paused. "But she's safe."

DuBois grunted.

Across the lot, the enforcer was being loaded into a squad car. But Slater was still out there.

Chapter 78

Thursday morning, 7:48 a.m.

When DuBois and his team arrived at the mall, the service corridors were still empty except for delivery trucks and early coffee runs. Unmarked cars boxed the exits. Uniforms staged out of sight. Search warrant signed.

As they headed toward the building, a patrol officer radioed. "Got a gray Toyota Camry leaving the back service drive with a matching description."

"Plate?" DuBois asked.

"Temporary tag."

"Take it."

As they neared the Camry, Slater's face was visible for a split second through the windshield, eyes scanning.

The sedan turned left, the wrong direction for home, but he could've been going anywhere.

"Move," DuBois said into his radio.

Two patrol units peeled off quietly, no lights or sirens yet. They wanted Slater to think he was clear.

Slater accelerated, creating distance. He must've seen the patrol units in the rearview because his brake lights flashed, and the engine roared.

"Now," DuBois said.

Sirens ripped open the quiet morning. Slater floored it. The sedan shot through the next intersection just as the light turned red.

Miller followed, threading between cars with inches to spare. Pedestrians shouted. Horns blasted. The sedan swerved into a parking structure entrance.

"Garage!" Miller barked into his radio.

DuBois swung wide and cut off the secondary exit. Inside the garage, the gray sedan screamed up the ramp. The concrete echoed, and tires shrieked.

Slater wasn't a trained runner. In his panic, he reached the top level and a dead end.

Slater tried to whip the car into a three-point turn, but it was too late. Miller's vehicle blocked the ramp behind him. DuBois' car slid sideways across the front. The perp was pinned.

For a split second, Slater stared at the gap between the vehicles as if he were calculating. Then he threw open the car door and ran. DuBois jumped out of his car and sprinted after him.

"Slater!" he shouted.

Slater bolted toward the stairwell. DuBois closed the distance fast, age be damned. Slater slammed through the stairwell door and stumbled down two steps at a time.

Miller pounded up from below. Slater saw him, froze for a moment, then turned back up. That was a wrong move. DuBois hit him head-on, shoulder driving into his chest. They crashed into the railing. Slater clawed at the metal, trying to stay upright.

"You don't want this," DuBois growled.

Slater swung an elbow and connected. DuBois barely flinched. He hooked Slater's arm, twisted hard, and drove him face-first into the concrete wall.

"Done," DuBois said.

Miller rushed up and slapped cuffs on him. Slater stopped fighting. That was the thing about men like him. They only fought when they were sure they could win.

Breathing hard, Slater turned his head just enough to speak. "You don't understand," he said.

DuBois hauled him upright. "Oh, I think I do."

They walked him back toward the cruiser.

Slater's eyes darted around, toward the road, toward anything that wasn't handcuffs. But there was nowhere left to go.

As they loaded him into the back seat, Miller leaned in close. "Is your wife still at her office?"

Slater didn't answer.

~~~

Inside the medium's office, Claire Hawthorne stood behind her desk, looking composed. She attempted a smile.

"Officers," she said smoothly. "Is there a problem?"

DuBois stepped aside so she could see through the glass. Slater was being placed into the police car. Her composure fractured, just a hairline crack. It was enough.

"We have a warrant," Miller said, presenting it to her.

She watched as officers moved past her, opening drawers, photographing files, bagging electronics.

"Vincent," she said softly to DuBois, as if they were acquaintances. "Surely we can speak privately."

"No."

~~~

Slater sat in the department's smaller interview room with his hands cuffed to the table. He didn't look like a criminal mastermind. He looked like a suburban husband who sold insurance.

DuBois stepped in, closed the door behind him, and took his time sitting down. "Attempted flight doesn't look good."

"I panicked," Slater replied. "You had half the county crawling around my wife's office."

"Yeah. That happens when your wife runs a side business brokering juvenile kidnappings."

"You don't know that," Slater said.

DuBois smiled. "Yeah, we do. We have surveillance video of you and Wilcox. We have financial exchanges. We have burner phone records linking you to Mendoza. And we have your vehicle appearing in traffic cameras near the transport yard when you approached Gibson and Mendoza. So, we're past 'You don't know that.'"

Slater's composure wavered, just a tick. "My wife has clients. People talk to her. That doesn't make her a criminal."

"No," he said. "But it makes you the errand boy."

"I'm not anybody's—"

"Lackey?" DuBois cut in. "That's the word you're looking for."

DuBois leaned forward, elbows on the table.

"I'm trying to figure out if you're the guy running this," he said, "or if you're just the one carrying the bags."

Slater didn't answer. Good. He was thinking now.

DuBois sat back again. "Let me help you out," he said. "If you're the mastermind, this is all yours. Planning. Execution. Cleanup. You're looking at everything that comes with that."

A beat.

"If you're the lackey... maybe you get lucky."

No response.

"Your wife's spiritual practice is expensive," DuBois said. "Wilcox paid cash, repeatedly."

Slater broke first. "This wasn't supposed to get violent."

DuBois just sat and let him talk.

"It was supposed to be simple," Slater continued. "A relocation, a scare, nothing permanent."

"Wilcox dead wasn't permanent?" DuBois asked.

Slater's eyes flicked up. "That wasn't us."

"Then who?"

"The muscle," Slater snapped. "He panicked. Wilcox refused to pay when they got the wrong kid, and things went sideways."

"We know it was you who recruited Mendoza."

"He was disposable."

"And the wrong kid?"

Slater's face hardened. "That wasn't our fault. Wilcox didn't have good information."

"You folded," DuBois said. "You're folding now."

Slater stared at the table. "This was all Claire's idea."

There it was. He had no remorse, just deflection.

"She saw Wilcox unraveling," Slater continued. "He was desperate. She told him she could fix it."

"How?"

"He paid," Slater said. "I handled logistics. She handled the client."

"And when it went wrong?"

Slater's eyes shifted. "She told me to clean it up."

DuBois leaned forward. "Meaning?"

"Containment," Slater said. "Loose ends."

"Like Mendoza and Gibson?"

"I didn't kill anybody. I wouldn't do that."

"Who did the killing?"

"That was Billy Noonan."

"The guy we nabbed last night at the warehouse."

"Yes."

"What about the little girl you kidnapped last night?"

Slater shook his head. "That wasn't my call."

"Of course it wasn't," he said. "You're just the lackey, right?"

Slater's head snapped up. "I handled logistics," he snapped. "She handled the clients."

DuBois gave a snort of disgust. "You gave up your wife in less than ten minutes."

Slater looked up sharply. "She's the one who promised Wilcox something," he snapped. "She's the one who said she could make his problem disappear. I just rounded up the help."

DuBois opened the door, then paused. "You're obviously not the mastermind," he said. "You're not even a good lackey."

Then he walked out.

Chapter 79

Thursday late morning

Claire Hawthorne sat perfectly upright in the interview room next door. Her hands were folded, her ankles crossed, and her expression was calm enough to pass for boredom. The fluorescent lighting did nothing to soften her.

DuBois took the chair across from her and read her the Miranda Rights. "Do you understand your rights?"

"I do."

"And you're choosing to speak?"

"For now."

DuBois studied her. "Your husband was arrested attempting to flee, among other things."

Hawthorne's eyes didn't flicker. "People panic when they're frightened."

"He's frightened of you."

That earned the smallest tilt of her head.

"He says you handled Wilcox," DuBois continued. "You made the promise. You set the expectation. He just managed logistics."

She adjusted the sleeve of her blouse. "Vincent," she said calmly, "my husband is not built for pressure."

"He folded fast."

"Of course he did." No denial, just dismissal.

"He says you sourced the job. That you identified the boy."

"That's absurd."

"He says when it went wrong, you told him to 'contain it.'"

Hawthorne let out a quiet breath. "You're quoting a frightened man trying to save himself."

DuBois leaned forward. "He gave you up."

She met his eyes. "No," she said softly. "He thinks he did."

"But you don't believe he will."

She smiled, not warmly. "You misunderstand our marriage."

"Please help me understand."

"Another time."

"You were paid," DuBois said. "For counseling, and you were paid cash."

"All legal. My clients value discretion."

"Wilcox valued revenge."

Irritation flashed in her eyes. "You think grief is revenge?"

"I think obsession can be."

Hawthorne folded her hands again. "Unless you have evidence, Detective, this is just narrative."

DuBois held her gaze. "We're building it."

She didn't blink. "I have nothing more to say."

"Your husband is giving us details. You might want to save yourself."

Hawthorne's expression didn't change. "He won't give you anything that matters."

DuBois stood. "We'll see." He walked to the door.

Behind him, Hawthorne spoke once more. "You're chasing shadows."

DuBois looked over his shoulder. "We're chasing you."

~~~

Outside, the sky had gone that dull violet color that made everything look softer than it really was. Inside the department, Slater was in a holding cell. Claire Hawthorne was still pretending composure would save her.

DuBois walked toward JP. He had called him earlier and asked him to stop by. JP was leaning against his truck, hat low over his brow.
~~~

"McCloud."

JP lifted his head slightly. "Vinny."

DuBois stopped a few feet away. "Are you good?"

"Dené's home, so yep."

DuBois nodded. "Slater's talking enough to hang himself, probably his wife too."

"Good to hear."

"I can't believe this came together because of a pen click," DuBois said. "And Slater's ticked about that. He said Noonan had a bad habit with that pen. He said Noonan was a long-time smoker and picked up the habit to keep his hand from reaching for a cigarette."

"That's good that he quit. Now he won't die from lung cancer while he rots in prison."

DuBois studied him. "You helped close this," DuBois said. "But you also went rogue for a minute."

JP's mouth twitched. "Yeah."

"You ever pull that again in the middle of an active hostage situation—"

"I know," JP said. "You'll charge me."

DuBois held his gaze. "Damn right. But you got Dené out. And you didn't blow the scene."

JP adjusted his hat. "They were about to run with her."

DuBois extended his hand. "Good work, McCloud."

He started back toward the building.

"Vinny," JP called.

DuBois turned.

"Truth's like a rattlesnake," JP said. "You can try to step around it, but sooner or later, it's gonna strike."

DuBois gave him a thin smile. "And this time?"

"This time" — JP tilted his head toward the building—"it bit the right people."

Chapter 80

Thursday night

The house was quiet again. Not the hollow quiet from before. This one felt heavier, like it was used up.

Dené was asleep, finally, on the couch in the living room. Morgan had insisted on staying beside her. Conner hovered until JP gently sent him away. Gene had retreated to his bedroom, muttering something about making coffee in the morning.

Sabre stood in the kitchen, hands braced against the counter.

JP was at the sink, rinsing dried blood from his knuckles.

"You're going to need stitches," she said.

"It'll close," he replied.

She watched the water swirl pink, then clear. The blood itself didn't unsettle her. It was how normal it looked in her kitchen.

JP shut off the faucet and dried his hands. "They've got Slater," he said quietly. "His wife is still pretending she's above it."

Sabre nodded. "She fed Wilcox's grief-induced obsession by kidnapping a child. How can people do that to other people?"

JP leaned back against the counter. "And when it went sideways, they tried to contain it, which made everything worse. DuBois said Slater claimed Wilcox refused to pay the final installment when they had the wrong kid. You can't really blame him."

"So, their solution was to silence him," she said. "And Gibson. Maybe Mendoza and Mateo too. How many people were they willing to kill?" Sabre looked toward the living room. "I can't even think about what could have happened to Dené if you hadn't saved her."

"Then don't think about it."

Sabre crossed the small space between them. "This started because a grieving father couldn't accept what had happened to his son," she said. "Because someone told him revenge would feel like closure."

She let out a breath that wasn't quite steady. "I represented Giovanni. I stood up in court and argued that what happened to Liam was an accident."

"That time the system worked," JP said.

"Did it, though?" she asked quietly.

"Yes. It did."

Sabre looked down at her hands. "Wilcox didn't think so."

"Wilcox was unraveling," JP said. "That's not on you."

"But it came to our house. It crossed into our family."

JP didn't know what to say.

"There were no more lines," she whispered. "No more walls between work and home. They watched us and took one of ours."

"They were desperate," JP said.

"I'm not sure I can do this anymore. Life isn't supposed to be this frightening."

Silence settled between them.

"Do you want to quit?"

"I don't want to be afraid every time someone rings the doorbell," she said. "I don't want Morgan promising not to *squeal*. I don't want Dené thinking she has to fix things."

"You didn't cause this," he said.

"I chose this," Sabre replied. "We have Dené living with us so she will be safe and loved."

"She is loved. And we did keep her safe." JP paused. "You're not suggesting we send her to live with her father, are you?"

"Absolutely not."

"Then what are you saying?"

Sabre looked at the shape of Dené under the blanket. "I think I need to step back from work."

JP let her talk.

"Not forever," she added. "But long enough to remember where the line is."

"You're talking about a leave of absence."

"Yes."

"You won't last," he said.

She almost smiled. "Maybe not."

He took her hands. "We finish this, clean, with no loose ends. And then you can decide if it was enough to trigger you to stop doing a job you love."

She nodded.

For the first time in weeks, the air felt like it belonged in her lungs. "This was revenge dressed up as justice," she said quietly. "And it almost took someone who had nothing to do with it."

JP squeezed her hands. "But it didn't."

Yet the cost had been close enough. And Sabre knew something had shifted. The system had been exploited. Her family had been targeted. And whatever came next, she would choose it, not react to it.

Also by Teresa Burrell

THE ADVOCATE SERIES

THE ADVOCATE (Book 1)
THE ADVOCATE'S BETRAYAL (Book 2)
THE ADVOCATE'S CONVICTION (Book 3)
THE ADVOCATE'S DILEMMA (Book 4)
THE ADVOCATE'S EX PARTE (Book5)
THE ADVOCATE'S FELONY (Book 6)
THE ADVOCATE'S GEOCACHE (Book 7)
THE ADVOCATE'S HOMICIDES (Book 8)
THE ADVOCATE'S ILLUSION (Book 9)
THE ADVOCATE'S JUSTICE (Book 10)
THE ADVOCATE'S KILLER (Book 11)
THE ADVOCATE'S LABYRINTH (Book 12)
THE ADVOCATE'S MEMORY (Book 13)
THE ADVOCATE'S NIGHTMARE (Book 14)
THE ADVOCATE'S OATH (Book 15)
THE ADVOCATE'S PHANTOM (Book 16)
THE ADVOCATE'S QUANDARY (Book 17)
THE ADVOCATE'S REFLECTION (Book 18)
THE ADVOCATE'S SABOTEUR (Book 19)
THE ADVOCATE'S TRIGGER (Book 20)

THE TUPER MYSTERY SERIES

THE ADVOCATE'S FELONY
(Book 6 of The Advocate Series)
MASON'S MISSING (Book 1)
FINDING FRANKIE (Book 2)
RECOVERING RITA (Book 3)
LIBERATING LANA (Book 4)

CO-AUTHORED STANDALONE

NO CONSENT
(Co-authored with L.J. Sellers)

From the Author

Dear Reader,

Thank you for reading my book. I hope you enjoyed reading it as much as I did writing it. Would you like a FREE copy of a novella about JP when he was young? If so, scan the QR code below and it will take you where you want to go. Or, if you prefer, please go to www.teresaburrell.com and sign up for my mailing list. You'll automatically receive a code to retrieve the story.

SCAN ME

Teresa

Made in the USA
Las Vegas, NV
21 August 2026

52522924R10194